Understanding Charles Seeger, Pioneer in American Musicology

Music in American Life

A list of books in the series appears at the end of this book.

Understanding Charles Seeger, Pioneer in American Musicology

Edited by

BELL YUNG AND HELEN REES

Foreword by

ANTHONY SEEGER

University of Illinois Press

Urbana and Chicago

Publication of this book was supported by grants from
the Bei Shan Tang Foundation,
the Society for American Music,
and the Henry and Edna Binkele Classical Music Fund

♾ This book is printed on acid-free paper.

Frontispiece: Charles Seeger in 1977 at his ninetieth birthday celebration
in Berkeley, California. Photo by Rulan Chao Pian.

Library of Congress Cataloging-in-Publication Data
Understanding Charles Seeger, pioneer in American musicology /
edited by Bell Yung and Helen Rees ; foreword by Anthony Seeger.
        p.   cm. — (Music in American life)
Includes bibliographical references and index.
ISBN 0-252-02493-1 (acid-free paper)
1. Seeger, Charles, 1886–1979—Criticism and interpretation.
I. Yung, Bell. II. Rees, Helen, 1964–   . III. Series.
            ML423.S498U53   1999
         780'.92—ddc21   98-58104
                CIP

C 5 4 3 2 1

CONTENTS

FOREWORD
Anthony Seeger

In 1977, to celebrate his ninetieth birthday, Charles Seeger gathered in Berkeley, California, members of his wide circle of friends, family, and associates to discuss his ideas. He did not want his nine decades celebrated with a Festschrift presented to him but rather with a discussion of his ideas in which he could be a lively participant. To those of us who participated, those were heady days—at once a family reunion, a warm return to the University of California at Berkeley, where he had begun teaching in 1912, and an assembling of former students and friends— among them many of the most renowned musicologists and ethnomusicologists from around the world. Most of us felt privileged to be there at this confluence of the personal and the professional, with the honored nonagenarian obviously having such a good time.

It was my impression, though, that Charles was frustrated by his inability to get people to be tough on his ideas and to discuss them head-to-head with him—even though that was one objective of the event. He had spent considerable effort revising a collection of his articles, *Studies in Musicology, 1935–1977,* which was overwhelmingly directed toward the more systematic ideas on which he was still actively working. He was still working on them at his death in 1979.

The "legend of the man" referred to in the introduction and the only in-print collection of his writings were a puzzling and difficult legacy. How did the essays illustrate his importance for the foundation of musicology and ethnomusicology? For nearly fifteen years many more people seemed to invoke Charles Seeger's name than read the man's ideas—an ironic situation for a person who wanted his ideas to be taken seriously.

The situation has changed in the past few years. Ann Pescatello's 1992 biography *Charles Seeger: A Life in American Music* (complemented by Judith Tick's 1997 biography *Ruth Crawford Seeger: A Composer's Search for American Music*), a second compilation of Seeger's essays and manuscripts, *Essays in Musicology II, 1929–1979,* published in 1994, and this collection of critical analyses fill three very different needs. The Pescatello biography presents the man rather than the myth: the man who like all of us was constantly trying to make moral and ethical choices and still have food to eat; the pragmatist who dealt with the political realities of budgets and bureaucracies and the complexities of domestic life. The second collection of essays complements the focus of the first (and suffers from the same systematic bias, thus omitting some of my favorite earlier essays). And *Understanding Charles Seeger, Pioneer in American Musicology* analyzes distinct facets of Charles's career, and places him in the context of the intellectual and social traditions of his times. It is more focused than the Pescatello biography and yet far broader than his own essay collections. The essays presented here focus on some things that he may never have recognized himself—yet that cry out to contemporary readers.

Charles Seeger wanted his ideas confronted directly while he was alive. Nearly twenty years after his death it is time to discuss them analytically as well—set in their historical context and read carefully for what he had to say then and what they may still contribute to discussions today. The editors and the authors are to be congratulated on the courage and thoughtfulness of their approaches, and readers should themselves move between the interpretations and the original publications, creating their own "Charles Seeger" in the process and figuring out how, and whether, to address any of his ideas themselves.

Scholarly writings are parts of an ongoing conversation with past authors, with our contemporaries, and with unknown future readers. We can take issue with Aristotle, bicker with Hegel, argue with Marx, reinterpret Charles Seeger, and put forward our own ideas with the assumption that, if we are lucky, people will be arguing with and through us in some unknown future. It is wonderful to see such interesting conversations with Charles Seeger get started at last.

PREFACE

The conception of this volume owes much to the three Seeger Seminars conducted by Bell Yung at the University of Pittsburgh in 1984, 1990, and 1994. Among the projects arising from the 1990 seminar were papers by Grimes, Rees, and Saavedra, which eventually went on to become a panel at the 1991 annual meeting of the Society for Ethnomusicology. These, together with Yung and Zbikowski's essays that were first read at the 1993 SEM annual meeting, formed the initial core of this collection. A concrete plan for putting together the volume was formulated by Yung and Rees in spring 1994. The corpus was then joined by Baranovitch's paper from the 1994 Seeger Seminar, subsequently presented at the 1994 SEM annual meeting, and Tick's essay read at the same meeting. Last but not least, Greer's essay completes the volume. We wish to thank all the authors for their cooperation in this long process, and Yung would particularly like to acknowledge the contributions of all the participants in the three seminars toward his thinking.

We wish to thank the two referees for the University of Illinois Press. Both Fred Lieberman and the second anonymous reader offered sharp, perceptive, and detailed comments that improved the manuscript greatly. We are grateful to Tony Seeger for writing the Foreword and to Rulan Chao Pian for Seeger's portrait.

Our gratitude finally goes to Judith McCulloh and Margo Chaney of the University of Illinois Press, whose expertise and patience facilitated the arduous process of transforming a multiauthored manuscript into a finished product.

INTRODUCTION
Bell Yung and Helen Rees

As early as 1923, Charles Seeger published an article in which he lamented the peripheral status and low standards of music as generally taught in U.S. universities and in which he argued eloquently for the adoption in this country of the term "musicology" to comprehend and replace such clumsy phrases as "'music history, music aesthetics, etc.'" (1923:98).[1] Seven decades later music in its various manifestations—performance, historical musicology, theory, composition, ethnomusicology, systematic musicology, music education—is of course firmly established in colleges and universities here, and American proponents of these subfields are both numerous and highly regarded internationally.

Throughout his long life Charles Seeger played a vital role in the development of the multifaceted realm of contemporary American musical scholarship: he helped establish university curricula, scholarly societies, and the fields of musicology and ethnomusicology; he saw the value of contemporary American musics at a time when the European classical tradition still dominated the academic imagination; and, central to this volume, he was an influential scholar-musician active in practically all areas of musical endeavor—performance, composition, theory, criticism, pedagogy, and musicology, both theoretical and applied. He along with musicologists such as Otto Kinkeldey was instrumental in the establishment of formal musical scholarship in the United States.

1

Seeger made a unique contribution to musicology by reason of his unprecedentedly broad activities and interests. Indeed Seeger's major theoretical articles draw on all his many musical experiences as well as on his readings in other fields. In fact, in such late articles as "The Music Process as a Function in a Context of Functions" (1966), it is impossible to separate his interest in the creative processes of music—itself informed by his multiple activities in composition, criticism, and folksong scholarship—from his passionate attachment to consideration of the social environment of music. Seeger's range of musical interests, together with his wide reading in such fields as philosophy, folklore, and anthropology, and his involvement in government cultural policy, truly makes him one of the twentieth century's pivotal figures in the reconciliation not only of critical and cultural musicology but also of academia and the world outside the ivory tower. The fact that the contributors to this volume include music theorists, historical musicologists, and ethnomusicologists, Americanists and non-Americanists, underlines the broad-based appeal of his work: divergences frequently become commonalities, with interlinked ideas drawing the reader out of small niches into the wider world of musical scholarship. Music scholars of all stripes—and indeed American social historians and folklorists—all can find food for thought in analysis of Seeger's work.[2]

Charles Seeger continues to be an influence on music and musicological research, as shown by the extraordinary frequency with which his name is invoked in a wide range of musicological literature. There is no doubt that he still provides great stimulus and inspiration and that he is "one of the giants of the history of our field" (Nettl 1991:268). Yet Seeger's writing is also criticized as difficult to read and understand. In Nettl's words, while it causes the reader to "'think big,' it does not tell one precisely how to proceed" (ibid.). He suggests, indeed, that Seeger's leadership resulted from his "charismatic style" rather than from any "substantive instruction" (ibid.:269). Kerman too underscores the common perception that Seeger's writing is difficult, observing that "reviewers must have either thrown up their hands at it or been scared away. . . . No one has read him . . . without being impressed by his penetrating sharpness and clarity of mind, and without being frustrated by his maddening penchant for abstraction" (1985:158). Graduate students faced for the first time with Seeger's essays and articles frequently voice the same complaint.

However, those willing to read with patience and care, an open mind and breadth of view, are rewarded with Seeger's insightful observations and original ideas. The authors of the eight essays in this volume are serious readers of Seeger, particularly of his early and often neglected writings. Focusing on various themes that long occupied Seeger's professional and intellectual life, the essays in this volume examine Seeger's work as composer, music theorist, critic, musicologist, music philosopher, and social activist. They both pinpoint the sources for many of Seeger's ideas and highlight his crucial role in the development of musicology and ethnomusicology as they stand today, in particular in the United States. Above all, they demonstrate the interrelation of the multiple and disparate strands of his thought, an essential step in evaluating Seeger's work and assessing his contribution in specific rather than general terms.

The experienced Seeger student is aware of two factors for a successful reading of his text. First, while Seeger writes with a philosopher's logic and a scientist's rigor, he is also a poet at heart. He often writes associatively, with his mind and pen seemingly hopping from one topic to another. These may be only tangentially related on the surface, but they are subsequently shown to be significantly connected. Such associative writing, which may flow along with the main text or be embedded in lengthy footnotes, may distract and confuse the reader, but it always proves to be intriguing, provocative, and inspiring to the patient and the acute. Seeger also exercises poetic license in his writing style, which has been criticized as grammatically awkward and semantically abstruse. Many passages certainly deserve such criticism, but some of these may be interpreted as his playful indulgence in the formalism of the verbal construction—the music of the prose?—in lieu of simple and straightforward discussion. In short, one needs to read Seeger with a touch of imagination and a sense of humor.[3]

Second, despite the amazing range of topics covered by Seeger's more than one hundred publications (including reviews and other writings), a few broad and fundamental themes resurface again and again. These are not repetitions, but treatments of the same issues from different perspectives and in different contexts. The reader comes to realize that many papers are thematically and chronologically linked in this way and that reading one helps the reading of others. Seeger makes these links explicit, in fact, in the chart entitled "Conspectus of the Organization of Musicological Study upon a Basis of the Systematic Orientation" (1977:12–13). Furthermore, Seeger's views did not remain stagnant but clearly evolved as his professional life went through various stages. Thus reading his earlier writings is not only critical in understanding the major articles of his later years, but also provides a historical context for some of the most important conceptual frameworks that he explored for several decades through scores of articles.

Born in 1886 and still actively lecturing and writing up to his death in 1979, Charles Seeger seems to have accomplished in his ninety-two years several lifetimes of work.[4] Among his achievements Seeger has been recognized as one of the most original thinkers in musical studies in the twentieth century. His ideas did not arise accidentally but developed from a rich experience of musical activities of many kinds: as composer, performer, teacher, scholar, bureaucrat, and inventor.

Seeger's composing and performing activities occurred early in his life. Graduating from Harvard magna cum laude in music in 1908, he immediately set off for Europe, where first he apprenticed as a conductor and then switched to the study of composition. He returned to the United States in 1911 to pursue an active career as a composer; in addition, as a pianist he formed a duo with his first wife, Constance Edson, a violinist, and performed extensively. He took an early interest in avant-garde composers and compositions; was active in the composers' circle in New York during the 1920s and 1930s; played a leadership role in the Composers Collective, a socially activist organization in New York City; and was most closely associated with composers such as Henry Cowell, Edgar Varèse, Charles Ives, and Carl Ruggles. His compositions date mostly from those early years.[5]

His career as a teacher began in 1912 when he accepted a professorship in music at the University of California at Berkeley and taught there for six years. Initially there was not even a music department or a full music curriculum, both of which Seeger built in the next few years. While in Berkeley, he designed and taught courses in musicology, a novelty in the United States at the time. In the 1920s he taught at the Institute of Musical Arts in New York City, the precursor of the Juilliard School of Music, and in the early 1930s at the New School for Social Research in New York City, and he took on private students, most notably Ruth Crawford, who became his second wife in 1932. Still later, in the 1950s and 1960s, he taught at the University of California at Los Angeles, where he exerted significant influence on a generation of future ethnomusicologists. After he retired from UCLA, he held visiting positions or guest lectured at Harvard, Cornell, Brown, and other universities in the East. Bell Yung was fortunate enough to be in his seminar when he spent a semester at Harvard in spring 1971.

Seeger was also an organizer. Not only did he build the Berkeley Music Department and play a leadership role in the Composers Collective, he was a founding member of some of the major musicological organizations in the United States and Europe: the American Musicological Society, the Society for Ethnomusicology, the International Musicological Council, and the International Folk Music Council (now the International Council for Traditional Music).[6] As an inventor Seeger is best known for the melograph, which he developed in the 1950s. His device eventually evolved into the more sophisticated machines of today. The melograph's display of a musical line offered the scholar a more objective transcription of music sound. More significant, it opened windows into fundamental issues of the concept of music and the scholarly study of music.

One of Seeger's strongest beliefs was that a musical scholar should not stay in the ivory tower. Carrying his conviction into action, he made a dramatic career turn when in 1935 he began work as a government bureaucrat in Washington, D.C., continuing until 1953. He first worked for the Resettlement Administration, which was part of President Franklin D. Roosevelt's New Deal, designed to revitalize the nation's battered economy after the Great Depression. The Resettlement Administration, or RA, was specifically created to relieve the poverty of rural and urban groups that either had not been reached by other federal agencies or lacked adequate political representation. At the RA, Seeger organized on a national scale musical groups and musical programs "to help homesteaders . . . to express themselves through music, . . . to encourage social integration, to act as a corrective to the disruptions suffered by people uprooted from their homes and thrown together in new communities by using familiar music idioms, particularly folk song" (Pescatello 1992:139). From 1937 to 1941, Seeger was deputy director of the Federal Music Project.

Seeger's next major bureaucratic role took him to the international scene. In 1939 as turmoil brewed in Europe the U.S. State Department, in order to increase cultural exchanges among the nations in the Western hemisphere, set up conferences on inter-American relations in four areas: philosophy and letters, education, fine arts, and music. The objectives were greater cultural cooperation and a better understanding of Latin American countries. From these conferences developed the Pan American Union. In 1941 Seeger was appointed director of the Union's Inter-American Music Center and chief of the Music and Visual Arts Division. His job was to promote the interchange of music and musical activities between the Americas, including the exchange of leading musicians and musicologists, publication and performance of musical works, building a library of printed music and sound recordings, sponsoring publications, and ultimately establishing the Inter-American Music Council. After the Second World War he was closely involved with the United Nations Educational, Scientific, and Cultural Organization (UNESCO) and its various affiliated musical organizations.

Probably Seeger's greatest long-term legacy will be his publications. Aside from a small corpus of published compositions, these include his editions of several volumes of folk music; reviews of books and records; and two years of concert reviews written under the pseudonym Carl Sands for the New York edition of the *Daily Worker*. Of greatest direct relevance to musical scholarship is of course Seeger's work as a musicologist, in which capacity he published approximately eighty papers. These may be grouped into the following categories, some of which overlap: contemporary composition and composers; the theory of the European art music tradition; the melograph; folk music; music of the Americas; "applied musicology," in which music is discussed in the context of education, government, the music industry, class structure, etc.; one important category within applied musicology, music education; and the philosophy of music, musicology, and ethnomusicology.

Despite the above grouping it is obvious that several themes pervade almost all of Seeger's articles, regardless of subject matter: the definition of music and musicology; the relationship between language and music as media of communication; language as the lens through which music is understood conceptually; theories of value; social responsibilities of the musician and the musicologist; and the myriad issues related to social contexts of music. The essays in this volume treat some of these categories and issues and discuss Seeger's work and thought in the context of his relations with contemporaries such as Carlos Chávez and Ruth Crawford Seeger. The sequence of essays is outlined below; however, each may also be read independently.

Seeger started his musical life engaged in performance, composition, and the teaching of composition; these activities could perhaps be said to have reached their fullest flowering in the compendium "Tradition and Experiment in (the New) Music" (ca. 1931), discussed in Taylor A. Greer's essay. Yet even here, where Seeger deals in depth with technical features of art music composition, he is inspired by extramusical intellectual stimuli. Greer demonstrates how Seeger draws on concepts formulated by the philosophers Johann Wolfgang von Goethe and Bertrand Russell to propose a novel compositional terminology and a new aesthetic that would aid experimental composers. This aesthetic promotes a balanced musical style that would be characterized by the harmonious use of what Seeger defined as the six functions of musical experience: pitch, dynamics, timbre, proportion, accent, and tempo. This aesthetic is shown to have inspired the third movement of Ruth Crawford's String Quartet, written in the same year as "Tradition and Experiment in (the New) Music." Seeger's experiments with his new terminology aimed both at the musical realization of the aesthetic principle of balance and at stimulating modern composers to discover new techniques and thus avoid the excesses of late romanticism. In this compendium philosophical and compositional inspirations and aims are inextricably linked.

Seeger's compositional and social concerns of the 1930s are drawn together in the essay by Leonora Saavedra. She demonstrates, moreover, that these concerns were by no means unique to him and his compatriots. The Mexican composer Carlos Chávez, well known to Seeger, faced similar issues and frequently sought similar solutions. Both men encountered a two-sided artistic problem as American art music composers: the need for a consistent compositional technique differentiated from the mainstream European; and the lack of an audience for their music. Through their experiences both Seeger and Chávez became greatly concerned with the roles of music and the composer in a class society and published many articles on the subject; and both sought answers from Marxist-oriented theories and organizations.

Robert R. Grimes's chapter examines the same period of Seeger's life from a different, though related, angle: the gradually evolving concept of "value" as it appears in Seeger's early writings. Grimes traces Seeger's interest in such writers on value as Georgii Plekhanov and Ralph Barton Perry and the increasing influence of Marxism on his work during this period. Grimes also notes the embryonic appearance of leitmotivs such as the relationship of speech and music and the dyads of fact and value, form and content, and internal and external value, which would continue to evolve throughout Seeger's life.

Grimes's essay pursues Seeger's intellectual development to the late 1930s, after which his increasing involvement with folk music and government administration led to new avenues of awareness and approaches to musical work. Helen Rees's chapter, on the relationship of folk music to some of Seeger's broader theoretical preoccupations, takes up where Grimes's essay leaves off. By the end of Seeger's life many people viewed him as a folk music specialist; he resisted this, insisting that his interest in folk music was only a "temporary bypath." Rees suggests that folk music was in fact far more than this, being demonstrably a major factor in the formulation of ideas in several seminal theoretical articles from the 1940s onward.

Judith Tick too deals with the influence of folk music on Charles Seeger's work, although from a different perspective. She focuses on the 1940 manuscript by Ruth Crawford Seeger, "The Music of American Folk Songs," a first-rate analysis of vernacular musical style that never achieved publication. Intended as an appendix to *Our Singing Country* (1941), the second anthology of traditional American music compiled by John and Alan Lomax, for which Ruth Crawford Seeger served as music editor, it was severely cut to meet the publisher's needs. Crawford Seeger's manuscript leads us to rethink the intellectual relationship between her and her husband: a comparison of its language and ideas with those occurring in publications by Charles Seeger demonstrates substantial shared thinking. Several major articles by Charles Seeger can be seen to have deep roots in Ruth's detailed study of singing style.

Several of the essays in this volume, including those by Grimes and Rees, touch upon Seeger's lifelong preoccupation with the relationship between language and music. Lawrence M. Zbikowski focuses on this relationship as outlined in the 1970 article "Toward a Unitary Field Theory for Musicology." Alone among the essays in this volume, Zbikowski's does not look back at how Seeger came by his ideas but forward at how one may use the insights of later scholars of linguistics and cognition to arrive at a new interpretation of Seeger's problematic formulation. Drawing on Gilles Fauconnier's theory of mental spaces and the concept of knowledge structures, Zbikowski proposes placing Seeger's theory within a broader theory of cognition in order to clarify the process of conceptualizing music. Endorsing the recent view that language does not acquire meaning from reference to objective reality, being constructed instead through cognitive processing, he argues that the principal barrier to realizing the fruits of the unitary field theory lies in the sterility of reference to the objective world. Given, then, that meaning is constructed rather than objective, Seeger's "linguocentric predicament" is greatly lessened, since the application of speech to music involves the mapping of connections between different conceptual domains rather than arrival at a "greater truth."

Most of the essays introduced so far dwell to some extent on Charles Seeger's frequent borrowing of extramusical ideas to stimulate his own creative thinking. Greer, Saavedra, and Grimes in particular highlight the contributions of a variety of philosophers to the evolution of Seeger's early thought. The last two essays in this volume, however, go beyond this, suggesting that we may attribute Seeger's novel approach to musicology at least in part to his thorough assimilation of path-breaking developments in two quite disparate fields, namely, anthropology and physics.

As Nimrod Baranovitch notes, well before the emergence around 1953 of the new field of ethnomusicology, Seeger was known for his emphasis on the social context of music and on the importance of looking beyond the great composers of the Western art tradition in musicological research. His approach certainly foreshadowed that of ethnomusicology, and he is often cited as one of the founders of the field—albeit one whose contribution is seldom identified in concrete terms. Baranovitch pinpoints direct influences on Seeger's early and middle writings (1933–53) from anthropologists such as Franz Boas and Alfred Kroeber, and he suggests that Seeger's introduction of anthropological thought into musicology—specifically the emphasis on society and on concepts such as cultural relativism, functionalism, and objectivism—helped lay the foundations for modern ethnomusicology.

Scholars have certainly remarked on Seeger's interest in social science, but no one has yet pointed out the influence of physical theories on some of his writings. Bell Yung's essay explores Seeger's excursion into two theories from modern physics: the particle-wave duality in atomic physics and the special theory of relativity. In these theories Seeger not only finds parallels between specific concepts in modern physics applicable to musical and musicological research methodology, but also invokes the fundamentally revolutionary approaches of modern physics to underscore his own revolutionary approach toward musical research.

Throughout Seeger's writings one senses that he is constantly seeking and exploring new ways to talk about music, to interpret music, and to understand the importance of music in society and in the life of the individual. He also comes across as a passionate Americanist, keenly interested in American art music composers and joining such figures as the Lomaxes in an increasing fascination with the many musics of the New World. Seeger not only contributed to the intellectual trends and institutionalization of musical scholarship as practiced in the United States today, but also championed the worth of American musics of all kinds. For both these reasons he may be seen as one of the true pioneers of American musicology.

As the essays in this volume show, many of Seeger's ideas were ahead of his time. They point to a new philosophy and methodology of musical research whose tenets and approaches have exerted a tangible influence over the last several decades, both direct and indirect, on the world of musical scholarship.

NOTES

1. Certain ideas in this article were stated ten years earlier, in 1913, when Seeger wrote an unpublished position paper called "Toward an Establishment of the Study of Musicology in America" (Pescatello 1992:55). Adoption of the novel term "musicology" for the academic study of music was also urged by Seeger's older contemporary Waldo Selden Pratt (1915).

2. One need only note the range of journals publishing obituaries for Seeger to have some idea of the regard in which he was held by scholars of different fields: such journals include *Ethnomusicology* (Rhodes 1979); *Journal of American Folklore* (Green 1979); *Musical Quarterly* (Robertson Cowell 1979); and *Yearbook of the International Folk Music Council* (Hood 1979). The potential breadth of his appeal is also shown in the journal *Chinoperl News,* in which the 1970 article "Toward a Unitary Field Theory for Musicology" is briefly discussed and introduced to a sinological readership (Lieberman 1975:127–33).

3. At a party after Seeger gave a talk at Cornell University in 1977, Bell Yung commented to Seeger that he was a poet at heart, upon which Seeger chuckled with obvious delight.

4. For a portrait of the man, his work, and his times, see Ann M. Pescatello's fine biography *Charles Seeger: A Life in American Music* (1992).

5. For Henry Cowell's appreciation of Seeger's compositional talents and for Seeger's discerning observations on the work of others, see Cowell (1962 [1933]).

6. So greatly appreciated were Seeger's contributions to the establishment of musicology and musicological societies in the United States that in 1975 the College Music Society named him an honorary founder (Lieberman 1976).

REFERENCES CITED

Cowell, Henry. 1962 [1933]. "Charles Seeger." In *American Composers on American Music: A Symposium.* Ed. Henry Cowell. 119–24. New York: Frederick Ungar.

Green, Archie. 1979. "Charles Louis Seeger (1886–1979)." *Journal of American Folklore* 92 (4): 391–99.

Hood, Mantle. 1979. "Reminiscent of Charles Seeger." *Yearbook of the International Folk Music Council* 11:76–82.

Kerman, Joseph. 1985. *Contemplating Music: Challenges to Musicology.* Cambridge, Mass.: Harvard University Press.

Lieberman, Frederic. 1975. "Some Contributions of Ethnomusicology to the Study of Oral Literature." *Chinoperl News* 5:126–53.

———. 1976. "Charles Seeger: Honorary Founder." *College Music Symposium* 16:149–50.

Lomax, John, and Alan Lomax, comps.; Ruth Crawford Seeger, music ed. 1941. *Our Singing Country.* New York: Macmillan.

Nettl, Bruno. 1991. "The Dual Nature of Ethnomusicology in North America: The Contributions of Charles Seeger and George Herzog." In *Comparative Musicology and Anthropology of Music: Essays on the History of Ethnomusicology.* Ed. Bruno Nettl and Philip B. Bohlman. 266–74. Chicago: University of Chicago Press.

Pescatello, Ann M. 1992. *Charles Seeger: A Life in American Music.* Pittsburgh: University of Pittsburgh Press.

Pratt, Waldo Selden. 1915. "On Behalf of Musicology." *Musical Quarterly* 1 (1): 1–16.

Rhodes, Willard. 1979. "Charles Seeger, 1886–1979." *Ethnomusicology* 23 (2): v–vi.

Robertson Cowell, Sidney. 1979. "Charles Seeger (1886–1979)." *Musical Quarterly* 65 (2): 305–8.

Seeger, Charles Louis. 1923. "Music in the American University." *Educational Review* 66 (2): 95–99.

———. 1966. "The Music Process as a Function in a Context of Functions." *Yearbook: Inter-American Institute for Musical Research* (Tulane University) 2:1–36.

———. 1970. "Toward a Unitary Field Theory for Musicology." In *Selected Reports* (University of California at Los Angeles, Institute of Ethnomusicology) 1(3): 171–210.

———. 1977. "Introduction: Systematic (Synchronic) and Historical (Diachronic) Orientations in Musicology." In *Studies in Musicology, 1935–1975.* 1–15. Berkeley: University of California Press.

Seeger, Ruth Crawford. 1940. "The Music of American Folk Songs." Ms. Ruth Crawford Seeger Papers, Music Division, Library of Congress, Washington, D.C.

1

The Dynamics of Dissonance in
Seeger's Treatise and Crawford's Quartet

Taylor A. Greer

In a tribute written in 1932 to his friend and fellow avant-garde composer Carl Ruggles, Charles Seeger makes a telling remark about his approach toward experimental composition: "A complete criticism . . . should have both its scientific-critical, or logical, section and its impressionistic, or rhapsodic, one. But in treating of Carl Ruggles, it is quite impossible to do justice by the former without writing a history of music and a manual of modern composition, not to mention a ponderous treatise upon musicological method" (1932:591). Notwithstanding his self-effacing tone, Seeger himself was in a good position to "do justice" to Ruggles's music, for he had just written a huge compendium called "Tradition and Experiment in (the New) Music" that combines all of the projects mentioned above. The recent publication of this work in *Studies in Musicology II* (Seeger 1994:39–273) was the culmination of a long music-intellectual journey that Seeger had embarked upon in his first teaching appointment at the University of California at Berkeley, in 1912, had continued in New York during the 1920s and 1930s, and had finally completed at UCLA during the 1960s. In many respects the treatise is at the same time a prophecy and a diary of that journey. At various junctures in this work he speaks as a composition teacher, as a critic, and finally as a philosopher. What for others might have been a pure exercise in philosophical reflection was for Seeger integrally connected with the daily work of the composer as well as the musicologist. For him, philosophical exegesis was inseparable from compositional genesis.

The treatise's interdisciplinary character is especially evident in his investigation of the basic elements of music, which appears in chapters 3 and 4. One of his central motivations for writing it was his profound discontent with the state of contemporary music in America during the 1920s. He believed that Scriabin, Stravinsky, and Schönberg were generally perceived as the leading experimental composers of the period, and for different reasons Seeger rejected the music of all three. By reexamining traditional musical parlance—the terms used to describe such things as pitch and rhythm—Seeger felt he could set the stage for a new conception of composition. At the same time he also felt compelled to question the underlying philosophical assumptions on which any theory of music was based. In the end Seeger's reappraisal of the way musicians talk about music is inseparable from his broader speculations about aesthetics and avant-garde composition.

Philosophical Background

Seeger's theory of musical criticism appears in the introduction and opening two chapters of the treatise. He proposes fourteen "principles" of criticism that he presents in the form of a continuous narrative combined with an explanatory diagram and various comments.[1] A close look at this list reveals that his aspirations are not limited to philosophy. The principles themselves can be divided into three groups: initial intuition (numbers 5–7), mediation between intuition and reason (numbers 1–4, 8–11), and finally a mix of historiography and compositional theory (numbers 12–14). Each group reflects the ideas of a contemporary philosopher who exercised some influence on Seeger's thought: Henri Bergson, Bertrand Russell, and Ralph Barton Perry.[2]

The seed from which everything grows in Seeger's approach to music criticism is the individual's spontaneous intuition. Following Henri Bergson, Seeger believed that the human faculty of intuition had a mystical character, for it precedes all acts of language. Yet, since intuition alone is fallible and may lead to an incomplete understanding of musical experience, it needs to be complemented by something else. Seeger's solution to this problem is a binary model of human knowledge in which two opposing mental faculties are balanced in equilibrium: reason is contrasted against intuition. Music criticism can be likened to a process of negotiation in which the critic must mediate between intuitive insight and logical analysis. The source for this ideal of mediation is the British philosopher Bertrand Russell, who in an early essay used it as a means of explaining religious experience, in particular, mysticism (Russell 1918).[3]

This same ideal of balance also serves as a foundation for a new aesthetic for experimental composition. To guide him in his aesthetic meditations, Seeger relies on yet another thinker—the eighteenth-century poet, critic, and philosopher, Johann Wolfgang von Goethe. Seeger invokes a distinction between style and manner that Goethe initially developed in an essay written in 1799 entitled "The Collector and His Circle," which outlines his aesthetic ideals (Goethe 1986:121–59).[4] According to Goethe most artists and art lovers exhibit one of two ways of thinking, which he calls manners: serious or playful. In the course of the essay he enumerates three different serious manners—imitators, characterizers, and miniaturists—that are then juxtaposed against three playful manners—phantomists, undulators, and sketchers—so as to create three pairs of opposites, or six in all. Having inaugurated this "mannered" catalog, Goethe then unveils an aesthetic principle whereby opposite manners become fused together. The highest ideal comes about only if all three pairs of opposites combine to create a grand synthesis, or what he calls style.

Reappraisal of Musical Materials

In his early treatise Seeger revives Goethe's aesthetic ideal, yet he also adapts it to suit his own musical ends. First of all he reinvents the opposition between style and manner so as to focus on the basic elements of musical experience rather than Goethe's abstract categories of serious and playful. Thus he focuses initially on a comprehensive method of description, a musical taxonomy, before considering any specific compositional applications. He draws a sharp distinction between two conceptions of musical sound: the raw, physical approach in which music, like any other sound, serves as the data for scientific measurement; and the manipulated approach, which treats music as a product of culture. He goes to great lengths to distinguish the scientist's from the artist's perspective of musical experience, contrasting the understanding that each has of the basic materials of the medium. Yet *both* conceptions play an important role in the treatise, as can be seen in the following comment: "It is of prime importance that the craftsmen have practically automatic control of this manipulation so that the elements of composition are not the qualities of the raw but of the manipulated materials. In other words, the experimenting with the *materials* must be practically completed before the experimenting with the *forms* can progress beyond an elementary stage" (Seeger 1994:90). A new, more refined method of description not only would clarify our theoretical knowledge of musical phenomena, it might eventually lead composers to new creative ideas.

The framework of his descriptive method conforms to that of Goethe's scheme of manners. Thus he defines six functions (or resources) of musical experience, which are divided into two groups of three: pitch, dynamics, and timbre, which fall under the general category of tone; and proportion, accent, and tempo, which belong to the general category of rhythm. In Seeger's mind a balanced musical style would be characterized by a harmonious use of all six functions. To indicate a change, or what Seeger calls "inflection," of any function, he coins the terms "tension" (an increase), "poise" (no change), and "relaxation" (a decrease). The resulting classification scheme can measure three values for each musical function, yielding a total of eighteen possible values in all.

Despite the apparent neutrality of Seeger's system of classification, however, the six functions that it describes do not enjoy equal status among composers. Seeger was acutely aware that the function of pitch has a certain priority over the other five simply because it lends itself to being measured and characterized in words. This priority was the source of some concern to him, for if a hidden bias existed in the very nomenclature of musical description, then it could conceivably influence the course that modern composition would eventually take. Cautioning that composers should avoid falling prey to such a bias, he offers a provocative remedy to overcome it.

Since in his judgment one of the flaws of nineteenth-century romanticism was that the pitch function had become "overdeveloped," the best way of compensating for this imbalance would be to refine the organization of the other five. In his words his goal was not "to transfer tonal practice bodily into the other functions, but rather taking the *method* of pitch organization, insofar as we can understand it musically, and seeing if it . . . yield[s] musical results" (Seeger 1994:90). He devises an experiment in which the terminology traditionally used to describe matters of pitch is reinterpreted as a means of measuring the nonpitch functions. He unveils the following list of terms:

1. gamut, both articulated and unarticulated
2. interval
3. scale
4. mode

5. chord
6. consonance and dissonance
7. tonality

Much of chapter 4 is organized as though he were carrying out some kind of grand theoretical experiment, testing old definitions against new functions. Since it is not possible in this space to review all of the results of Seeger's terminological experiments, this essay focuses on the hypothetical analogues for the concepts of "gamut" and "consonance and dissonance." For convenience the information concerning consonance and dissonance is summarized in figure 1.1.

According to Seeger the functions of dynamics and timbre were so poorly understood that the terms borrowed from pitch nomenclature were of limited use in describing them. The chief problem was that there existed no universally accepted unit for measuring differences in gamut for either function. In spite of this shortcoming Seeger proposes provisional definitions of the consonant and dissonant use of dynamics and timbre, though his comments about the latter are somewhat sketchy.[5]

	CONSONANCE	DISSONANCE
DYNAMICS	a) no change in loudness in all parts b) constant change in loudness in all parts	a) frequent and sudden shifts in dynamics b) simultaneous increase and decrease in loudness within different parts
TIMBRE		
PROPORTION	durations which form a ratio between 1 and a whole number > 1	durations which form any other ratio
ACCENT	regular accentual pattern	irregular accentual pattern either in one part or between multiple parts
TEMPO	gradual change in tempo	sudden change in tempo

Figure 1.1. Analogues of consonance and dissonance for the nonpitch functions

Changes in dynamics can be articulated, as with the terms *fortissimo, forte, mezzo forte,* etc., or unarticulated, as with *crescendo* and *diminuendo.* Seeger's way of adapting the distinction between consonance and dissonance for this function is to focus on the rate of change itself and the relationship between contrasting rates of change in different parts within a given texture. Hence "consonant" dynamics indicates either no change or a constant change in loudness, both of which during the past two centuries have become the norm. By contrast the concept of dissonant dynamics denotes either a sudden alternation between loud and soft in a musical texture or a simultaneous increase and decrease in dynamics within different parts of a texture. This distinction becomes the seed for an entire movement of Ruth Crawford's String Quartet.

Of the five functions considered, proportion is the one most conducive to pitch nomenclature. By proportion Seeger means the relationship between two groups of durations, either successive or simultaneous, assuming the two share a common beat or pulse. Seeger's strategy is to borrow the acoustical model traditionally used to explain intervals and then to adapt it to rhythm. In his adapted model a proportion between two durations, like that between two frequencies, may be expressed as the ratio of two whole numbers. Seeger then takes the pitch/proportion analogy one step further by proposing a harmonic series of durations as a basis for distinguishing between proportional consonance and dissonance. Figure 1.2 displays proportional intervals both in their melodic (successive) and chordal (simultaneous) forms (Seeger 1994:102). Consonant proportions occur between each pair of measures at (a) and within each measure at (b). Each ratio consists of one and a whole number greater than one (e.g., 2:1, 3:1, 4:1) and can be likened to a fundamental measured against one of its upper partials. Dissonant proportions are ratios of whole numbers that cannot be reduced to a consonant proportion and thus correspond to the relation between two upper partials, as shown in figure 1.2(c) and (d). Throughout this section of the treatise Seeger's ideas about proportion bear a strong kinship with those of Henry Cowell, as presented in his book *New Musical Resources,* which he wrote in the late teens and published in 1930.[6] Recent critics have attacked this analogy. For instance Daniel S. Augustine argues that since the perception of rhythm is fundamentally different from that of pitch, any analogy between the harmonic series and ratios of proportion is bankrupt (Augustine 1979:54–58).

The two remaining aspects of rhythm, accent and tempo, are intimately linked with proportion. Accent consists of two elements: the rela-

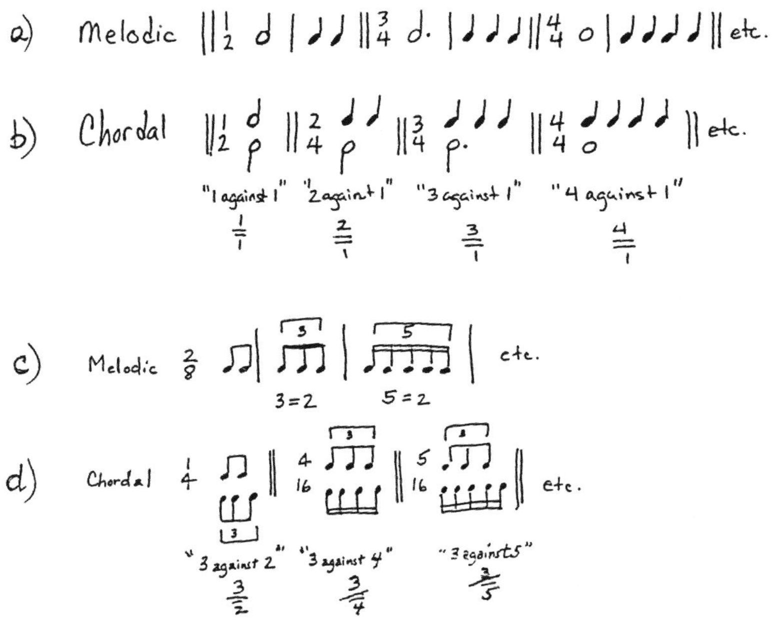

Figure 1.2. Examples of consonant and dissonant proportions (Reprinted with permission from Charles Seeger, *Studies in Musicology II, 1929–1979*, ed. Ann M. Pescatello, 102, © 1994 by the Regents of the University of California Press)

tive amount of stress a given beat receives in relation to the beats preceding and succeeding it; and the interval of time between beats that receive the greatest stress (Seeger 1994:104). Since of all the functions accent is the least likely to be perceived as a gamut, much less an interval or scale, Seeger focuses on the pattern created by a succession of accents. Consonant accent is a regular pattern either in a single voice or multiple voices; dissonant accent refers to irregular accentuation in one part or cross accenting between two or more parts.

As regards tempo, Seeger observes that sensitivity to differences in tempo is not as highly cultivated in Western musical culture as that of differences in pitch. Although objective measures of tempo do exist, such as metronome markings, most musicians ignore them in favor of a relative and therefore less exact approach. Directions such as *piu mosso* or *meno mosso*, for example, indicate neither exact tempos nor exact changes of tempo. As a result Seeger is content to focus on the rate of tempo change. Gradual changes, either increasing or decreasing, are classified as consonant, extreme changes as dissonant. He also compares the ratios between two tempos using the same definitions of consonance and dissonance as he did for proportion. For example, if a slow introduction is followed by an allegro movement two or four times as fast, the change is consonant. If the ratio is closer to 2:3 or 2:5, the spans of time are in a dissonant relationship.

Seeger's ultimate goal in this section of the treatise is to find a comprehensive framework for comparing a broad range of musical materials. As it turns out, one of the problems he encounters when hypothesizing such things as an interval of dynamics or a scale of tempo is the absence of a viable unit of measure within each function. Indeed this absence is in part what in later chapters will fuel his attempt to discover a musical calculus for all six functions. Furthermore his terminological experiments also led him to discover the degree to which different musical dimensions depend on one another: a dramatic change in one function often creates a change in another. Thus a truly comprehensive system of description would need to take these interrelationships into account.

Crawford's String Quartet

Within the treatise Seeger does not consistently provide musical examples to illustrate the new terminology he imagines. Most of the examples he does present are in conjunction with the three rhythmic functions. As far as dynamics and timbre are concerned, for the most part he is content merely to suggest hypothetical analogies to pitch nomenclature. The third movement of Ruth Crawford's work "String Quartet 1931" is useful in this connection, for her treatment of dynamics and accent serves as one way in which Seeger's theoretical speculations can be realized in compositional practice.[7] The genesis of this quartet took place in the fall of 1930, when as the recipient of a Guggenheim Fellowship she was living in Europe. It is fair to say that during this period she was immersed in Seeger's ideas about experimental composition. Not only had she been studying privately with him in New York City the previous year, but she also had worked intensely with him on the treatise itself during the summer of 1930, helping him type and edit the manuscript (Gaume 1986:119–21).

The third movement is an essay in dynamic counterpoint, that is, a polyphonic texture in which the independence of the parts is determined by the treatment of dynamics rather than of pitch and/or rhythm. There is a constant change in dynamics in all the parts such that until the climax at m. 75 no two instruments have the same dynamic marking at the same time: while one is growing, the other or others are receding. Crawford creates this contrapuntal effect by means of various canons of crescendos and decrescendos. The first canon appears in the opening duo between viola and 'cello beginning at m. 3 and continuing until m. 13 (see the excerpt in figure 1.3). Throughout this section the viola reaches the peak of its crescendo when the 'cello, by contrast, is at the bottom of its decrescendo and vice versa. The dynamic range in these ten measures is rather limited: between ppp and p. But as the ensemble grows with the other two instruments' entering—the second violin at m. 13 and the first violin at m. 19—Crawford increases this range, reaching mezzo forte at m. 21.

Crawford's canonic treatment of dynamics in this excerpt shows one way in which Seeger's hypothesis of pitch analogues leads to a new compositional device. Since at every moment each instrument is at a different stage in the cycle of crescendi and decrescendi, the net result is a dissonant use of dynamics.

But Crawford's careful control of dynamics also helps shape the movement's rhythmic contour. In mm. 13–18 the second violin, viola, and 'cello all display the same pattern in dynamics: a gradual process of swelling and shrinking that takes four beats for each instrument. Since the entrances are staggered, a succession of crescendi appears in every measure whereby each of the three instruments reaches its climax on a different beat. The pattern is as follows:

instrument	VA	V2	VC	—
beat	1	2	3	4

Throughout most of the five measures the same three pitches appear, F♯, B♭, B—a fact that suggests that listeners can focus their attention on the subtle nuances within a single function: dynamics.

Yet Crawford's intricate treatment of crescendos also creates corresponding patterns of accent and proportion. The crescendos described above accentuate the first, second, and third beats within mm. 13–18. Although Seeger's new terminology does not account for such a rhythm, it seems appropriate to classify it as consonant. It is significant that when Crawford finally introduces the first violin at m. 19, it climaxes on the fourth beat—the only beat that up to this point has not received an accent. The new rhythm implied by the succession of crescendi would also be considered consonant: a continuous pulse of quarter notes.

Figure 1.3. Ruth Crawford, "String Quartet 1931," third movement, mm. 1–24 (© 1941 by Merion Music, Inc. Used by permission)

What is striking about the third movement of Crawford's quartet is the contrast between the way Crawford approaches dynamics and rhythm—a dissonant pattern of changes in volume among the four parts and a consonant pattern of accents created by those changes in volume. There is an overall balance of musical functions whereby a constant flux in one function is counterbalanced by less activity among the others. When viewed in the context of Crawford's own conception of compositional ideals, this kind of equilibrium is no accident. In a letter written in 1948 to Edgard Varèse, who had asked her to define her musical "credo," she writes:

1. Clarity of melodic line;
2. Avoidance of rhythmic stickiness;
3. Rhythmic independence between parts;
4. Feeling of tonal and rhythmic center;
5. Experiment with various means of obtaining at the same time organic unity and various sorts of dissonance. (Neuls-Bates 1982:310)

In this list of aesthetic desiderata, the crucial element is the fifth. In a single sentence Crawford juxtaposes two sharply contrasting, if not contradictory, principles that Seeger had proposed in the treatise more than seventeen years before: extended dissonance and organic unity. In her mind, exploring new types of dissonance within a single musical function was inseparable from trying to achieve some kind of unity over an entire work.

These observations, though hardly a comprehensive analysis, suggest that the sense of balance exhibited in Crawford's quartet can be interpreted as a musical realization not only of Goethe's ideal of style but also of Seeger's philosophical theory of mediation. In sum, this movement is far more than some exercise in "dissonation" of a neglected resource; indeed, it reveals how Crawford was able to transform a set of abstract aesthetic ideas into a refined work of art.[8]

Conclusion

In this essay I have investigated three areas: a summary of Seeger's philosophical theory of balance; an overview of his abstract experiments for exploring musical resources that had previously been neglected; and a brief analysis of a section from Crawford's String Quartet that realizes some of Seeger's experiments. In closing, I would like to reconsider

Seeger's philosophical theory, especially in light of Crawford's aesthetic meditations mentioned above. The following questions can be raised regarding this theory's overall historical impact: In what ways did Seeger's philosophical project shape individual works written by ultramodernist composers between the wars? In what ways did it contribute to the aesthetic principles shared by the ultramodernist composers as a group?

In answer to the first question, analytical observations of a short section of the third movement of a multimovement work offers little basis for generalization. Rather, my brief discussion of the quartet serves as an initial step to help stimulate other, more detailed analyses of the relation between philosophical theory and compositional method. Indeed, it bears mentioning that more comprehensive studies of movements as well as entire works by Crawford, Ruggles, and Cowell have begun to appear in recent years.

Before considering the question of what aesthetic concerns the ultramodernist composers may have shared as a group, it is important to consider a potential contradiction in Seeger's adaptation of Goethe's ideal model. The relation between theory and practice is paradoxical: although the ultimate end he seeks is balance, the means he recommends to achieve this end is manifestly *unbalanced.* It seems rather ironic that the one composer who had the benefit of studying closely Seeger's theories about the ideal of balance, Ruth Crawford, wrote several works that were distinguished by the imbalance among functions.[9]

This paradox is a direct consequence of his discontent with nineteenth-century mannerisms. His search for pitch analogies reveals that he was reacting against the traditions of the past as much as he was trying to inaugurate a new "music of the future." If composers were ever to throw off the yoke of the romantic tradition, they had to try cultivating those musical elements that their nineteenth-century predecessors had neglected. For Seeger the various terminological experiments in the treatise were merely one part of a pedagogical discipline designed to lay the foundation of a new style of composition that he had already unveiled in an essay published in 1923. "Such a set of disciplines would serve, in a way, as a temporary substitute for the unattainable style they aim eventually to establish and at the same time would serve as a corrective for the mannerisms against which they revolt. Work in them would, indeed, be half stylistic and half manneristic" (Seeger 1923:430). Viewed in the context of the entire treatise, these disciplines include a theory of melodic form proposed in chapters 7–9 and a regimen of dissonant counterpoint presented in chapters 10–17. Thus, he articulates two aesthetic models: the first, an ideal goal of perfect balance; the second, an intermediate goal based on imbalance, which he believes in the long run will help composers achieve the first.

The aesthetic of balance that Seeger urges composers to attain is anything but a pure philosophical construction; it is defined in relative rather than absolute terms. His aim is not to exhort composers to write music that employs all six functions for their own sake. Rather his recommendations are based on a historical view of the nineteenth century: he encourages his contemporaries to employ musical functions that previous composers have neglected. If a composer's music succeeds in cultivating new aspects of the neglected functions but fails to create an overall balance among all six, then Seeger's goal will have been achieved. In sum, his notion of synthesis is shaped as much by historical factors as by a purely philosophical abstraction of balance.

With this in mind, it is useful to consider Joseph N. Straus's comment regarding the aesthetic principles shared by such ultramodernist composers as Ruggles, Cowell, and Crawford. "Ultra-modern music, then, is characterized by two deep, and deeply contradictory, impulses: one toward heterogeneity and multiplicity, the other toward integration and unification. It pushes both terms of the dichotomy to their outermost limits" (1995:219–20). This observation captures well the ferment of creativity found in ultramodernist music in which new concepts of form and order often appear alongside experimentation for its own sake. Such a paradox is certainly present in the fifth part of Crawford's compositional "credo" cited above, in which she juxtaposes the word "experiment" with the notion of organic unity. Yet when one views these paradoxes and contradictions in the context of Seeger's pair of aesthetic models—one of balance, the other of imbalance—they seem easier to reconcile. What may appear as contradictory or paradoxical features in a single composition can also be interpreted as an aesthetic way station, a moment of purposeful imbalance along the path toward achieving Seeger's ideal vision of balance. While it would be a mistake to conclude that the ultramodernist composers were united by their devout faith in Seeger's compositional prescriptions, it is important to acknowledge that his peculiar blend of philosophical and musical speculation was one among many sources of inspiration for some of the leading experimental composers in America during the 1920s and 1930s.

Ultimately Seeger's faith in the union between theoretical speculation and artistic practice was a reflection of his own protean personality.
The portrait of Charles Seeger that emerges from this study is as much
that of a philosopher as of a composer or musicologist. For him it was
inconceivable that the study of experimental composition would not lead
directly to questions about historical method and the nature of human
knowledge. In "Tradition and Experiment in (the New) Music" they create a rich interdisciplinary tapestry. Indeed the title of the treatise itself
reflects the breadth of his aspirations: he was as eager to question the
traditions of the past, whether they took the form of language, art, or even
knowledge itself, as he was to renew them.

NOTES

1. Seeger uses the word "principle" rather loosely: some statements in this
eclectic list are closer to being hypotheses or speculations than true principles
within a formal system. For a complete exposition of the fourteen principles, see
Seeger (1994:65–83).

2. For more details regarding how these philosophers influenced Seeger's
thought, see Greer (1998).

3. Seeger refers to the same collection of essays by Russell in two different
autobiographical reminiscences. See Seeger (1970:20; n.d.). Seeger also mentions
Russell's collection in his "Preface to a Critique of Music" (1965).

4. Seeger explicitly mentions Goethe as his source in his explanation of the
importance of showmanship in contemporary music (see Cowell 1933).

5. Regarding timbre, Seeger observes that whereas "consonant" tone quality
is the rule in single melodic lines, "dissonant" tone quality became fashionable
in polyphonic textures during the nineteenth and early twentieth centuries. He
finally concludes that until a concept of gamut is developed for this function, it
is premature to describe the phenomenon of timbre with pitch-based terms
(1994:100–101).

6. The degree of influence that Seeger may have had on Cowell or vice versa
is still a difficult question to address, since Cowell's private papers (now on
deposit at the New York Public Library) had been inaccessible for so long. For
more information see the 1996 edition of Cowell's treatise, with notes and an
accompanying essay by David Nicholls.

7. Other analyses of this movement can be found in David Nicholls's work
(1983, 1990), Ellie Hisama's essay (1995), and in Joseph N. Straus's insightful treatment (1995).

8. For more detailed studies of the relation between Seeger's theoretical speculations and Crawford's music, see Nicholls (1990:89–133), Tick (1990:405–22), and
Straus (1995).

9. In addition to the third movement of the String Quartet, the *Piano Study in Mixed Accents* (1930) stands as an example of her fascination for a limited number of musical functions.

References Cited

Augustine, Daniel S. 1979. "Four Theories of Music in the United States, 1900–1950." Ph.D. dissertation, University of Texas.

Cowell, Henry. 1996 [1930]. *New Musical Resources.* Cambridge: Cambridge University Press.

———, ed. 1933. *American Composers on American Music: A Symposium.* Stanford, Calif.: Stanford University Press.

Gaume, Matilda. 1986. *Ruth Crawford Seeger: Memoirs, Memories, Music.* Metuchen, N.J.: Scarecrow Press.

Goethe, Johann Wolfgang von. 1986. "The Collector and His Circle." In *Essays on Art and Literature.* Trans. Ellen and Ernest H. von Nardroff. 121–59. New York: Suhrkamp.

Greer, Taylor Aitken. 1998. *A Question of Balance: Charles Seeger's Philosophy of Music.* Berkeley: University of California Press.

Hisama, Ellie M. 1995. "The Question of Climax in Ruth Crawford's String Quartet, Mvt. 3." In *Concert Music, Rock, and Jazz since 1945: Essays and Analytical Studies.* Ed. Elizabeth West Marvin and Richard Hermann. 285–312. Rochester, N.Y.: University of Rochester Press.

Neuls-Bates, Carol, ed. 1982. *Women in Music: An Anthology of Source Readings from the Middle Ages to the Present.* New York: Harper and Row.

Nicholls, David. 1983. "Ruth Crawford Seeger: An Introduction." *Musical Times* 124 (July): 421–25.

———. 1990. *American Experimental Music, 1890–1940.* Cambridge: Cambridge University Press.

Russell, Bertrand. 1918. *Mysticism and Logic and Other Essays.* London: Longmans and Green.

Seeger, Charles Louis. 1923. "On Style and Manner in Modern Composition." *Musical Quarterly* 9 (3): 423–31.

———. 1932. "Carl Ruggles." *Musical Quarterly* 18 (4): 578–92.

———. 1965. "Preface to a Critique of Music." *Primera Conferencia interamericana de etnomusicologia: Trabajos presentados.* Cartagena de Indias, Colombia, February 24–28, 1963. Washington, D.C.: Pan American Union.

———. 1970. Interview with Vivian Perlis, March 16. Oral History, American Music, Yale School of Music.

———. 1994. *Studies in Musicology II, 1929–1979.* Ed. Ann M. Pescatello. Berkeley: University of California Press.

———. n.d. "Foreword." In "Principia Musicologica." Ms. Box 51, Charles Seeger Archives, Music Division, Library of Congress, Washington, D.C.

Straus, Joseph N. 1995. *The Music of Ruth Crawford Seeger.* Cambridge: Cambridge University Press.

Tick, Judith. 1990. "Dissonant Counterpoint Revisited: The First Movement of Ruth Crawford's String Quartet." In *Words and Music in Honor of H. Wiley Hitchcock.* Ed. Richard Crawford, R. Allen Lott, and Carol Oja. 405–22. Ann Arbor: University of Michigan Press.

2

The American Composer in the 1930s:
The Social Thought of Seeger and Chávez

Leonora Saavedra

In March 1934 Charles Seeger published the article "On Proletarian Music" in the New York journal *Modern Music* (Seeger 1934). As a member of the Composers Collective of New York, Seeger was involved at that time with composing music for the working class. A few months later Carlos Chávez published in the Mexican newspaper *El Universal* three articles in which he analyzed the role of music and the composer in society: "El Arte en la Sociedad," "El Arte Occidental," and "El Arte Proletario" (Chávez 1934a, 1934b, 1934c). These articles were intended to prepare the audience for the performance of *Llamadas,* his proletarian symphony for workers' chorus and orchestra, at the opening of Mexico's Palacio de Bellas Artes on September 29, 1934. In these essays Seeger and Chávez addressed from their own perspectives a number of issues concerning the social role of the composer of Western art music within a class society and the problem of composing for the nonruling classes.

The publication of these articles a few months apart is more than a puzzling coincidence. As composers of Western art music in America,[1] Seeger and Chávez confronted a similar set of problems and perspectives. For example, their concern for the role of music and the composer in society had its origins primarily in the need both felt for a personal compositional style and technique, and secondarily in the lack of an audience for the new, more personal type of music they attempted to create.

In attempting to solve this problem both distanced themselves from the European musical tradition. Partly because of the social consciousness prevalent in the artistic milieu to which they belonged and partly because of their personal tendency to comprehend phenomena within a broad historical perspective, Seeger and Chávez developed a notion that musics are culture bound and, eventually, that American composers should create a music of their own, culturally and socially rooted. They both turned to social analysis to understand their individual roles and developed consequently a philosophy of history and a theory of historical change that helped them carve for themselves, theoretically at least, a potential place in music history. In order to accomplish this they needed to develop a series of theoretical tools and models that clarified and guided their activities, not only as composers, but, equally important, as critics and public functionaries. Although they were not always able to apply these models successfully, many of the ideas that were part of their social thought in the 1930s remained important concepts in their subsequent theoretical work, even after their particular concerns changed and their attitude toward social causes became less militant.

~

In the 1920s a number of American artists made pilgrimages to Europe, seeking not only new artistic directions but also the feeling of belonging to a rich intellectual tradition (Howe 1966; Pells 1973; Susman 1966, 1970). Most returned, paradoxically, with an incipient consciousness that the tradition they sought to emulate and had regarded as universal was in fact a local one. The Western European tradition was itself undergoing a crisis that helped artists in the Americas to demystify it. American artists found an explanation for and a solution to this paradox in the development of two forceful ideas. One pertained to the inescapable interrelatedness of things, so that culture was now viewed as consisting not only of art but of all the things the inhabitants of a common geographical area do, the ways they do them, and the ways they think and feel about them, their values, and their symbols. The second one, related to the first, was the idea that specific cultures do produce specific forms of art. This idea eventually resulted in a call for the creation of a "national" culture for the American countries, whose characteristics should be recognizable as such by the majorities. Thus artists were faced with the problem of determining how to produce an American culture and what and how much to preserve from the mother culture (Seeger 1962:22; Chávez 1924b). One possible answer to this question was to insert art in its social milieu, a milieu that would be the source of its legitimacy and of its difference.

The need for art to belong culturally—and therefore socially—was complicated by the feeling that artists of the time had that society itself either was disintegrating into its component parts, as in the United States during the Depression, or else had already disintegrated and now required a new social order, as in postrevolutionary Mexico. The question thus was raised of how artists and intellectuals might function socially and politically in an environment that affected them deeply but provided them with no stable role. In the late 1920s and early 1930s intellectuals in both countries, guided by a new belief in the active social power of art and culture, sought radical alternatives to the economic programs and the political, social, and artistic preoccupations that had prevailed since the turn of the century. Socialism, radical political thought tinted with Marxism, and Communist organizations seemed to free American artists of their historical isolation from public affairs, giving them the feeling of being affiliated with a progressive force, the working class, through which they could make an impact on society at large. The Communist Party of the United States became a significant social force by organizing and sponsoring cultural groups, while in Mexico both the Communist Party and the government provided artists with meaningful social roles by encouraging the development of styles that might inculcate in the minds of peasants and workers a consciousness of their history and social class.

Besides sharing with many other artists in Mexico and the United States the awareness of being at an artistic and historical crossroad, Seeger and Chávez also shared in part the artistic milieu of New York in the late 1920s and early 1930s.[2] They both published in and presumably read the journal *Modern Music*. Chávez's music was performed by the League of Composers and other new music organizations in the United States and was regularly reviewed in that journal by, among others, Marc Blitzstein, who was also a member of the Composers Collective. They had several friends in common, including Aaron Copland, who occasionally attended the Composers Collective's meetings, and Henry Cowell, who had been Seeger's student and introduced him to the collective. Seeger's acquaintance with Chávez's music, which he reviewed often for various publications, dates from the 1920s (appendix 1). Their working relationship and friendship, if not tight, would go on until at least the late 1940s. In the early 1930s they communicated concerning their common interest in experimenting with new methods of teaching composition and in developing a specifically American way of composing modern fine-art music (appendix 2). But even though they shared a circle of friends with strong social ideas, it has not been documented if Seeger and Chávez ever exchanged their thoughts on proletarian music or if they read each other's essays on this topic. However, in 1934 both Cowell and Seeger received copies of Chávez's proletarian symphony, *Llamadas* (appendix 3).

Most important, Seeger in the United States and Chávez in Mexico were both confronted with a similar initial set of contradictions. In the first place they were increasingly aware of the elitist nature of the musical tradition in which they had been trained, and both knew that in the lives of the masses on the continent this tradition played a very small role. On the other hand, they were conscious of the widening distance between the language of modern composers and the taste of the bourgeoisie, who historically had been their audience. Both phenomena contributed to their social isolation and pushed them into thinking in terms of the relationship of music to social groups within a single society. Second, both believed in the value of technical expertise as well as in the high quality of the music composed within the Western fine-art tradition, and each was convinced that this quality would eventually become apparent to whomever approached it, including the working class. Yet each had to face the fact that the tradition in which they had been trained was undergoing a crisis due to the expansion and gradual abandonment of the tonal system, and neither was comfortable with the alternatives offered by the new trends that had emerged.

Confronted with this set of contradictions, both men wrote between 1923 and 1934 several texts in which they analyzed the problems of modern composition in America (Seeger 1923, 1930, 1932, 1994; Chávez 1924a, 1924b, 1925, 1928, 1929a). The main leitmotivs in these writings are the importance of compositional technique; the different alternatives to nineteenth-century European romanticism that were available to a modern composer; the relationship between technique and inspiration (in the process of composition) and between technique and emotion—content, value—(in the moment of listening or of criticism); a transformation of the methods for teaching composition; and finally, for Chávez the relationship with the public and for Seeger the problem inherent in teaching and talking about music by means of the spoken language. Understanding the concerns and ideas of Seeger and Chávez at this time is indispensable for understanding their work on music and society within the global context of their theoretical discourses.

Between 1929 and 1930 Seeger finished writing a text that was a product of his composition lessons, "Tradition and Experiment in (the New) Music" (Seeger 1994). It was divided into two parts, a speculative treatise on musical composition and a manual on dissonant counterpoint. Seeger did not publish this work as a whole, but parts of it were reworked and published as articles for journals and encyclopedias (see Pescatello 1994b:10). In his introduction Seeger assessed the options available to a young composer. In his view the great romantic tradition of nineteenth-century Europe underwent a revision in the period 1900–1914 through a series of small revolutions. In 1930 he saw three main parties of composers, which he defined in terms of their approach to a dichotomy that would worry him at this time and ever after: their compositional technique and the values embodied in their music. These parties were the neoclassicists, who "would have us either reject a good deal of the new material or else cast it into historical similarities" and for whom "objectivity" and "lack of expression" are the catchwords; the neoromanticists, who "wish to feel free to use ordinary material, but draw the line at any systematization of it" and who "wish 'soul,' 'spirit,' 'meaning,' 'intention' to be mystical determinants of technical and critical procedure"; and finally a third group, "which presents no uniform front and is therefore difficult to name." Seeger presented the first two parties as the conservative ones "who wish to revive practices partly abandoned" and the third one as "the more radical element, which wishes to concentrate upon a further development of the innovations already established" (1994:52). Seeger had a hard time describing the values present in the music of this last group.

For Seeger experiment in the radical group's *manner* of composition had produced an embarrassment of technical riches that nobody was able to master. Each individual composer or group had emphasized the development of just a few of the six music resources (pitch, timbre, dynamics, accent, proportion, and tempo), thus creating an imbalance that needed to be corrected in order to produce a true grand *style* out of several manners (for his definition of "style" and "manner" see Seeger 1923: 423). Despite his criticism of the radical group, Seeger avowedly sided with them (Seeger's comments on the treatise are quoted in Pescatello 1994b:10) and agreed with their aims as he described them: "if we are to hear a new music comparable to the music of Palestrina, Bach, and Beethoven, it will be less through a musical pre-Raphaelite movement or timorous anti-intellectualism than through a systematic overhauling of all the elements in the situation—materials, methods and values" (Seeger 1994:52).

Seeger had the intellectual habit, in his theoretical discourse, of describing phenomena in terms of dichotomies, and more often than not his prescription and his prediction for the future was for there to be a balance between the two elements of the dichotomy. At the time of the treatise on composition, Seeger was interested in achieving a series of balances—between tradition and experiment, between the different resources of music, and between precept and imitation in teaching composition and in the traditions of writing music and of talking about it that correspond to imitation and precept (Seeger's interest in balance is described in Greer 1994). Finally, Seeger was very concerned with finding a balance between "objectivity" and "personal expression," between "mysticism, emotionalism and aestheticism" and the logical and rational (see Seeger's objections to Joseph Schillinger's *System of Musical Composition,* quoted in Greer 1994:37). Seeger gave the "welling up of strivings" of the romanticists 50 percent of the credit in any composition and wrote: "that it should be systematized is not suggested here. But there is nothing . . . to show that methodical thinking cannot be harmonized with it. Indeed, is it not from men who have both the heart and the head that the greatest art has always come?" (1994:52).

The fact that Seeger did not think that the inspired element of composition should be systematized did not prevent him from theorizing about it since, in his view, equal emphasis should be placed on composing and on valuing what is composed. In 1923 Seeger understood the process of composition to be made up of three stages: a period of prevision (the knowledge of the possibilities of the technique as well as the maturing of critical judgement); a period of vision or inspiration (direct artistic outpouring, partly at least defying analysis in words); and a period of revision in terms of the first process. It is important to note that Seeger lays equal emphasis here on the relevance of technique and of critical judgment. He continues this description of the compositional process with the following paragraph:

> In composition of the intellectual or deliberately methodical type, the second period tends to be dominated by the first and much modified by the latter. In composition of the opposite type, it tends to dominate the others. Thus Schoenberg's music even at its best (and a great deal of Bach) is something we admire. It satisfies our curiosity and stimulates our intellectual life. But it does not stimulate a lively emotional reaction, and, as an afterthought, we often blush that we 'like' music that moves us so little. And so, Puccini, even at his best moments, stirs our vitals—we grow

hot and cold, feel tears and choking sensations—but after it is over we are apt to have contempt for ourselves having been moved by what we cannot admire. (1923:428)

A combination of these two extremes—Seeger thought—has been present before in all grand styles, but rarely when, as in the present times, there is no great style.

That paragraph is significant for what it reveals about one of Seeger's concerns at the time: the role of critical judgement in composition and the inevitable problem of having to use speech to talk about music. Indeed in that paragraph Seeger starts by talking about music as it is being composed and concludes by talking about music as it is perceived or judged in criticism. For Seeger the interplay between emotion and reason, musical technique and musical value, takes place in a continuum that goes from the compositional process to the music, to the perception of music, and finally to its criticism in speech. Composers, in the very act of composition and in their works, make a statement in the language of music about technique and about musical value; not only do they make critical judgments as they go, but what they compose embodies value: "musical fact and musical value, then, do exist and are expressed in music primarily as musical technique and musical style." However, "they have to be spoken about as two separate things because language cannot present them, as music does, as one thing" (1994:64). This continuum then exists alongside two others, one in which musical fact and musical value go from being an inseparable entity to being separate, and a second one that goes—to put it in Seegerian terms—from that which cannot be spoken about to that about which we must and should speak in criticism.

To summarize, modern compositional technique should be balanced by equally developing all musical resources. However, the crisis in modern composition, as Seeger saw it, was not only of technique but also of musical values and of valuing. He examined this crisis in some detail in his article on Carl Ruggles: "The fundamental critical desideratum has been stated, namely, the achievement of the grandeur, the complete convincingness, the sublimity that inheres in the best work . . . the technical means by which the material of an art which has in recent years drifted so far from such an ideal is to be re-induced to its service, is interesting and involves critical determinations throughout the process" (1932:584). Therefore composers as they compose and especially as they revise their compositions should exercise continuous critical judgment of the values of their music and ask themselves "is this good, is this beautiful, is this sublime?" while trying to find the adequate technical means to express these values. This continuous valuing is also the task of the composition teacher and of the critic and must regrettably be done in speech. This Seeger would later call the "linguocentric predicament." One of the tasks that he saw for himself from this point on in his life was to carry on a critique of the technical and the critical nomenclature about music and to elaborate a theory of musical fact and musical value, which he started in the first part of "Tradition and Experiment in (the New) Music." In the next few years Seeger would increasingly put the blame for this crisis of valuing not so much on the musical valuing of the composer himself as on the lack of exalted values in society in general. In the writings of his "proletarian period" he would try to find through social analysis a cause, an explanation, and a solution to both the linguocentric predicament and the crisis of content and technique in modern composition.

In examining Chávez's "pre-proletarian" writings, it is important to note that he was largely self-taught. He resented Western European music, which was presented as being the only model of real beauty in music, and Western European compositional technique, which was presented as *the* technique of music. In a series of articles written in what Seeger would surely call a rhapsodic tone (Chávez 1925, 1928, 1929d, 1929e, 1932a, 1932c), he objected to a system of teaching composition in which composing was equated with applying rules for harmonic and melodic writing derived from styles that had been created and exhausted in themselves, whether those of Palestrina, Wagner, or Schoenberg. He revered an artist's individuality and his ability to learn and detach himself from tradition, and he valued, for example, Varèse's originality over Schoenberg's craftsmanship (1925). Chávez's main concern in the early 1920s was thus the development of a consistent compositional technique, one that would be unique to him.

Chávez believed in perfect congruence between technique and content: "Technique is nothing more than the vivid result of a particular idea. If the idea changes, the technique is compelled to change with it. Technique is, in fact, the idea itself converted into stable value" (1928:29). Like Seeger (1923:423) he believed in the organic development of a composition out of basic material: "External form unfolds from the center of a work of art; the whole inner substance, when objectified, is nothing more than the external form. . . . The means of objectifying works of art are tangible sounds . . . and their attributes. The strength, the singular energy of these means lies precisely in the degree of perfection to which they develop all that is contained in the internal substance" (Chávez 1928:28). But unlike Seeger he did not think that the breach between experimental composition and the existing music theory could be bridged. Chávez thought that compositional technique was individual, something not to be learned by precept or even by imitation, but by the sheer exercise of a musician's creativity as he worked with music's tools and materials: "Let [the apprentice] see the elements of the problem; secondly, let him be helped to set it for himself, to perceive the different forms possible and to visualize the different results. But let him in no way be taught to solve the problem. The known devices and rules for solution lead to results that are too much alike. . . . The potentialities of the materials and the use of tools are infinite" (1928:31).

In the late 1920s Chávez turned to social analysis to explain how people's need for a theory on music making was a result of music having become a product that meets a social demand: "When man first made music it was out of a spontaneous necessity that resulted and was satisfied in musical terms. Later music developed into a custom, thus meeting a permanent demand. It was after this happened that it became a product—and then there arose all the problems of producing music. Facing the need for a more developed music, the musician sought increasing knowledge of those elements and processes required to solve the initial problem" (1928:30).

Chávez's conception of music as a social product corresponding to a social demand moved sharply to the center of his artistic and social concerns when in 1928 he returned to Mexico City after almost a decade of lengthy sojourns in Europe and in New York. Indeed he realized that 70 percent of Mexico City's professional musicians—the potential performers of his music—were in virtual unemployment, in a world in which public concerts of art music were almost nonexistent (1929d). In his own description Chávez found most of the urban population drawn to light forms of popular music of little quality; they were not at all interested, understandably, in the music of the professional French- and German-trained composers but equally were not ready for experimental fine-art music of the sort he was trying to write. He faced, in short, a world lacking the audience that, as he would later say, made the existence of composers and other professional musicians socially necessary and justifiable.

Chávez at first made plans to return to New York. But after ten years of civil war Mexico was in need of strong cultural leaders, and he instead became conductor of the newly created Symphony Orchestra of Mexico and accepted appointments to be director and composition teacher of the

National Conservatory and, a few years later, head of the Department of Fine Arts of Mexico's Ministry of Education. Chávez saw these appointments as an opportunity to build a rich musical life into which he hoped most of the country's population would be drawn. In 1929 he diagnosed Mexico's musical needs as follows: all social classes must be taken into consideration; musical production must be in agreement with society; good professional performers should be trained in schools; the musical taste of the average audience should improve; and a larger audience should be built who would benefit spiritually from art and would render inevitable the existence of professional musicians (1929d).

Chávez started focusing on art as a social good, such as food or clothes, or, as a political economist and certainly a Marxist would say, as a commodity with a potential exchange value because of its use value (1932b). He increasingly conceived the interplay between music and musical life in terms of a free market: music is a product that must satisfy a need, which in turn must grow if there is to be more music. He hoped that state-sponsored institutions such as the National Conservatory would produce good musicians, closely in touch with the educational and spiritual needs of all social classes, and would facilitate the circulation of musical goods to all the population, thus stimulating an increase in the demand. On the other hand, he thought that performers and composers should not survive if what they produced was not what society needed.

Concerning Mexican music itself, Chávez saw a multiplicity of musical needs and an embarrassment of riches in genres and styles (1929e, 1930b). He observed the disparity between the foreignness of music in the tradition of Western fine art and the immediacy of Mexican folk music. He saw the advantages and shortcomings of both and concluded that neither of them was truly representative of what Mexico was (1930b). Unlike Seeger, who thought that the problem with modern music was one of balancing value-as-content and technique, Chávez left this problem to the individual composer and worried instead about how the composer was to produce music that had a true social function and thus met the spiritual needs of a whole country. His concern then shifted from the development of a personal style to that of a national style. He set himself to the task of composing and teaching others how to compose music that could speak to the majority: peasants, Indians, and workers, as well as the middle classes. However, it was by no means clear how and why conservatory-trained composers could be the spokespersons for all social classes. His analytical skills focused sharply on understanding the historical process by which things had become the way they were and on finding the theoretical and practical solution to the predicament in which fine-art music in Mexico seemed to be.

Seeger's immersion in social analysis was also the result of being personally confonted by his own social role as a composer. At Berkeley in the teens he had encountered social misery, political agitation, and socialism. He had also faced personal conflict because of his political beliefs and had had shortly thereafter a psychological breakdown that he eventually overcame. In the 1920s he gave up composition even though he continued to teach it. Among his composition students was Ruth Crawford, later his second wife, who played a major role in the writing of the composition treatise at the end of the decade (Pescatello 1994a:19–21). Seeger's divorce from his first wife, Constance, and his relationship with Crawford led among other things to the termination of his teaching engagement at what would later become the Juilliard School of Music. As he would say many years thereafter: "by about 1932 or 1933, an event of importance happened in which this compositional interest, the teaching interest, the musicological interest, the social situation and the concern with the misery of people, the increasing disillusionment with teaching, the very sharp decrease in my personal income, and of course a number of lesser strands, all became focused in one point" (1972:209–10). Cowell introduced him to a group of composers who were "trying to do something about the Depression," recalling "the days in Berkeley when we [Seeger and Cowell] thought that we were to blame because we couldn't connect our music with the social situation" (ibid.).

The regular members of the Composers Collective and their occasional visitors represented a considerable portion of the talented, professionally trained New York–based composers of the United States in the 1930s.[3] Some of them were already well known, and many were also members of, or had their music performed by, organizations of composers and performers that aimed to turn contemporary composition in the United States into a major and legitimate cultural force. From a political standpoint the composers regarded their music as a weapon in class struggle; as composers, however, political music gave them an opportunity to be anchored in the social reality of their country. Seeger and Ruth Crawford took the collective, in his own words, very seriously. Years later Seeger would spell out the connection between his activities at the collective and his previous concern for modern composition: "The upshot of the situation was that both Ruth and I felt that here was the missing link in the book ['Tradition and Experiment in (the New) Music'] that

I had written. The book that I had written was predicated on the valid-ity of a theory of composition which was entirely intrinsic to music—that is, oblivious to any extrinsic influences. I had indicated in the preface of the book that of course outside events did influence music, but we hadn't the slightest idea how" (1972:211). As Seeger has declared, Communism in the United States in the 1930s had around it the aura of early Bolshe-vism, which proclaimed the need for experimentation in all the arts. Contemporary technique was revolutionary in itself. Thus the compos-ers in the collective devoted themselves to writing music for the work-ing class, even picketing songs, using dissonant chords or complicated rhythms (ibid.:213). With this perspective Seeger once again took up composition.

Again, Seeger's activities within the Composers Collective and Chá-vez's at the head of Mexico's musical institutions were then mostly the result of intense reflection on an artistic crisis and therefore did not take place in an intellectual vacuum. On the contrary they were complemented by a program of essays and other written documents in which each, push-ing forward his social analysis, sought the theoretical clarity he seemed to need in order to act. In these writings Seeger and Chávez borrowed a number of concepts from Marxism or from Marxist-oriented theories. First, Marxism provided both Seeger and Chávez with a theory that ac-counted for how society is structured and how its different parts relate to each other, thus allowing them to find within this social structure a place for themselves and for their bourgeois and proletarian audiences. Second, the Marxist concept of human society as a comprehensible whole leads to the view of art as a product of society and one determined to an extent by the characteristics of the society that produces it. For Seeger and Chávez this concept implied too that different kinds of societies produce different kinds of art with different social functions and, to carry the analysis further, that different social groups or classes within the same society produce different kinds of art. They therefore saw in class soci-ety an explanation for the elitist nature of fine-art music and for the breach between them and a broader audience. Finally, Marxism, a true offspring of nineteenth-century German philosophy, also claims, as Seeger recog-nized, that society evolves in an ordered series of events and processes that allow, if understood correctly, the prediction of the outcome of cer-tain historical situations (Seeger 1934:121). Since Seeger and Chávez were both prone to understanding phenomena in their historical perspective and to speculating on further developments, this notion was useful to them in assessing the role they felt called to play in the development of both modern music and a larger (proletarian) audience.

Thus with the help of some Marxist-oriented concepts Seeger and Chávez developed in the 1930s their own theory of history and of historical change. Both men held linear, evolutionist notions of history (not incompatible with Marxism) and believed that musical technique "progresses" in accordance with the progress of society. Seeger, for instance, held that "among those tribes whose conditions of economic life seem farthest back in the evolutionary scale from us the arts seem to be least developed" (1935:22).[4] Similarly Chávez believed that people had progressed from using pentatonic scales to the diatonic system and then to scales with ever smaller intervals (his main formulation of a theory of historical change in the use of scales is in Chávez 1937). On the other hand, both dreamed of a bygone golden era of tribal societies in which social organization had been communal, with music holding an important and generalized social function and the making and employment of musical objects being closely integrated in their social production and use. Significantly in these societies professional musicians did not exist as a separate social group, or at least there had been no significant difference between the music made by professionals and that practiced by the people.

Both Seeger and Chávez projected onto these idealized societies a state of affairs that they wished would return. In ancient Greek and Aztec societies, argued Chávez, art played a political role that is now lost. In one and the same social class, the art practiced by its members is considered as their own by them, while every other art is foreign (1929b). In a society without classes such as (so Chávez believed) the Greek or the Aztec, art is by definition only of one kind, that which is practiced by professionals and amateurs alike. An artist is then first among equals. His art is at the service of the rites and public celebrations of society, which identifies with this art because it is the expression of collective life (1929c). Chávez notes that for the same reason "among the ancient Mexicans music was not an individual expression indispensable to the life of the spirit but a concern of an entire state organization" (1962:170).

Seeger, in turn, returned to "primitive cultures" in order to understand the process by which one art, language, in which average individuals have phenomenal proficiency, dominates individual and social life and predominates over another, music, which performs a function far inferior in scope and power. The person of primitive cultures, Seeger stressed, is a well-rounded individual, not a worker specializing in one field to the exclusion of others (1935:22), and "the arts are integral elements in the work, play, ritual, etc. of the group. What we call the two arts of music and language are virtually one process. (Demand the singing of the melody without the words or vice versa—it cannot be done). Similarly, there is little or no distinction between the idiom [language or music] in general use and the set construction or art-work in it" (1935:24). This last concept was especially important for Seeger: in this ideal, primitive world musical products (set constructions) would be socially integrated as an undifferentiated part of everyday music language, and therefore all the people would be equally proficient in producing music. Thus, in a society in which music would not have a separate social function, there would be no need to value music in terms of speech.

A very different situation arises within a class society. Both Seeger and Chávez understood music making as music production and considered the appearance of professional musicians the result of the social division of labor. But, being Americans trying to understand cultures that resulted from the clash of societies already with a differentiated class structure, Seeger and Chávez understood *class* society as a result only of the coming together of two separate cultures through war, trade, or intermarriage, and ignored Marxist theories that propose that the appearance of different social classes within the same society is in itself due to social division of labor and to the development of technology and increase in production rate in some of the labor areas (Seeger 1935:22–23, Chávez 1929e; cf. Engels 1962:302–27). Thus they hardly ever questioned class society in itself, and their analyses remained at a superstructural level.

These two separate cultures and their arts may exist side by side quite intact for a long time, claims Seeger, and the music of the ruling culture will tend to center in seats of government while that of the more primitive strains tends to spread over the countryside. Eventually hybrid forms will tend to crop up in the intermediate localities and among different new classes. Seeger conceived the process of acculturation between the different kinds of idioms in a continuum going from primitive strains to folk or country, to popular or city, to professional or refined art (1935:23–24). This theory, of course, is extremely schematic and simple, but in it Seeger begins to associate musical idioms with geographical areas, social groups, and social functions and to conceive of these factors as the main determinants of the idiom practiced by a group or an individual.

Concerning the art of urban workers in the twentieth century, Seeger describes the situation as follows: "The first generation drawn into the factories brought with it more or less well-established peasant or folk cultures, including language and music idioms and a repertory of set constructions in them. But the children of these immigrants knew little of, and cared less for, this culture. The life was too hard to admit much time for its pursuit and it was obviously unsuited to the changed conditions of industrial struggle. The third generation lost all trace of their ancestral folk heritage yet no new thing rose to take its place . . . popular arts [are] characterized by all the weaknesses and none of the strength of professional art" (1935:28).

Like Seeger, Chávez understood the multiplicity of regional types of music in Mexico as the result of the encounter of the European and Indian cultures. This multiplicity was not only due to differences in social class and ethnic background, but also to strictly musical factors. With European music came the predominance of the major and minor scales over the pentatonic music of the Indians (Chávez 1930a). None of the surviving strands of either one, he says, stands for the true collective art, which will only come from a balance between the different types of music. Chávez disapproved of popular, urban art. He regarded it as being generated by the bourgeoisie, whose moral condition it reflected and who used it as an instrument to impose its tastes, habits, and beliefs upon the ruled classes. But, unlike Seeger at this time, he acknowledged the existence of a rich tradition underlying Mexican peasant and Indian art, and he did believe that peasants are prolifically creative and produce art that is not only of great beauty, but also functional, in immediate fulfillment of a social need. The problem with their art, Chávez writes, is that it suffers from the same limitations and miseries under which they suffer as a class (1934c). He admires the vigorous, spontaneous first impulse of this art, but he finds no strong conceptions in it and, faithful to nineteenth-century ideas of the value of organic form, finds no development of its basic material or inner substance. Thus Chávez approaches here Seeger's idea that the crisis in modern composition is partially one of technique, of having to choose from and balance a multiplicity, in this case, of tonal systems in order to develop musically the vigorous first impulse of folk art. Seeger, in turn, concludes that the strong values he misses in modern society are to be found in proletarian art, to the service of which modern technique should be put.

Concerning the composers themselves, both authors argue that the ruling class ceases to produce its own art much as it ceases to produce its other needs, and instead it employs professional artists for this purpose. A high degree of specialization naturally appears in the work of these professionals, whose pieces of fine art establish a new type of social function: the spiritual enrichment of the ruling class at the expense of the working classes. Their works become the property of the ruling classes, who withhold them from the masses. At this point in their theory of historical change, Seeger and Chávez find themselves needing to explain the professional composers' closeness to as well as distance from the ruling class and to find in this very explanation the conceptual tool that will allow them to explain why and how modern composers are to become the artistic spokespersons of the nonruling classes.

In Seeger's view composers belong to the proletariat, the "modern concept" of which he expands to accommodate artists to the point of mistaking a social class for the structural organization of society: "[Proletariat] designates primarily the virtually propertyless members of modern industrial society, especially the workers in the basic industries of production and the agencies of communication, transportation and distribution. These form the essential *structure* of society. But secondarily it comprises many white-collar workers and intellectuals, including musicians and other artists. These form the *superstructure* of society" (1934:121). Compare Seeger's understanding of structure and superstructure with Marx's classic formulation: "In the social production of their life, men enter into definite relations that are indispensable and independent of their will, relations of production which correspond to a definite stage of development of their material productive forces. The sum total of these relations of production constitutes the economic structure of society, the real foundation, on which rises a legal and political superstructure and to which correspond definite forms of social consciousness" (Marx 1962:362–63).

As for music itself, and language, these are employed in class society as media for the production of set constructions (pieces) that now stand apart from the idiom in which they are produced. From this it follows that it is possible for the ruling classes to understand an idiom without being able actually to produce anything in it. Seeger wrote: "The strength of professionalized art is found in the works of exceptional mastery that were possible only under the conditions of exceptional specialization. The weakness of this art is found in the fact that its social function involves well-rounded, complete musical activity on the part of a mere handful of exceptional poets and musicians. . . . The great majority of people who come in contact with this art are involved in a one-sided, incomplete musical activity—they listen . . . only. Thus professionalized art and its pale reflection, popular art, take on the character of commodities, produced for consumers who are not themselves producers" (1935:28–29).

The idea that pieces of music can become independent from the idiom in which they are produced and that the technique involved in their production is a matter that eventually concerns only those who produce them becomes the theoretical tool that enables Seeger to condemn bourgeois fine-art music socially without compromising his belief in the value of technical expertise—and therefore to justify his attempts and those of the collective to compose music for the proletariat. Seeger's idea of the historical importance for a social group of making its own music is in itself certainly one of his most valuable insights and one that proved to be very useful to him in his later work on the relationship between musical styles—or idioms—and social groups.

Proceeding from this analysis, Seeger offered the following historical explanation for the state of affairs he had described in the introduction to his treatise on composition. As music ceased to be the generalized language that most of society had been able to use and as the ruling classes, unable to make their own music, no longer shared the idiom of the contemporary composers, these composers started alienating themselves from society and produced a "rebel musical art" that obviously no longer reflected the values of the bourgeoisie. Since the producers of music are drawn from the ruled classes, elements hostile to the purposes of the ruling classes may creep into the little understood fabrics of the nonlinguistic arts. As a result musical technique was able to continue to travel the "revolutionary paths" that had once been followed by the bourgeoisie as a rising class and "a basic contradiction set up between the stabilized and the still revolutionary factors. . . . By 1914, both in language and in music, the vanguard of the bourgeois art was in many ways completely out of line with prevailing developments in economic, political and social theory and practice. The music especially lost support and was in a fair way to dying" (Seeger 1935:27–28).

Although revolutionary and full of promise, contemporary technique reflects conflicting tendencies between form and content, skill and taste, and technique and value, and no composer can use it as a comparatively balanced whole. Partly caused by and partly causing a preoccupation with technical detail, content in composers' music has, in Seeger's words, "been lost sight of." He believed that composers no longer exercise critical judgment in terms of the values they want their music to embody, and when they do, they concentrate on the criticism of a few musical resources. He further maintained that contemporary composers are unable to express values such as the grand and the sublime because these values do not characterize the social system in which they and their art flourish (1932:580, 1934:123).

Since the ruled classes, in turn—Seeger erroneously thought—lost with industrial society their own musical heritage around the turn of the twentieth century, the "music-hungry" masses offer the professional musician a new audience, unrivaled in size and in potential for development (1935:30). The proletariat, on the other hand, knows what kind of content it wishes to have in the music it hears but lacks the musical technique needed to express it. In this situation, writes Seeger, "the obvious thing to do is to connect the two vital trends—proletarian content and the forward looking technic of contemporary art music. It can be done and is being done" (1934:125). Thus Seeger saw in this connection the solution to two crucial problems confronting composers: the lack of an audience and the crisis in twentieth-century compositional value.

Seeger saw two possible ways of relating music to the working class, ways in which some of his leitmotivs can be recognized. Since the ruled classes have been exploited "very largely by linguistic techniques . . . [they] must fight for their freedom partly with language, but . . . with a special kind of language, namely, one that definitely puts limits upon itself" (1935:30). Language, therefore, must be checked by, among other things, "the linguistic study of music—musicology—which must be made to bend its efforts to the freeing, rather than the further imprisonment, of music by language" (ibid.:31). The second way to which Seeger points in this article is "through increasing musical activity by the masses for their own ends" (ibid.).

Seeger's theory of how music functions in class society had a counterpart in practice. In 1934 he attempted to predict the outcome of the historical situation in which he was immersed, and conceived a three-period process whereby society would evolve from having music *for* the proletariat to having music *of* the proletariat (1934:122–26). He then set himself to some self-appointed tasks in this process. For example, in the already emergent first period, the proletariat hears and performs great bourgeois music of the kind that embodies proletarian, revolutionary values. In the 1930s Seeger contributed as a critic under the pseudonym of Carl Sands to the newspaper the *Daily Worker.* Many of his contributions were meant to be a guide for composers and workers to those values that were suitable to be retained from bourgeois music and those that needed to be found in the music for the working class. Thus, in criticizing both the technique and the values of the music he reviewed, he fully embraced what he must have perceived at that time as the social role of the critic.

As it has been remarked, Seeger used words such as "grand," "strong," "sublime," and "tumultuous" to describe these values and condemned "the morbidity, the servile melancholy, the frenetic sexuality, the day-dreaming flight from reality that permeates much of the music of the nineteenth-century" (1934:123). Seeger used these terms in a rather schematic and propagandistic way. But propaganda was hardly Seeger's only aim. In light of Seeger's lifelong preoccupation with value, these articles take on a different dimension. Seeger truly believed in the importance of valuing, and he did not shrink from the difficulty of doing it, and doing it in speech. Valuing and reflecting on valuing was for Seeger the only way of coming to terms with this problem: "Criticism has not the objectivity of science nor the subjectivity of mysticism. Its task is to mediate between the two. . . . Broadly speaking its method is the reverse of the method of science. It starts with the assumption of *principles*. These are statements in the form 'such-and-such is valuable' or 'good,' 'right,' 'great' . . . terms with opposites such as 'bad,' 'wrong,' 'small'. . . . When particular instances of music-making are referred to these principles, statements of *opinion* may be made; but these, like working hypotheses of science, must have authoritative acceptance before they can be accepted as judgements or dicta" (1994:62–63). Thus what he was searching for in those articles was in the end what he would later call "arbitrage general": common sense and social consensus.

In the second period—which was just beginning in the 1930s and overlapped the first—professional composers, such as Seeger himself and other members of the collective, would compose new music for the proletariat to perform, thus modifying, at least in theory, the social function of professional music. Thus the collective's compositions were to serve as a link "from above down," to use Seeger's terminology, between this idiom and the workers while the workers' own musical activity may be seen as a link "from below up"—and certainly one in agreement with Seeger's idea of the importance for social groups of being musically competent. In this sense the musical activity of the workers' organizations and the role of the collective in them can be considered as an interesting historical experiment in attempting to build new social conditions in which fine-art music would be consumed, therefore transforming its social function.

The third period, according to Seeger, would be that of the music of the proletariat in which content would predominate. It was therefore to be expected that its first stages would show "the usual phenomena of technical crudity." Seeger concludes "On Proletarian Music" with an interesting account of the dialectics of technique and content and their relationship to other realms of the superstructure. At the end of the third period, he says, general revolutionary content "becomes associated with a new technique, that technique develops in a new way and in turn throws a new light on the generalized notions of content. This new light—musical revolutionary content—reacts again upon the general content. In this two-way relationship, technique and content become identified and then we have art products of the highest type" (1934:126).

In 1934 Seeger described the music of the collective and the performances of it by workers in New York in terms that can only be judged excessively optimistic (1934:125). In fact, as Seeger would later admit in his "Reminiscences of an American Musicologist," the working-class audiences of the 1930s had a hard time recognizing this music as their own (1972:219). It would be incorrect, however, to surmise that the composers of the collective were unconcerned with the technical difficulties their music presented to its intended performers and audiences. Indeed Seeger intimated that the collective had a method of sorts for dealing with such difficulties. Already in "On Proletarian Music" he urged that "if something unusual is done in one department it is wise to risk little in others at that time" (1934:125). Similarly he later recalled that "[This] was one of the things we tried to do in the Collective: to use ordinary fragments of technique in an unusual way, because we thought that was revolutionary and therefore suitable for the workers to use. We didn't give them those same patterns in the usual way, which was what Broadway did . . . we took those same formulas, simply used them differently, and hoped that we were doing something revolutionary. Lots of the compositions . . . had unusual harmonic progressions in them, but usual chords. Or if there were some unusual chords, they put them in conventional patterns" (quoted in Dunaway 1980:164).

Unlike Seeger, Chávez did not try to account for the contradiction that may be perceived between the works of professional composers and the values of the bourgeoisie for which they are produced. In the three articles written just before the performance of his proletarian symphony in 1934, Chávez tried to find in Marxist-inspired social analysis the theoretical justification for the new role he advocated for composers. Given Mexico's nascent new social order, he felt compelled to justify the need for art in itself. Thus he stated that art is a human product and, giving a curious twist to Engels's statement on freedom as man's knowledge of his own needs, that art is a product that contributes to man's freedom in that it contributes to culture and to man's mastery of his own environment (Chávez 1934a). Concerning the music itself, Chávez was content to write that art possesses something that allows it to transcend its social origins (a concept with which Marx would have agreed) and safeguard its nobility from moral corruption at the hands of the bourgeoisie (1934b). On the other hand, finding support in Marx's ideas on the relationship between the economic structure and the political and ideological superstructure of society, Chávez stated that art is not the product of an individual but that it is inevitably determined by the real conditions in which human beings live.[5] An artist, Chávez concluded, is an unconscious spokesman for his culture and that is the way he is acknowledged by the living social mass.

To Chávez, concerned with the development of Mexico's concert life, the main problem of the relationship between the bourgeoisie and professional music appeared to lie in the circulation of musical products, and it was through the understanding of the sociology of music that he would find a theoretical social place and role for the modern composer. Unlike Seeger, Chávez did try to find a reason for the inclusion of composers in the proletariat based on the way composers produce their social life: taking as his point of departure the Marxist definition, again, of work as the activity that creates wealth, Chávez equates workers and artists as the only two creative and productive forces of society. Borrowing Marxist terminology, he states that the artist, being a propertyless worker in capitalist society, is forced to sell his labor power to the bourgeoisie in exchange for a very low salary, and he has no control over the way in which his work is distributed.

The idea that composers are propertyless workers, producers of artistic wealth, allows Chávez to sever their ties to the bourgeoisie and to place them—in his theoretical model—within the proletarian class they now need to serve. He draws two corollaries from this, one pertaining to the area of the circulation of musical products, the other to their production. Fine art, he writes, is deliberately kept away from the masses by the bourgeoisie in an attempt to keep them in an ignorant, spiritually impoverished state (1934c). Chávez, like Seeger, believed that the proletariat should be given the opportunity to be exposed to the most forceful and morally enlightening of the music of the past (the works of Beethoven, for example, and not of Chopin)—which meant becoming acquainted with the tradition of Western fine-art music. The inability of large audiences to appreciate both fine-art music and the artistic innovations of twentieth-century composers was simply a function of their lack of experience with it. With repeated exposure, Chávez believed, the public would gradually develop a taste for it.

Concerning the production of musical objects, Chávez urged composers to develop a class consciousness as propertyless workers, to give themselves the means for the circulation of their products, and, in anticipation of an historical time when society—and also music—would be reunified, to develop the strong original impulse of proletarian art in order to become the vehicles for the expression of collective feeling, giving Mexican music the collective quality it lost with the conquest of the Aztec empire (1934c).

Like Seeger, Chávez saw as fundamental the need to integrate proletarian content (vigor, spontaneity) with contemporary technique. However, in his view the main problem with which composers were confronted involved not matters of content and technique, but the dominance of diatonic-based tonality at the expense of other tonal systems—whether ancient Western or present non-European—that ought to be a part of the cultural heritage of humankind (1930a, 1936:37–38). Chávez thought to find here an opportunity to cut loose from a compositional technique dominated by Western European music. He dreamt of a unified technique in which musical elements from both the "refined" art of Western civilization and that of "primitive" communal societies, especially present-day Mexican Indian, would be drawn together: "It will never be necessary for [the students], for lack of a background of their own, to imitate European musical forms and formulae. It is not that they will go on arranging folk-tunes, or writing music in imitation of folk music. Rather the elements of that music that find response in their own feelings will assist them in creating their own idiom, giving it color and vitality, rhythmic vigor and harmonic variety" (1936:39).

The use of melodic materials from or modeled after Mexican Indian music is only the most superficial manifestation of this syncretic style at which Chávez was aiming. Much more crucial was his attempt to formulate a system for the organization of tonal and harmonic materials based upon the use of non-Western scales, a system that would be his own personal alternative to the disintegration of the tonal system in European music. The rudiments of this system, in which a repertory of harmonic intervals was derived from the melodic intervals of a particular scale, were formulated by Chávez in *Toward a New Music: Music and Electricity* (1937). He organized research centers to provide him and his composition students with information on music, scales, and instruments from "all continents." But faithful to his idea of a hands-on method for teaching composition, Chávez thought that the system would emerge from the composer's own work with melodic and scalar materials and from an acquaintance with European and Mexican Indian musical instruments within the composition workshop at the National Conservatory.

Thus, for Chávez, as for Seeger, the solution to both the crisis in twentieth-century Western music and the lack of a social role for modern composers lay in relating their music in more than one way to the nonruling classes. Like the composers in the collective, Chávez engaged in a series of enterprises from "above down" and "below up." He wrote refined concert pieces based on Mexican Indian scales and using Mexican Indian instruments; he made "unadulterated" concert versions of traditional mestizo music; and he composed simple, Mexican-sounding music for workers' choruses to sing on bourgeois stages. He urged the state to recognize the need for a music that would be by the proletariat and for the proletariat. He started schools in which the working class would learn of class struggle while studying solfège. Finally, through performances with his orchestra, he provided bourgeois and proletarian audiences alike with multiple opportunities for a systematic exposure to twentieth-century music.

These public enterprises did not last long, however. Chávez lost his appointments at the National Conservatory and the Fine Arts Department in 1934 and discontinued his concerts for workers six years later. He did continue at the head of the Symphony Orchestra of Mexico through 1947 and managed to create a large audience for fine-art music. But his audience was a bourgeois one, and even this gradually was lost to several newly founded orchestras with more conventional repertoires. In this sense Chávez's social experiments were a failure. Yet his preoccupation with music within society was the starting point for the development of a refined conception of musical life in terms of demand, supply, and distribution of musical products that would prove to be very useful to him.

As for Seeger, by the late 1930s he as well as other members of the collective were advocating the need for the composers to immerse themselves in the traditional music of the working class in order to produce not only proletarian but true American music. Many of them were consistently using materials from jazz and popular or folk music in their music for the concert hall or the stage. Seeger wrote: "Plainly, if we are to compose for more than an infinitesimal fraction of the American people, we must write in an idiom not too remote from the one most of them already possess—their own musical vernacular. . . . The people of America cannot, and for a long time to come will not be able to make much high art music. . . . If therefore a composer is going to sing the American people anything new, if he is going to celebrate his oneness with them . . . if he is going to teach them that their undoubtedly limited musical tastes and capacities, crippled as they have been . . . can develop to a higher level, he must first get upon a common ground with them, learn their musical lingo, work with it and show he can do for them something they want to have done and cannot do by themselves" (1939:149).

Scholars have often wondered why the composers of the collective did not turn to folk music as a model for their own "protest songs" since all of them had had some exposure to it in the early thirties. Some have tried to find an explanation in the collective's "anti-Americanism" and in the changing attitudes in the Communist Party throughout the decade. Considering, however, that the collective's aim was not only to write music to be used by the proletariat as a weapon in class struggle, but also to relate themselves to society as composers of Western fine-art music and even to alter the social function of professional music in order to help overcome the crisis in modern composition, to compose in the idiom of folk music, which was not composed with the most revolutionary musical technique nor expressed the values Seeger was looking for, was not a possible choice. In this sense the whole experience of the collective was a failure, and for Seeger—as a composer—a real defeat. Writing for the proletariat simply did not provide him with the content or technique he needed, and he soon abandoned composition for good. It was only later through his work as a scholar and cultural administrator that Seeger effectively addressed the social and aesthetic concerns that had arisen in his precollective years.

~

Thus Seeger and Chávez both failed to give fine-art music a new social function and to provide art music composers with a new social role. To an orthodox Marxist the impossibility of radically altering a domain of the superstructure without a previous transformation of the economic structure of society would have been self-evident. Indeed, according to the Marxist theory of historical change, social revolutions occur only when the development of productive forces itself turns social relations into their fetters, and social change is needed to allow this development.

The main problem with the analyses produced by Chávez and Seeger—to stay within the frame of the classic Marxism they seem to have been handling—was their lack of understanding of what the proletariat really is and of the relationship between the economic structure and the superstructure of society. The proletariat is indeed a class that has nothing but its surplus-producing labor power to sell. Since the means of production are the private property of the capitalist class to which labor power is sold, this class retains control over the product and, most important, over the surplus. But composers, poor as they may be, are by no means members of the proletariat. A thorough analysis of the social class to which composers belong would have led Seeger and Chávez to the conclusion that art music composers sell not their labor but their products, and they do so in a free market.

Composers, when they produce, enter in social relations with other people who buy and consume their works, and these relations (and not the people, as Seeger thought) are part of the economic structure of society. But their works themselves, in general, create relatively little surplus and are not appropriated by the ruling classes for the same reasons that these appropriate proletarian labor force (as Chávez thought). Artworks contribute to the creation of social consciousness and are part of an intellectual, social, and political life that reflects and, most important, helps hold in place the specific mode of production of material life—and therefore the social relations—of any given society. Artworks, consequently, belong to the superstructure of society and are ultimately conditioned by the economic structure. The key word here is ideology: in classic Marxism art, not being scientific, is part of an ideology in which the values and beliefs of the ruling class predominate. But Marx himself conceded art a certain degree of independence from the constraints imposed by the economic structure of society, an independence upon which he did not have the time, and probably also not the means, to elaborate. Thus what Seeger and Chávez would have needed is a theory of how the economic structure and the superstructure of society relate to each other and of how the domains that mediate between art and the rest of society are articulated. Neither Marx nor the Marxist theory of their time provided them with such a tool.

Nevertheless, in the course of trying to examine the links between art and society, Seeger and Chávez came to understand music as a social product with a social function rather than as the suprasocial creation of an individual mind. Moreover, they developed something close to a sociology of music in which music products are seen as embedded in and to some extent conditioned by a network of consumers and producers, who belong to specific and sometimes opposed social groups that do use

art to establish relations of power either to each other or to their surroundings.

Chávez's conception of musical life in terms of demand, supply, and
distribution of musical products helped him articulate the premises for
much of his activity within Mexico's musical life in the 1940s, including
the founding of Mexico's National Institute of Fine Arts—still the ruling
institution of its artistic life—and the development of a state-sponsored
model for Mexico's musical life (Saavedra 1989). In any event, Chávez's
writings of the early 1930s allow a better understanding of his search for
a real social function for concert music and for a unified, collective musical style.

In Seeger's case too the experience of his "proletarian period" left a
mark on his subsequent theoretical work. The relationship between the
different musical styles, or idioms, and the different social classes became
the subject of further research for him (1977f [1966], 1977d [1957]). From
his "proletarian period" came some of the criteria that he would continually use to define an idiom: what is the social class or group of the music
makers and consumers? Is the music produced in a style that is technically within the reach of the majority of this group? Do the producers
produce for themselves or for another group? (see, for example, a systematic application of these criteria in the definition of idiom in Seeger 1977b
[1949]). The notion of idiom as related to social classes and social functions, in turn, would become a functional category and a working definition in a number of studies. Then, too, the idea of the historical importance
for a social group to produce its own music recurs throughout his work.
Finally, in his later work on the music of the Americas he developed his
ideas on the interaction between the different musical idioms into a veritable theory of the acculturation between the social groups that were
drawn together on this continent (1977c [1952], 1977e [1961]). To the end
Seeger constantly toyed with the idea of—the prediction of—an American music in which an integration of most idioms would be achieved.

Both Seeger and Chávez were men with acute personal needs and
strong drives to perform a social role. Their creative output, their theoretical work, and their need to transform their surroundings were integrated in a homogeneous whole, such that one cannot be understood at
the expense of the others. In Chávez's case an understanding of stylistic
change in his music and his involvement with nationalism becomes
impoverished when regarded as a matter of aesthetic choice instead of
placing these phenomena within his much broader conception of national art as a system in which national—and not nationalistic—music

is produced, distributed, and consumed by the Mexican people. Like-wise, the trend in recent scholarship on Seeger has been to focus exclu-sively on his scholarly work, especially on those of his writings that make him the founding father of ethnomusicology. And yet his scholarly out-put cannot be fully understood without taking into consideration his original concern for composition, his constant preoccupation with the integration of fine-art music (especially that of the American countries) to society, and those elements in his scholarly output that are closer to a philosophy and to a sociology—rather than to an anthropology—of music. Moreover, from the time of his involvement with writing music for the proletariat on, Seeger never withdrew to a scholarly ivory tower. If his theoretical and critical thinking was so crucial for the understand-ing of his praxis during his "proletarian period," it is to be expected that his scholarly output will not be fully understood unless correlated, for example, with his activities as a public functionary in subsequent years.

Almost every single effort that Chávez and Seeger made to under-stand music involved a criticism that was directed toward its transfor-mation, a transformation that more often than not involved social change. A thorough understanding of Chávez's and Seeger's work will be achieved only in the light of their need for an integration between theory and praxis and between their artistic or scholarly output and their social con-cerns.

APPENDIX 1

From Seeger to Chávez

[Stationary letterhead] Unión Panamericana
Unión de Repúblicas Americanas
Wáshington [*sic*], D.C., E.U.A.
[Typed] August 18, 1943
AIRMAIL

Dear Carlos:

Thank you for your letter of August 10th which arrived this morning. I hasten to tell you that I have already acknowledged receipt of the excellent photograph of the first page of your Piano Sonatina to Mr. Ortega, under date of July 26. It is exactly what I wanted.

You will remember that when you were in Washington we discussed the possi-bility of your sending to the Pan American Union some scores by the younger Mexican composers such as Blas Galindo, Moncayo, etc., so that we could copy the parts and obtain performance in the United States. Our Music Copying Project is in full swing, and I would be glad to have some of these works copied if the composers are agreeable. We would accept the works for copying with the understanding that permission for performance upon non-commercial programs such as those of the Union, of the United States Government, or non-profit institutions, could be taken for granted as given by the composers. We would, however, refer all requests for commercial performance either to the agent of the composer in the United States, or to the composer himself. I would like to say in this connection that when scores and parts are available, performance with a fee is not difficult to obtain. It would be, then, to the advantage of the young composers to have their works handled in this way.

I am especially pleased to print the facsimile of the Piano Sonatina. This is the first work of yours that I became familiar with, and I remember with pleasure your playing it with me in the little room in Greenwich Village some years ago [emphasis added].

With warmest and friendliest greetings,
Your friend
[Signed] Charles Seeger
[Typed] Charles Seeger
Chief

(México, Archivo General de la Nación, Fondo Carlos Chávez, Caja Correspondencia 12, Expediente 53)

APPENDIX 2

From Seeger to Chávez, undated

[Typed] My dear Chávez:
Circumstances may take me to Mexico this summer and I am wondering if there would be any chance of giving a series of lectures upon music either in connection with the Conservatory or independently. My pronunciation is still fairly good and my lectures could be translated ahead of time with the help of my father, who is a good linguist. The titles would run:
 1 Tradition and Experiment in Musical Idiom
 2 Music and Language
 3 Critique
 4 Technique
 5 Consonance and Dissonance
 6 Scale and Mode
 7 Harmony—Tonal and Rhythmic
 8 Form—The Motif
 9 " —The Phrase
 10 " —The Whole

I would stress especially the means by which we may develop in the Americas some independence of European traditions. The material would be for musicians. It is the content of my book which I hope to have published next winter some time—an attempt, the first of its kind, I believe, to lay out a plan for the writing of music in any idiom occidental or oriental so that it will progress from any given point.

Hoping to hear from you and with best regards
[Handwritten] Sincerely Charles Seeger
[Typed] 204 1/2 West 13th St
New York City

∽

From Chávez to Seeger

May 16th, 1932
Mr. Charles Louis Seeger
204 1/2 West 13th. Street,
New York City, N.Y.
U. S. A.

My dear Seeger:

I was very glad to hear from you and learn that you are coming to Mexico this Summer. I think the series of lectures you are planning would be of interest for a group of musicians in this city. The Conservatory will make some arrangements—publicity, hall, programs—in case you care to be presented by us, which we are glad to do. Nevertheless we are not in condition to offer you any fee.

Looking forward to see you soon, I am,
Most cordially yours,
Carlos Chávez.
[Handwritten signature] Ch

(México, Archivo General de la Nación, Fondo Carlos Chávez, Caja Correspondencia 11, Expediente 28)

APPENDIX 3

From Henry Cowell to Chávez

[Stationery letterhead] THE NEW SCHOOL
FOR SOCIAL RESEARCH
66 W TWELFTH ST NEW YORK
[Typed] Oct 12'34

Dear Carlos:

Are you still interested in the idea of a magazine for new musical problems, in Spanish and English? I have been sorry that this idea did not develop better already, and I think that it is time to begin such a periodical. Adolph Weiss is very much interested here, and has the support of experienced literary people; Seeger, Crawford, Riegger and Becker and myself all helping.

I read with great interest that you have composed a Proletarian Symphony. I have enormous interest in writing music for the proletariat, and would like to know whether you have any music suitable for performance here by worker' [sic] chorusus [sic] and clubs? I would like to have it, if you have [emphasis added].

Always warmly yours,
[Handwritten] Henry

∿

From Chávez to Cowell

[Typed] December 12th, 1934
Mr. Henry Cowell,
66 W. 12th Street, New York City, N. Y.
U. S. A.

My dear Henry:

Yes, of course I am still interested in the idea of a magazine in spanish [*sic*] and english [*sic*] for the cause of music. I will, if you like, gladly take care of the spanish [*sic*] part. I wait for your suggestions and details. It will be difficult to count on financial support from Mexico to start with, although I think the magazine may sell, in time, all over Latin America.

I am sending to you my last symphony Llamadas, a proletarian work that is and has been sung already by various hundreds of workers and children [emphasis added]. I will greatly welcome your idea of the work. I am sending to you, also, a collection of seven plates of H. P. just recorded here. It is not yet out for sell [sic] but it will be soon.

Under separate cover you will find my last piece, just written a few days ago, "Spiral," movements for violin and piano, that I am submitting to you for publication in New Music. I would like to hear from you soon to this respect. I have a copy of the orchestral score of H. P. ready. I remember I took up with you the matter of giving you this manuscript for publication in New Music which I did not do before because I did not have the copy ready. Are you still interested in such publication?

I am going on with my work here, always hoping to space the time to go and visit my friends in New York.

With my best wishes to you and hoping to see you soon, perhaps, I am,
Most affectionately yours.
[Signed] Carlos Chávez
[Typed] Carlos Chávez

(México, Archivo General de la Nación, Fondo Carlos Chávez, Caja Correspondencia 3, Expediente 48)

~

From Seeger to Chávez

[Stationery letterhead] Unión Panamericana
Unión de Repúblicas Americanas
Wáshington [*sic*], D.C., E.U.A.
[Typed] December 11, 1945

Dear Carlos:

Thank you for your letter of November 15. In accordance with your wishes, I shall discourage initiation of work upon the band instrumentation of ENERGIA and urge Lt. Thurmond to wait for the publication of your Corrido EL SOL toward whose appearance I look with much interest. Now that we are on this subject, I want to tell you that the Pan American Union has no copy of your LLAMADAS for chorus and orchestra in the edition of the Palacio de Bellas Artes, México, 1934. *You sent a copy to me personally at the time of publication* [emphasis added]. I would gladly have presented this copy to the Union, but I lent it to someone, and the work has never been returned. Do you happen to have a copy you could send us, or, if not, any idea how we could obtain one?

With warm personal regards and the Season's Greetings,
Cordially,
[Signed] Charles Seeger
[Typed] Charles Seeger
Chief, Music Division

(México, Archivo General de la Nación, Fondo Carlos Chávez, Caja Correspondencia 12, Expediente 49)

NOTES

The portion of this essay dealing with Charles Seeger's involvement in the Composers Collective is partly based on interviews conducted by the University of California at Los Angeles Oral History Program. Grateful acknowledgment is given to the Regents of the University of California and the UCLA Oral History Program, Department of Special Collections, Charles E. Young Research Library, for permission to quote from "Reminiscences of an American Musicologist," © 1972 by the Regents of the University of California. All rights reserved. Used with permission.

1. In this essay the word "America" will be used in its geographically—and politically—correct sense.

2. A glimpse at this musical scene and its cross-cultural tendencies can be caught from, for example, Carmona (1989), Cowell (1962 [1933]), Lott (1983), Meckna (1985), Oja (1979), Root (1972), and Rosenfeld (1928).

3. Literature on the Composers Collective includes Reuss (1971a, 1971b, 1979) and Dunaway (1977, 1980).

4. Note that Seeger did not feel completely comfortable with the theory of progress; in his writings he refers to it as a working hypothesis subject to empirical demonstration (1935:20–21). Still, he used it to understand historical change at this time and later on. See, for example, Seeger's discussion of "complex" and "simple" (1977a [1940]: 247).

5. "The mode of production of material life conditions the social, political and intellectual life process in general. It is not the consciousness of men that determines their being, but, on the contrary, their social being that determines their consciousness" (Marx 1962:363).

REFERENCES CITED

Carmona, Gloria, ed. 1989. *Epistolario Selecto de Carlos Chávez.* Mexico: Fondo de Cultura Económica.
Chávez, Carlos. 1924a. "Querer es Poder: Cuarto Editorial de Música." *El Universal* (Mexico City), September 21.
———. 1924b. "La Importación en México." *La Antorcha* (Mexico City), October 11.
———. 1925. "Editorial de Música." *El Universal* (Mexico City), January 4.
———. 1928. "Technique and Inner Form." *Modern Music* 5:28–31.
———. 1929a. "The Two Persons." *Musical Quarterly* 15:153–59.
———. 1929b. "El Arte Popular y el No Popular." *El Universal* (Mexico City), June 12.
———. 1929c. "El Fin Extrartístico en el Arte Popular." *El Universal* (Mexico City), June 18.
———. 1929d. "La Música, la Universidad y el Estado." *El Universal* (Mexico City), July 3.
———. 1929e. "Instituciones Artísticas." *El Universal* (Mexico City), July 16.
———. 1930a. "El Conservatorio en 1929." *El Universal* (Mexico City), January 5.

———. 1930b. "La Música Propia de México." *El Universal* (Mexico City), October 8.

———. 1932a. "Composición Musical." *El Universal* (Mexico City), January 28.

———. 1932b. "Vocación Artística." *El Universal* (Mexico City), January 30.

———. 1932c. "Formación de Artistas." *El Universal* (Mexico City), February 6.

———. 1934a. "El Arte en la Sociedad." *El Universal* (Mexico City), September 27.

———. 1934b. "El Arte Occidental." *El Universal* (Mexico City), September 28.

———. 1934c. "El Arte Proletario." *El Universal* (Mexico City), September 29.

———. 1936. "Revolt in Mexico." *Modern Music* 13:35–40. (Revised and translated version of "Composición Musical" [January 28, 1932] and "Formación de Artistas" [February 6, 1932].)

———. 1937. *Toward a New Music: Music and Electricity.* Trans. Herbert Weinstock. New York: Norton.

———. 1962. "The Music of Mexico." In *American Composers on American Music: A Symposium.* 2d ed. Ed. Henry Cowell. 167–72. New York: Frederick Ungar. (Translation of "La Música Propia de México" [October 8, 1930].)

Cowell, Henry, ed. 1962 [1933]. *American Composers on American Music: A Symposium.* 2d ed. New York: Frederick Ungar.

Dunaway, David K. 1977. "Unsung Songs of Protest: The Composers Collective of New York." *Folklore* 5:1–19.

———. 1980. "Charles Seeger and Carl Sands: The Composers' Collective Years." *Ethnomusicology* 24:159–68.

Engels, Frederick. 1962. "The Origin of Family, Private Property and the State." In *Karl Marx and Frederick Engels: Selected Works in Two Volumes.* Marxist-Leninist Institute of Moscow. 2:170–327. Moscow: Foreign Languages Publishing House.

Greer, Taylor A. 1994. "Critical Remarks." In Charles Louis Seeger, *Studies in Musicology II, 1929–1979.* Ed. Ann M. Pescatello. 27–42. Berkeley: University of California Press.

Howe, Irving. 1966. "A Memoir of the Thirties." In *Steady Work: Essays in the Politics of Democratic Radicalism, 1953–1966.* New York: Harcourt, Brace & World.

Lott, R. Allen. 1983. "'New Music for New Ears': The International Composers' Guild." *Journal of the American Musicological Society* 36:266–85.

Marx, Karl. 1962. "Preface to 'A Contribution to the Critique of Political Economy.'" In *Karl Marx and Frederick Engels: Selected Works in Two Volumes.* Marxist-Leninist Institute of Moscow. 1:361–65. Moscow: Foreign Languages Publishing House.

Meckna, Michael. 1985. "Copland, Sessions and Modern Music: The Rise of the Composer-Critic in America." *American Music* 3:198–204.

Oja, Carol J. 1979. "The Copland-Sessions Concerts and Their Reception in the Contemporary Press." *Musical Quarterly* 65:212–29.

Pells, Richard. 1973. *Radical Visions and American Dreams: Culture and Social Thought in the Depression Years.* New York: Harper and Row.

Pescatello, Ann M. 1994a. "Foreword." In Charles Louis Seeger, *Studies in Musicology II, 1929–1979.* Ed. Ann M. Pescatello. 19–26. Berkeley: University of California Press.

———. 1994b. "Introduction." In Charles Louis Seeger, *Studies in Musicology II, 1929–1979.* Ed. Ann M. Pescatello. 1–16. Berkeley: University of California Press.

Reuss, Richard A. 1971a. "American Folklore and Left-Wing Politics: 1927–1957." Ph.D. dissertation, Indiana University.

———. 1971b. "The Roots of American Left-Wing Interest in Folksong." *Labor History* 12:259–79.

———. 1979. "Folk Music and Social Conscience: The Musical Odyssey of Charles Seeger." *Western Folklore* 38:221–38.

Root, Deane L. 1972. "The Pan-American Association of Composers (1928–34)." *Yearbook for Inter-American Music Research* 8:49–70.

Rosenfeld, Paul. 1928. *By Way of Art: Criticisms of Music, Literature, Painting, Sculpture and Dance.* New York: Coward-McCann.

Saavedra, Leonora. 1989. "Los Escritos Periodísticos de Carlos Chávez: Una Fuente Para la Historia de la Música en México." *Inter-American Music Review* 10:77–91.

Seeger, Charles Louis. 1923. "On Style and Manner in Modern Composition." *Musical Quarterly* 9:423–31.

———. 1930. "On Dissonant Counterpoint." *Modern Music* 7:25–31.

———. 1932. "Carl Ruggles." *Musical Quarterly* 18:578–92.

———. 1934. "On Proletarian Music." *Modern Music* 11:121–27.

———. 1935. "Preface to All Linguistic Treatment of Music." *Music Vanguard: A Critical Review* 1:17–31.

———. 1939. "Grass Roots for American Composers." *Modern Music* 16:143–49.

———. 1962. "Carl Ruggles." In *American Composers on American Music: A Symposium.* 2d ed. Ed. Henry Cowell. 14–35. New York: Frederick Ungar.

———. 1972. "Reminiscences of an American Musicologist." Oral History Program, University of California at Los Angeles.

———. 1977a [1940]. "Contrapuntal Style in the Three-Voice Shape-Note Hymns of the United States." In *Studies in Musicology, 1935–1975.* 237–51. Berkeley: University of California Press. (Reprinted from "Contrapuntal Style in the Three-Voice Shape-Note Hymns," *Musical Quarterly* 26:483–93.)

———. 1977b [1949]. "Professionalism and Amateurism in the Study of Folk Music." In *Studies in Musicology, 1935–1975.* 321–29. Berkeley: University of California Press. (Reprinted from *Journal of American Folklore* 62 [244]: 107–13.)

———. 1977c [1952]. "Music and Society: Some New-World Evidence of Their Relationship." In *Studies in Musicology, 1935–1975.* 182–94. Berkeley: University of California Press. (Revised from *Proceedings of the Conference on Latin American Fine Arts, June 14–17, 1951*. 84–97. Austin: University of Texas Press.)

———. 1977d [1957]. "Music and Class Structure in the United States." In *Studies in Musicology, 1935–1975*. 222–36. Berkeley: University of California Press. (Reprinted from *American Quarterly* 9:281–94.)

———. 1977e [1961]. "The Cultivation of Various European Traditions of Music in the New World." In *Studies in Musicology, 1935–1975*. 195–210. Berkeley: University of California Press. (Reprinted from "The Cultivation of Various European Traditions in the Americas." In *Report of the Eighth Congress of the International Musicological Society, New York, 1961*. 364–75.)

———. 1977f [1966]. "The Music Compositional Process as a Function in a Nest of Functions and in Itself a Nest of Functions." In *Studies in Musicology, 1935–1975*. 139–67. Berkeley: University of California Press. (Reprinted from "The Music Process as a Function in a Context of Functions." *Yearbook, Inter-American Institute for Musical Research* 2:1–36.)

———. 1994. "Tradition and Experiment in (the New) Music." In *Studies in Musicology II, 1929–1979*. Ed. Ann M. Pescatello. 39–273. Berkeley: University of California Press.

Susman, Warren. 1966. "Thirty Years Later: Memories of the First American Writers' Congress." *American Scholar* 35:495–516.

———. 1970. "The Thirties." In *The Development of an American Culture*. Ed. Stanley Cobman and Lorman Ratner. 179–218. Englewood Cliffs, N.J.: Prentice-Hall.

3

Form, Content, and Value:
Seeger and Criticism to 1940

Robert R. Grimes

Throughout his long and distinguished career, Charles Seeger often spoke of the need for critical studies in musicology, the need for musicology, which he defined as the linguistic study of the art of music, to deal with the notion of value in music. Although the question of value is a recurring theme beginning with his earliest musicological writings, it is not always clearly evident to what Seeger was referring when he spoke of value in the context of music. But his concern with the concept of musical value was not only theoretical; in the first half of his musicological career it was profoundly personal as well. The date 1940 itself is not arbitrary; his growing acquaintance with folk music, beginning with his work for the federal government in 1936, led to many changes in the ways in which Seeger thought and spoke about music. These changes gradually manifested themselves in Seeger's more theoretical writings, and his article "Systematic and Historical Orientations in Musicology" (1939a) marks a turning point in Seeger's development.

This period of Seeger's life starts with his college education at Harvard, class of 1908. Although he began his musical career with the goal of becoming a composer or conductor, a few years spent in Europe following college dissuaded him from pursuing a career in conducting. Following his return to the United States, Seeger was invited to become head of the newly created music department at the University of California at Berkeley. The pressures of administration and teaching during these years (1912–18) left him with little time or energy to pursue composition, although a few short works of that period survive. After a brief and rather unsuccessful tour designed to bring music "to the people," he settled in New York, teaching part time at various New York institutions and giving private lessons. His involvement with leftist causes reached its peak in the 1930s with his participation in the Composers Collective, a specialized branch of the Pierre Degeyter Club, the music wing of the American Communist party. The goal of the collective was to develop a revolutionary workers' music. In 1934 and 1935 Seeger also served as the music critic for the New York edition of the *Daily Worker,* using the pseudonym Carl Sands. He left the movement somewhat suddenly in late 1935, moved to Washington, D.C., and began working with the Roosevelt White House, first in the Resettlement Administration and later with the WPA.

∾

Many of Seeger's comments in reference to his undergraduate education at Harvard University are strongly critical of the type of education he received there. Nevertheless, he did come into contact with some of the leading scholars of the day. In his senior year Seeger studied Chaucer with George Lyman Kittredge, noted as one of the leading scholars of English literature of the period (Reuss 1979:224). In a series of lectures on Chaucer, delivered in 1914 (six years after Seeger worked with him) and later printed, Kittredge made comments that would not sound foreign coming from the lips of Seeger himself: "The chief difference between the fourteenth century and our own, in intellectual matters, lies, I think, in a different attitude toward specialization. Our tendency is to exhaust one subject, if we can, and ignore the rest; theirs was to aspire to an encyclopædic grasp of the universe . . .—the man of intellect read everything he could lay his hands on; he did not confine his interests to his specialty, even if he had one" (Kittredge 1946 [1915]: 7–9). Whether it was the influence of Kittredge or not, Seeger could not be accused of a myopic view of music and musicology, and he continually read in a variety of fields, from science and linguistics to anthropology and philosophy. In his years teaching at the University of California at Berkeley, discontented with his grasp of contemporary intellectual thought, Seeger made a determined effort to educate himself through reading, discussion with fellow faculty, and attending university seminars in a wide range of subjects.

During the Berkeley years Seeger was already wrestling with concerns that would seemingly push him to search for answers through much of his life. In an interview in 1974 Seeger noted that as early as 1917, "I had had difficulty making out the connection between this fine art of music and society at large. I did not know enough anthropology to answer the question, 'What's the use of it? Are we just writing music for a small elite class?' If that's so, I'm not interested in it; music must mean something more than simply a luxury of an elite class" (quoted in Mead 1981:223). Throughout his career Seeger would be associated with many persons and movements and read and quote from many authors associated with various schools of thought or political movements. But Seeger was, seemingly, less interested in the labels or even ends of such movements or schools than in what they might contribute to the development of his own thought, to solving the various dilemmas that he encountered in his study of music and its contexts. He once noted that "if anybody or group run along beside me, I give them loyalty in proportion to whatever of my goal they share with me" (Pescatello 1992:116). His frequent association with Marxist movements and thought is perhaps best understood as the result of a concern common to Marxist theorists and Seeger: the desire to implement social change for the good of society as a whole, especially the powerless, the concern that intellectual life not be trapped in the "ivory tower." This concern can be seen in Seeger's days at Berkeley, when he was awakened to the plight of the migrant farm workers, and in the 1930s in his reaction to the Great Depression. While he admitted that his music meant a great deal to him, he continually questioned its value to society (Seeger 1972:140).

Seeger's reading in the Berkeley days included the dialectical materialist Georgii Plekhanov (1856–1918). Indeed Seeger recalled that, in the first musicology course he taught at Berkeley, Plekhanov's "On the Materialist Conception of History" was required reading (Seeger 1972:426). In this review essay Plekhanov tries to show that all history and historical change is fundamentally rooted in social relations, or social psychology. The spirit of the times reflects the values and beliefs of the dominant economic class; a change in the economic structure changes these beliefs and values.

> When we say that a given work is fully in the spirit of, for instance, the Renaissance, that means it is fully in keeping with the predominant temper of those classes which called the tune in social life. Society's psychology does not change until a change takes place in the social relations.

People become accustomed to certain beliefs, certain concepts, certain intellectual devices, and certain ways of satisfying definite aesthetic needs. But if the development of the productive forces leads up to any substantial changes in society's economic structure and, in consequence, in the relations between social classes, then the psychology of those classes also undergoes change, and, together with that psychology, so do the "spirit of the times" and the "character of the people." This change is expressed in the appearance of new religious beliefs or new philosophical concepts, new trends in art or new aesthetic needs. (Plekhanov 1976:233)

Plekhanov's deep belief in the basic connections among economic forces, social relations, and intellectual and aesthetic systems may have been one of the elements of the essay that attracted Seeger (figure 3.1). It certainly is a theme borne out in many of his later works. Plekhanov, as did Seeger and many others in the early twentieth century, abandoned the notion of ars gratia artis.[1] The idea that art exists for its own sake is, according to Plekhanov, the result of the artist's isolation from society. Plekhanov further stressed the notion that the greatness of an artwork is the result of an artistic form that corresponded with an idea of value contained within the form.[2]

While Seeger would later abandon the "great works" theory of music history, he often admitted that he was in these early days still very much captivated by it. But the emphasis that Plekhanov places on the link between art and the social milieu is, if not the source of Seeger's views on the matter, at least very similar to views Seeger held throughout his years in New York City. Plekhanov's dialectic of form and idea is also mirrored in Seeger's distinction of form and content that will be discussed later in detail. By rooting value in the social context Seeger was able to resolve the dilemmas raised by rooting aesthetic value in the beautiful as did his colleague, the philosopher Arthur Pope, whose lec-

Figure 3.1. Plekhanov's conception of social and artistic change

tures he attended; "What he called the 'philosophy of the beautiful,'" Seeger recalled, "was all right in itself, but as I said, music is not all beautiful. Some of it isn't beautiful and I was left pretty much high and dry there" (1972:111).

In the Berkeley years the greatest influence on Seeger's thought concerning value seems to have come from a series of lectures delivered at Berkeley in the spring of 1918 by the Harvard philosophy professor Ralph Barton Perry (1876–1957). Although Perry was already a young professor at Harvard during Seeger's student days, Seeger does not appear to have had any contact with him until Berkeley. "His [Perry's] first lecture was an eye- and ear-opener to me. There *was* such a thing as the study of value! . . . the value aspect of the history of music was just as much in my mind as was the scientific. . . . That I could transfer from literary criticism [presumably learned from Kittredge] to music criticism was clear. . . . But the apparatus of literary criticism fell far short of what I wanted the apparatus of musical criticism to be" (1972:112–13).

Perry's series of lectures was printed later in the same year under the title *The Present Conflict of Ideals,* and in the preface the author notes that he was publishing them in "virtually the same form" as they were delivered (1918:iii). Although the series of lectures does deal heavily with value theory as Seeger recalled, they were to a greater degree a philosopher's response to World War I, an issue in which Seeger was also profoundly interested at the time. Nevertheless they do present in an early form the basic value theory that Perry would develop throughout his career. The importance of Perry's thought to Seeger's own is demonstrated in Seeger's later essays on value, such as "The Musicological Juncture: Music as Value" from the 1960s, in which Seeger quotes extensively from Perry's work (1977:57ff.).

Value for Perry consists in interest, the interest that an individual and/or society places in a particular thing. He provides as an example the case of a miser and his interest in gold; it is this interest that makes gold valuable. Yet interest is also a fact: "If one wishes to know what is valuable one must discover these facts-of-interest" (1918:369). At the same time, however, one must be concerned with what the object of interest is. It may not be tangible, as is the miser's gold; it may be, as Perry suggests, an aspiration, such as "the lasting peace for which the world now longs," and one must distinguish between value as a fact of aspiration and as an independent fact. For Perry this is precisely why one must be rooted in a realist philosophy (as opposed to an idealist philosophy); it allows one to root oneself in a realistic knowledge of the way things are, and the disillusionment that may result "in no way forbids the hope that they may be otherwise, and is indispensable to the firm and patient adoption of the means by which they may become otherwise" (ibid.:369–70). Perry's reflections on the nature of value prove to be a key to unlocking some of the processes through which Seeger would work in coming to his own definition of musical value (figure 3.2).

Seeger's departure from Berkeley and eventual settlement in New York City was followed by the beginning of his published theoretical writings. In "On the Principles of Musicology" Seeger notes that the general agreement "that there is a 'mysterious' quality in music that allows us to place upon it a value for which we cannot logically account" is an assumption neither "logically sound or musically acceptable" (1924:244, 247). By "musically acceptable" he seems to refer to the problem of linguistic bias; any formulation in words of the grounding of this value will be made within the limitations of speech categories, and there is no justification for assuming that they correspond to intrinsic musical categories. Seeger stresses that "to the musician, *music is music*. Music is not something else, whether it be expressed by one word or a host of them" (ibid.:247). At this early stage of dealing with value, he is left with postulating the equal value of speech and music, which, while making clear Seeger's basic view, does little to advance the discussion from the "mysterious quality" with which he began.

In an article on Carl Ruggles and his music Seeger advanced at least the terminology of the issue. He distinguishes "the facts of the medium" from "the values they embody." He equates the facts of the medium with technique and points out that technique is not an individual talent, but "a communal, a manifold thing." In keeping with both Plekhanov and Perry, Seeger does not want these two elements viewed as separate entities but rather two interconnected facets of the same entity. Technique,

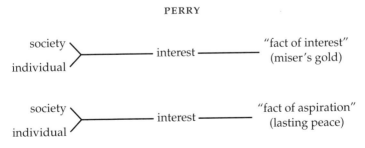

Figure 3.2. Perry's theory of value

moreover, is not the invention of a single individual, but rather the workings of an individual within a tradition, and he suggests that Ruggles's weakness in technique is not his fault, but rather an accident of the time in which he lives, a time when musical technique as a common style has disintegrated. "We cannot say that the man makes the times or the times make the man. It is nip and tuck between them" (1932:589).

"Musical value, and the expression and communication of it, is primarily the function of the composer—only secondarily should we look for its exposition in language," Seeger (1932:590) wrote of Ruggles's work. Yet when Seeger does attempt to deal with value in the linguistic context, he implies that there are actually two branches of value: the "social usefulness of his aims or his deeds," which he will later call the social function, or extrinsic value of music, and "conviction—sheer arrogant assertion—of value," which he later refers to as intrinsic musical value. When trying to describe this intrinsic value in Ruggles's music, Seeger employs poetic, metaphorical language: words and phrases such as "fantasy," "rhapsodic," and "intimations of the sublime." But Seeger's primary concern in relation to value is that the music itself be allowed to speak: "every composition embodies, among other things, a critique of the arts of its day, a revision of its criteria, a revaluation of its values" (ibid.:590–91). Thus music must communicate (although Seeger never directly states this here), but communicate in a fashion that is not necessarily homologous with speech. Already evident is the formation of some of the major Seeger dyads: Fact-Value and Technique [Form]-Content, and, in a very different relationship, the two types of value, external and internal.

If there was any doubt that Seeger did *not* consider form and content opposites, or even complements, but the same entity viewed from a different perspective, it would be banished by Seeger's definition of content contained in his next publication, "Music and Musicology," an encyclopedia entry: "The communicable *content* of music is predominantly the sound itself—the *forms* of the tonal and rhythmic manipulation" (1933:143, emphasis added). To demonstrate this, Seeger notes that the sound of language may be changed while still preserving the meaning; in music this same process is impossible. In short, music is untranslatable into another music, let alone translatable into speech.

Seeger clearly states in this article that musical value depends upon criteria that engage both the individual and society at large and ideally do so with some degree of balance between the two. Yet in his own day he perceived an "absolutism in values on the part of individuals but disregard of values in collective undertakings" (ibid.:145). That is, there was a lack of musical value rooted in the social context. The criteria for a value judgment include both intrinsic (musical) and extrinsic (extramusical) elements, which also require balance for proper criticism to take place.

This discussion of value, while filled with insight, is also somewhat confusing, largely because Seeger seems to change the vantage point from which he views musical value so often. If one confronts a particular musical piece, one can value it in a number of ways. First, the musician may value it as composer, performer, or listener. As composer the musician understands the piece as an expression of an intrinsically musical value judgment of an individual (within, however, a tradition and an idiom from which it cannot be artificially separated). As such it is both a value and a statement about value and what is valuable. As listener the musician experiences the piece first as an expression of an intrinsically musical value judgment and second, depending on the listener's own value judgment, a value (or nonvalue). As performer, the musician stands in a middle ground as both the medium conveying the value and critic on the purely musical level. Up to this point there is no need for reverting to speech in the valuing process, thus avoiding the linguistic dilemma. Second, however, the musician may (or perhaps better, must) also view a musical piece from an extramusical dimension, that is, in terms of the value of the musical piece to society. Seeger deals with this dimension in much greater depth in a later essay.

Finally, the musician may view a musical piece from the linguistic dimension, which may be expressed in impressionistic or scientific veins (Seeger 1933:146). Scientific discourse deals with the fact, the musical piece, the object of interest. Impressionistic discourse deals with the value, the relation to society, the interest itself. But for the linguistic dimension to move to the musicological dimension, it is necessary that the scientific discourse be constantly checked against the internal musical dimension of the musical piece. Although Seeger himself did not publish charts and diagrams in this early stage of his work, a Seegerian diagram may facilitate understanding Seeger's view of music value.

Figure 3.3 suggests that music as fact is a "concrete" aural entity, an object of interest. Music as value is more functional; it is the act of having interest in the entity, the reason why the fact is valuable. Obviously, these do not indicate separate referents but rather two dimensions of the same thing: one cannot take interest in a thing that does not exist.[3] The universe of language, however, is only indirectly connected to the universe of music; this suggests that through scientific discourse musicology tries to reflect the object (technique), while impressionistic discourse attempts to capture the function (content). The left half of the diagram is more fully developed in musicology because it is by nature static and structural; the right half, because of its dynamic and functional nature, is much harder to convey within the speech process.

The valuing of music is further complicated by the fact that nonmusicians as well as musicians can value it. The nonmusician will employ extramusical criteria to the valuing process, and these can take various forms.[4] They include nonmusical experts in acoustics or history who deal with the music fact from their own nonmusical expertise, the musical taste of the musically untrained, and extramusical valuing by institutions such as government or church. Obviously these criteria may also be used by musicians as well, but they differ from the musical criteria in that they exist in the universe of language and take interest in (i.e., value) the music fact from that viewpoint, rather than from within the universe of music.

Seeger's next article, "On Proletarian Music" (1934), furthers the discussion of the function of music in society and the nature of musical content. It is also a somewhat difficult article because it is so heavily slanted toward Marxist ideology. It is unclear if this article is simply Seeger's own thought or if he was cajoled into highlighting the Marxist element; however, Seeger admits that at least once during this period he was persuaded to add Marxist material to an otherwise purely theoreti-

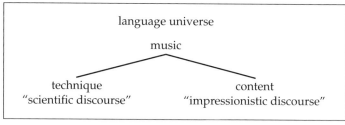

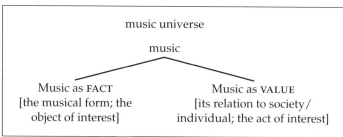

Figure 3.3. Music in Seeger's linguistic and musical universes

cal article.[5] This article was published during the height of Seeger's involvement with the Composers Collective and the *Daily Worker*, which must be kept in mind when analyzing it.

In the article Seeger uses his familiar dichotomies: form and content, technique and value, skill and taste (1934:122).[6] But he begins by explaining the explicitly Marxist terms"structure" and "superstructure" that he will later employ in a musical sense. The proletariat, the unpropertied members of a modern society, form the structure of society; the superstructure of society is made up of the "white-collar workers and intellectuals, including musicians and other artists" (ibid.:121). Returning to a content-technique dichotomy,[7] Seeger suggests that content is characteristic of the structure of society, while technique is characteristic of the superstructure of society. This lines up well with his basic argument: the proletariat knows the sort of music that it wants but lacks the technique to produce it. The musicians understand the musical-technical side but are only slowly becoming aware of the proper content for the music they produce, and they are learning this from the proletariat. Thus the musician's main task is to translate this content of the proletariat, which exists mostly in the linguistic universe, into value, which exists in the musical universe, rescuing modern music from what Seeger viewed as composers' empty obsession with technique and lack of value (figure 3.4).

Seeger suggests that all great musical styles begin with an awareness of the proper content of music and only then discover the proper technical dimension, and he gives as examples such styles as plainchant and early romanticism. This is, of course, exactly the opposite of what Seeger had seen happen in twentieth-century music: "In the subjectivism of Schönberg, for instance, as in the objectivism of Stravinsky and Hindemith, there is almost equal lack or weakness of content" (1934:124). This, Seeger suggests, is largely due to the decadence of bourgeois art music and society in general.[8]

SUPERSTRUCTURE	White collar Intellectuals Musicians	TECHNIQUE
STRUCTURE	Proletariat	CONTENT

Figure 3.4. Music and social structure in "On Proletarian Music" (1934)

The major difficulty with Seeger's argument is his assumption that
the proletariat knows the content—the revolutionary content—it wants
in its music. Clearly even the Composers Collective, which included to
one degree or another many distinguished musicians, had difficulty in
deciphering exactly what sort of "revolutionary content" the proletariat
desired.[9] Indeed the collective's slogan, "National in form: revolutionary in content," posed sufficient problems in its first half alone for the
men who were the experts at form and technique.

It is interesting to note that at this point Seeger sharply distinguishes
technique and content: "basic content . . . is largely non-technical and
even non- or extra-musical" (1934:125). In later works, as in his earlier
works, he stresses the interconnectedness of these two dimensions of
music. In this work Seeger also (and for obvious reasons) stresses the
social function of music: "Art, then, is always and inevitably a social function. . . . It is a social force. It is propaganda" (ibid.:126). It is interesting
to note that years later, speaking about this period of his life, Seeger soft-
ened his view but still held to the ubiquity of propaganda: "I've always
claimed for years that you can't talk without there being an element of
propaganda in it" (1972:480).

In 1933 and 1934 the question of musical value appears to have been
an especially gripping issue for Seeger. In February 1934 Seeger addressed the New York Musicological Society on the topic of "The Method
of Criticism." A published abstract describes the talk as "a systematic
exposition of the sources of the criteria for musical value in their relation to impressionistic and scientific criticism of music" (*Bulletin* 1933–
34). Seeger's contribution to Harvard University's *Records of the Class of
1908* for 1938 further emphasizes the importance of these years. "Whereas
in 1915 it had centered around the futility of one ivory tower, aestheticism, the focal point in 1933 was the futility of another, the studio where
one tried to lift oneself by the bootstraps of technique. . . . 1933 provided
the answer I have never been able to formulate for myself, for the times
thundered a veritable cultural ultimatum that few could fail to hear.
'Culture first, form afterwards'" (quoted in Pescatello 1992:130).

In 1935 Seeger, together with Amnon Balber and Max Margulis,
founded a music periodical entitled *Music Vanguard*. An anonymous introduction to the first issue, written in a style that almost certainly marks
it as the work of Charles Seeger, explained the purposes of the new journal.

[Musicology] needs to be rescued from the exclusively backward-look-
ing attitude of the old-fashioned, historical method. There are values in

the past that should not be allowed to perish; but these may be irrelevant or even pernicious to our minds unless their relation to the vastly more important values of making the music of today and tomorrow is correctly interpreted. Contemporary composition and mass music-making—the development of music from the narrow art for the few into a truly universal one—these should be the focal point of interest for a vital critique and theory of music. (Anonymous 1935:2)

Although stated in a more scholarly style, it is similar to Seeger's other statements regarding value at this time. The introduction also stresses the need for music education, not so much to create new audiences as to create a population of "literate" music makers, a theme that will continue through Seeger's later writings and work pertaining to music education organizations. His concern for music literacy, in terms of the ability to make music, is important for Seeger above and beyond his concern for the proletariat; it is fundamental to his conception of the proper working of any musical culture. In later works Seeger stresses the importance of music as an alternate mode of perceiving reality, an idea he has hinted at in works even before this period; for example, in 1933 he suggested that a "social order in which the functions now exercised by language could be performed by musical tones and rhythms is not inconceivable" (1933:143).

In that same first issue of *Music Vanguard*, Seeger authored an article entitled "Preface to All Linguistic Treatment of Music." In this article Seeger presupposes his distinctions of form and content and adds little to their understanding. In terms of the social function of music and its relation to language, however, the article contains a great deal of new information. Seeger suggests that in his day "the cultivation of music *as a social function* has sunk to a level below any known in history" (1935:18). Seeger views this as the inevitable result of the formation of classes in society: "While the arts of the ruled retain their generalized social function, those of the ruling class lose them" (ibid.:23). This happens, Seeger argues, because the ruled become the ones who must produce and perform the music of the society, while the rulers are the arbiters of aesthetic judgment; it is the ruling class (and the urban culture) that sets the standards for "fine art" in a society. Furthermore, "professionalized art and its pale reflection, popular art, take on the character of commodities, *produced for consumers who are not themselves producers*" (ibid.:29). This inevitably leads to a loss of the social function of the music, which results in a stale and lifeless musical culture. This is the state in which Seeger perceives Western music as having languished through most of the twentieth century. The salvation of Western music lies, for Seeger, in recapturing the social function of music composition and production, which, given his dialectical materialist position, means destroying the structures of the present social class system.

Although the final published form of "Systematic and Historical Orientations in Musicology" appeared only in 1939, Seeger delivered a paper by this title as early as October 1935.[10] Seeger is less concerned with a political or propagandistic agenda by this time, and it shows clearly in his work. While he is not denying the problems music faces in an industrial society, the Marxist asides are noticeably absent. In this article Seeger does not really add anything to his discussion of value except to introduce some new terms that will be found in his later discussions of value and criticism in music: "The method of criticism cannot flee subjectivity. This is, perhaps, its central axis—the relating of the subjective and the objective" (Seeger 1939a:127). This article seems to mark a turning point for Seeger: he has shed Marxist terminology, he seems sure of himself in speaking of value and critical method, and he has learned to value yet another dimension of music.

∾

The more concrete critical writings of Seeger include his work in 1934 and 1935 as music critic for the *Daily Worker* (New York edition) under the pseudonym Carl Sands. While there is a great deal of pure propaganda contained within this writing, there is also a good amount of solid theoretical and practical discussion of music contained within it.[11]

Seeger's first article for the *Daily Worker* (January 2, 1934, 5) reveals one of his central concerns during the mid-1930s. His review of a concert by the Pierre Degeyter Club orchestra (the musical wing of the Communist party) begins with a discussion of Vivaldi's Concerto Grosso in A minor.[12] "Technically it is good study material, . . . [but] the content (or meaning) lies within the narrow confines of early eighteenth century court life." Seeger was often concerned with evaluating the music of the past, trying to find a means of separating music of value, which should be preserved from empty music, or music of value only to another time. For example, in the same review he notes that Bach's Double Concerto for Two Violins is greater than the Vivaldi because of Bach's greater technical mastery; but more important is the content of the second movement: "Here is serene joy, delicate, but of immeasurable strength, one of the great heritages of the musical past. It belongs to all men. It transcends its epoch."

At the same time, however, Seeger notes that "Composers and players give only part of the music. The rest is given by the audience—by the audience as a whole. . . . Above all, music is a social experience." Thus it appears that the musical experience is not completed for Seeger until it is received by an audience. Yet "only indirectly, by association, can music give us facts. But directly, and very directly, it gives us aims." Seeger has already equated the terms "aim" and "value" in this article. In this instance Seeger appears to be using the term "fact" in a different sense than elsewhere, in its common usage as a piece of specific information. But more interesting is his claim that value may be directly mediated to the audience through music, not requiring a translation into the linguistic universe.

Important facets of Seeger's value theory and of his relationship to the workers' movement come to light in his review of Ray and Lida Auville's *Songs of the American Worker* (1934) a book of southern mountain songs collected by the Auvilles, who, after settling in Cleveland, had joined the Communist Party and fashioned new "workers'" lyrics to traditional songs. Seeger's review, while somewhat critical of the work, more importantly lays down practical points concerning "the principles and standards of revolutionary music criticism and of proletarian music style" (January 15, 1935, 5). Seeger is concerned about the relative importance of texts versus music in the revolutionary song. What element is more important? He had clearly answered that question in an early review for the *Daily Worker:* "It is essential that the music of workers' songs as well as their words should be revolutionary in character" (January 16, 1934, 5). Yet from Seeger's discussion of the question, it would appear that there was strong sentiment leaning toward the content of the lyrics as the most important element: "as some say, the music is a mere vehicle—a mere sauce—for the words . . ." (January 15, 1935, 5). Not surprisingly Seeger holds for the equal importance of the text and the music and warns of the conflict between language value and music value, which is his chief criticism of this collection of songs. In the Auvilles' work Seeger found that "for every step forward in the verse one takes a step backward in the music. That one is unaware of it makes it all the more dangerous." Seeger does not seem able to specifically explain what the musical value in this music should be and allows that at the present time the words probably *are* more important for revolutionary content, a situation that he hopes will soon change through the work of Hanns Eisler and various New York composers. It is perhaps most interesting to note that even at this rather late date Seeger still associated

American folk tunes with bourgeois culture, far from the ideal content of proper music. On January 2, 1936, just weeks after Seeger's relationship with the *Daily Worker* ended, a regular columnist for the newspaper printed an article strongly criticizing Carl Sands [Seeger] for his treatment of the Auvilles' work. Referring to their work, Mike Gold wrote:

> It is the real thing, folk song in the making, workers' music coming right out of the soul. . . . Really, Comrade Sands, I think you have missed the point. It is sectarian and utopian to use Arnold Schönberg or Stravinsky as a yardstick by which to measure working class music. . . . Not to see what a step forward it is to find two native musicians of the American people turning to revolutionary themes, converting the tradition to working class uses, is to be blind to progress. . . . It may shock you, but I think the Composers Collective has something to learn from Ray and Lida Auville. . . . (January 2, 1936, 5)

In an article of March 1935, Seeger noted that revolutionary criticism will "begin with the examination of the role of the [musical] organization in its environment and from this extract the standards of judgment upon which to formulate constructive criticism, of a frankly partisan nature, both of composition and of performance" (March 22, 1935, 5). While not denying the importance of technical and stylistic detail, he insisted they must be viewed as "contingents or resultants of the larger, more fundamental processes of which they are a part." Criticism cannot merely view a musical piece through the historical past and its present worth but must also view it "as a dynamic process of present growth and future development."

Seeger's review (November 23, 1934, 5) of William Dawson's *Negro Folk Symphony* demonstrates his concern for content in a concrete fashion. While calling the work outstanding among the new works presented at the concert of the Philadelphia Orchestra, he is also strongly critical of it. Seeger notes that the symphony, "based upon Negro folk-music . . . is not great music; it is not new music . . . because it is by a professor." He implies that Dawson's concern for form and technique saps the strength out of the musical resources he employs. He finds the first movement a "sterile intellectualization of no moment. Has he ever heard the music of Africa? . . . Superb music as complex as masterful as any in the world."[13] While Dawson shows promise, he is "enmeshed in the love of old and dead gods," presumably referring to the technique and form of the bourgeois musical tradition. In other words Seeger is reiterating his earlier statement: form must rise out of content, not govern it.

The premier of a choral work by Roy Harris, *A Song for Occupations!* provided Seeger with another opportunity to stress the need of rooting content in social function. Harris's composition seems to have been intended as an answer to members of the Pierre Degeyter Club who questioned Harris's assertion that composers wrote for society's sake. Seeger suggested that Harris really had no idea of what took place in society: workers "don't have 'occupations' and are not 'happy' in them. They have JOBS—some of them" (December 6, 1934, 5). Although Harris has a fine technical understanding of music, his music fails in Seeger's view because of a lack of understanding of society: "The technique is doing all it can. But there is little or no content."[14]

Seeger closes this review by suggesting that Harris "try writing some revolutionary mass songs," an exercise the Composers Collective was often engaged in. Interestingly Seeger seems to imply that the real function of these songs for the composer was to "clean you up better than you would believe," that is, that the exercise of writing such songs could retrain the bourgeois-influenced composer to begin in the area of content and social function of music rather than in formal and technical dimensions. Seeger himself wrote a number of these songs and even published a few, including one with the somewhat unlikely title of "Lenin, Who's That Guy?" Years later he described the song as "typical of the good, creative thought of those days" (Dunaway 1980:164).

Only after leaving New York, the Composers Collective, and the *Daily Worker* did Seeger really turn to folk music, although one can point to numerous moments in his life that prepared him for this interest. In an article published in 1939, "Grass Roots for American Composers," Seeger echoes his advice of 1934, suggesting that the professional composer "has an enormous amount of bias, professional pride and hokum to get rid of" (1939b:148). But now Seeger suggests that the solution is to be found not in the proletariat, but in the rural folk musician. By approaching the folk musician humbly and ready to learn, one may begin to "find content of an American character" (ibid.:144); this was a radical change in the man who had tried to bring classical music to the people in a countryside tour twenty years earlier.

~

How, then, did Seeger conceive of musical value in his early works? The concept was a gradually evolving one. For Seeger in his early writings value is the dynamic form of content; it is the act of valuing. Content, a more static term, is the link between internal and external, between the purely, intrinsically musical and the social function of music. The content from the composer's or performer's standpoint might be considered the reason why a person composes or performs either a particular piece of music or even music in general. Confronted by the world and its processes, the musician seeks to communicate, to address the reality he or she experiences, and does so through the universe of music. A music without content, without value, is an empty and meaningless form—technique without substance. At the same time it must not be supposed that content can exist without form; it is precisely the welding together of the two elements that makes music great or, perhaps better, worthwhile.

Nevertheless it must be stressed that Seeger conceived of music as an activity, not a static entity. He emphasized that "to *make* music is the essential thing—to listen to it is only accessory." Thus the value that music possesses must be rooted not simply in the musical composition, but in the musical activity and the effects of that musical activity. "The main question, then, should be not 'is it good music?' but 'what is the music good for'; and if it bids fair to aid in the welding of the people into more independent, capable and democratic action, it must be approved" (Seeger and Valiant 1980 [1937]: 179–80).

Seeger's need to know the relationship of his music to society—to the world—was a major impetus to his reflection on the nature of music. His theory of value seems to be his answer to that questioning, yet his conception of musical value continued to evolve and develop in his later writings. Referring to his time in New York City, Seeger later said: "We didn't realize until years afterward that those days when we just seemed to be wasting time we were really getting started on our second lives" (Gaume 1986:103). Coming to a basic understanding of the value inherent within music, the value that links the musical artifact with the process of human civilization, was essential for the development and expansion of the practical and theoretical work of Charles Seeger. And although he would continue to wrestle with the question of musical value in more and more sophisticated terms, he had found that music is something more than the luxury of an elite class.

NOTES

An earlier version of this essay was read at the Society for Ethnomusicology meeting in Chicago, October 13, 1991. I am grateful for the feedback I received at that time and from continuing discussions of Charles Seeger and his conception of music with a number of my fellow authors in this volume. I also wish to thank the Regents of the University of California and the University of California at Los Angeles Oral History Program, Department of Special Collections, Charles E. Young Research Library, for permission to quote from "Reminiscences of an American Musicologist," © 1972 by the Regents of the University of California. All rights reserved. Used with permission.

1. Seeger, in the foreword to "Journal of a Field Representative," gave as his first rule: "Music, as any art, is not an end in itself, but is a means for achieving larger social and economic ends" (Seeger and Valiant 1980 [1937]: 179).

2. See the discussion of Plekhanov's aesthetics in Petrovic (1967).

3. One should remember Perry's distinction of an independent fact (here, a musical piece) and a "fact of aspiration." Seeger does not speculate as to what a musical fact of aspiration might be, although one might hazard the guess that it could consist of something like Seeger's desire for a universal music-making ability.

4. For purposes of this discussion, the hypothetical nonmusician will have no intrinsic musical criteria to employ in valuing music. In reality the nonmusician will have some degree of musical ability on which to draw.

5. In his dissertation, "American Folklore and Left-Wing Politics" (1971), Richard Reuss reports that in an interview with Seeger (who used the pseudonym Carl Sands) on June 7, 1967, Seeger disclosed that "under pressure, Carl Sands reluctantly added a few lines espousing Marxist musical theory to an otherwise non-political article entitled 'Preface to An [sic] All Linguistic Treatment of Music,' which in the given context distorted the sense of his concluding remarks" (78). Reuss was aware that Seeger and Sands were the same person, although Seeger had not yet publicly revealed it, but did not include this information in his dissertation. By referring to Sands as the author of an article published under Seeger's name, he seems to have unwittingly disclosed the identity of Carl Sands. But in a letter of June 18, 1971, to Reuss, Seeger denied being forced to add anything to the article but claimed that he had "learned" to do so (quoted in Pescatello 1992:116).

6. Seeger sometimes uses the alternate form "technic" and at other times the more usual "technique"; there does not appear to be any significance in the distinction. Seeger had used the terms "skill" and "taste" in previous articles, especially "Music and Musicology," but this is the first time he formally links them to the other dichotomies.

7. One should notice that Seeger often exchanges terms among these parallel dichotomies; earlier in this same article he contrasts content with form and technic with value. This suggests that Seeger saw the parallel terms as very similar.

8. Seeger appears to be strongly influenced by the writings of the German socialist musician-author Hanns Eisler. A year after this article was published, Seeger met Eisler during his tour of the United States and attended his lecture entitled "The Crisis in Music," March 1, 1935 (in Grabs 1978:114–19). Eisler holds that "If a composer today claims that his music has no social or political func-

tion, he merely reveals his ignorance of these functions" (ibid.:115). Seeger suggests a similar sentiment in the final paragraph of the article under discussion. Although there are many similarities in the use of both terminology and clichés, Seeger's basic value theory of music seems to be his alone.

9. Among the musicians with some degree of affiliation with the collective were Elie Siegmeister, Henry Cowell, Marc Blitzstein, Aaron Copland, Jacob Schaefer, and Earl Robinson.

10. An abstract appears in the *Bulletin of the American Musicological Society* (June 1936): 5.

11. For convenience's sake, all quotations followed by a date and page number refer to the New York edition of the *Daily Worker*.

12. Pierre Degeyter was the composer of the "Internationale," the anthem of the international Communist movement.

13. Whether Seeger's review had any effect on Dawson is not known. Dawson did, however, revise this work in 1952 following a trip to West Africa, where he studied the indigenous music. See the liner notes by George Jellinek to Stokowski's recording of Dawson's symphony (Varèse Sarabande, VC 81056).

14. In fairness to Harris it should be noted that he dedicated the work to the workers of the world, who, he wrote, "are the most important part of any civilization." Howard Taubman, reviewing the concert for the *New York Times,* called it "music of assertive vigor, rhythmic audacity and sonorous strength" (January 28, 1934, 24). But thirty-seven years later Harris's work still upset Seeger. In a letter to Richard Reuss, Seeger admitted that in the mid-1930s "I had been something of a Roy Harris myself not so long before that time. Perhaps not so much of an opportunist. And certainly not a careerist" (quoted in Pescatello 1992:116).

REFERENCES CITED

Anonymous. 1935. "Introduction." *Music Vanguard* 1 (1): 1–2.

Auville, Ray, and Lida Auville. 1934. *Songs of the American Worker.* Cleveland: John Reed Club.

Bulletin of the New York Musicological Society. 1933–34.

Dunaway, David K. 1980. "Charles Seeger and Carl Sands: The Composers' Collective Years." *Ethnomusicology* 24 (2): 159–68.

Gaume, Matilda. 1986. *Ruth Crawford Seeger: Memoirs, Memories, Music.* Metuchen, N.J.: Scarecrow Press.

Grabs, Manfred, ed. 1978. *A Rebel in Music: Selected Writings of Hanns Eisler.* New York: International Publishers.

Kittredge, George Lyman. 1946 [1915]. *Chaucer and His Poetry.* Cambridge, Mass.: Harvard University Press.

Mead, Rita H. 1981. *Henry Cowell's New Music, 1925–1936.* Ann Arbor, Mich.: UMI. Research Press.

Perry, Ralph Barton. 1918. *The Present Conflict of Ideals*. New York: Longmans, Green and Co.

Pescatello, Ann M. 1992. *Charles Seeger: A Life in American Music*. Pittsburgh: University of Pittsburgh Press.

Petrovic, Gajo. 1967. "Plekhanov." In *The Encyclopedia of Philosophy*. Vol. 6:349. New York: Macmillan.

Plekhanov, Georgii. 1976. *Georgii Plekhanov: Selected Philosophical Works*. Moscow: Progress Publishers.

Reuss, Richard. 1971. "American Folklore and Left-Wing Politics." Ph.D. dissertation, Indiana University.

———. 1979. "Folk Music and Social Conscience: The Musical Odyssey of Charles Seeger." *Western Folklore* 38 (4): 221–38.

Seeger, Charles Louis. 1924. "On the Principles of Musicology." *Musical Quarterly* 10 (2): 244–50.

———. 1932. "Carl Ruggles." *Musical Quarterly* 18 (4): 578–92.

———. 1933. "Music and Musicology." In *Encyclopedia of the Social Sciences*. 11:143–50. New York: Macmillan.

———. 1934. "On Proletarian Music." *Modern Music* 11 (3): 121–27.

———. 1935. "Preface to All Linguistic Treatment of Music." *Music Vanguard* 1 (1): 17–31.

———. 1939a. "Systematic and Historical Orientations in Musicology." *Acta Musicologica* 11:121–28.

———. 1939b. "Grass Roots for American Composers." *Modern Music* 16 (3): 143–49.

———. 1972. "Reminiscences of an American Musicologist." Oral History Program, University of California at Los Angeles.

———. 1977. "The Musicological Juncture: Music as Value." In *Studies in Musicology, 1935–1975*. 51–63. Berkeley: University of California Press.

Seeger, Charles Louis, and Margaret Valiant. 1980 [1937]. "Journal of a Field Representative." *Ethnomusicology* 24 (2): 169–210. (Reprinted from the Resettlement Administration [Washington, D.C.] publication by the same name.)

4

"Temporary Bypaths"?
Seeger and Folk Music Research

Helen Rees

Though Charles Seeger published dozens of articles on all manner of musical subjects, he is now often associated with the study of folk music. However, in a letter to Richard Reuss written in 1971, Seeger inveighs against those who would classify him as a folk music specialist: "Folklore and folk music are only temporary bypaths for me and I sometimes rile up a bit when I am referred to as a student of folk music. . . . I make this sole and last appeal *not* to represent me as a student of folk music except as a necessary fulfillment of the ordinary task of the musicologist as I see it, namely, the study of *all* the music of a culture, a geographical area, or the whole world" (quoted in Reuss 1979:222). This complaint articulates a sensation that grows upon anyone who reads a substantial amount of Seeger's scholarly output: namely, that it is possible neither to view Seeger's articles on folk music independently of his overall theoretical and applied musicological work nor to consider the complex insights of his later years (the 1940s on) as unaffected by his work on folk music. As Reuss puts it, "the discovery of the existence of a viable and dynamic folksong tradition in twentieth-century America served as a major catalytic force in the shaping of Seeger's pan-musical and philosophic worldview" (ibid.).

This essay uses specific examples to examine the validity of Reuss's assertion. The first half shows how the preexisting theoretical preoccupations evident since the 1910s, 1920s, and 1930s framed and informed Seeger's work on folk music. The second half demonstrates that Seeger's discovery of American folksong contributed actively, materially, and discernibly to some of the most sophisticated and influential theoretical concerns of his later years.

Because Seeger's writings were inevitably influenced and inspired by whatever experiences his life and work caused him to encounter, it is useful to bear in mind the chronological framework within which his articles on folk music were written. Although he had made sporadic mention of the subject during his years teaching at the University of California at Berkeley (1912–18), it apparently did not occupy his attention during his subsequent residence in New York (1921–35) until the latter stages of his involvement with the Composers Collective:[1] it was only in the mid-1930s that Seeger began to take a serious interest in folk music as a live art form. He seems to have been inspired by its social relevance: as he commented, "I began to see the point: people make the music that they want to make" (quoted in Dunaway 1980:167). The chance to use folk music to help destitute communities came with his employment by the Resettlement Administration and the Federal Music Project from 1935 to 1941; and as head of the Music Division of the Pan American Union from 1941 to 1953, he had to deal with all kinds of music, including folk. During these periods he began to produce a large number of articles and reviews to do with folk music, and he continued to do so thereafter, both while at UCLA in the 1960s and during the years of retirement until his death in 1979. Apart from articles, lectures, and essays dealing directly with the music, its application, and study, there are also many record and book reviews and work as editor or music arranger of folksong collections. In addition, many writings dealing mainly with other topics draw at least some of their inspiration and examples from the world of folk music. As with the rest of his output, the articles that deal with folk music, and the preoccupations that pervade them, range from the highly abstruse to the extremely practical.

By the time Seeger started showing a serious interest in folksong in the 1930s, many of the leitmotivs that pervade his later work were already established as serious theoretical and practical concerns. His interest in folk music did not exist in isolation, but rather added a new source of data to his evolving frames of reference. Frequently, therefore, Seeger sought to embed his writings on folk music within a wider thematic context.

One of the most ubiquitous issues to arise in Seeger's publications is the necessity for a functional approach to musicology to complement the structural. His discussions of function tend in two distinct, if not unrelated, directions: first, the examination of musical processes rather than static artifacts; and, second, the consideration of how a music fits into and interacts with its extramusical setting—how it functions in society.

To take the first direction first, it is worth noting at the outset that many of Seeger's early discussions of the structure/function dichotomy use the terminology "historical" and "systematic" rather than "structural" and "functional." He himself in a late article explicitly relates these two dichotomies to one another, suggesting they may be viewed interchangeably (1977i [1966]: 340).[2] In its history/system guise this dichotomy rears its head as early as 1924, when Seeger declares, "we should emphasize a *systematic* orientation in musicology, corrected, when necessary, in the light of *historical* considerations. By a 'systematic' orientation I mean a facing of music *as it is*—as the craftsman and artist faces it in the actual process of working in it—at least to this extent, that one is quite free of concern as to *how it came to be* as it is" (1924:248–49). Practically the same point is made in 1939, when Seeger complains of the predominance of the historical viewpoint, which studies how music was and how it came to be like that; the systematic, he feels, is sadly lacking: "we have practically [no studies] of how [music] is! Nor of *how it came to be as it is*! Much less, of *how it is going to be* or of *how it is coming to be what it is going to be*!" (1939b:124).

Probably Seeger's most comprehensive article devoted specifically to the structure/function dichotomy is "The Music Compositional Process as a Function in a Nest of Functions and in Itself a Nest of Functions" (1977j [1966]). Here he sets out very clearly what he understands by these two terms: "structure" refers to discrete entities such as physical artifacts and patterns of belief, behavior, population distribution, and social class in the group that makes the artifacts; in the musical sense the most obvious example of a "structure" is the musical piece. "Function," by contrast, refers to ongoing processes: traditions of making, using, and believing; intensity of activity; and "the relative dependence and interdependence of the traditions of a culture, and to their combined operation in the culture as a whole and in the living bodies of their carriers" (1977j [1966]: 141). He feels that modern academic discussion in the humanities tends to emphasize structural rather than functional elements, probably because writing about discrete tangible objects is easier than identifying processes. As he puts it, structures "seem to 'stay still' while one contemplates them" (ibid.).

Precisely how Seeger applies the functionalist approach to folk music may be seen in the 1958 article "Singing Style":

> It must be admitted that it is easier to isolate *what* is sung than *how* it is sung. A repertory consists of artifacts presentable objectively in written and printed form—songs, melodies, words, *ragas,* modes, etc. These, being structural in character, are easily talked about. A singing style, on the other hand, consists of a complex of dispositions, capacities and habits built into the bodily processes and personality of the individual carrier of a song tradition when he is very young by the social and cultural environment into which he is born and by which he is nurtured. Being functional in character it is more difficult to talk about. (1958b:4)

"Ongoing processes" surface frequently as objects of Seeger's interest and provide fertile ground for a functionalist treatment. This happens, for instance, in his discussions of the "four idioms." As early as 1938 he defines "three main currents of activity" in American music: "folk," "academic or 'high art,'" and "popular" music (1938:411). By 1940 this has expanded to "four idiomatic types": "primitive, fine art, folk, popular and their hybrids" (1940b:1), thereafter usually referred to as the four "idioms" (see, e.g., 1954, 1965, 1977j [1966], 1980). Despite this careful system of categorization, Seeger refuses to view any of these "idioms" as existing unchangeably in a vacuum, either musically or contextually— he emphasizes the need to include the total musical picture in the study of any one of them, describing the relationship among them as "a reciprocal two-, three-, or even four-way activity of give-and-take within the social body as a whole" (1965:132). Similarly the article "Versions and Variants of 'Barbara Allen'" (1977k [1966]) compares many different folksingers' renditions of one song. In that it deals primarily with discrete entities, it could have emerged as a completely structuralist treatment; yet Seeger, ever alert to processes that might affect the object of his study, gives substantial room to the potential impact on the recordings at his disposal of such items as commercial hillbilly records, radio programs, and printed materials.

It is in record reviews that one finds a very practical application of this interest in process. For instance, in a review from 1949 of four records issued by Decca as part of their folksinger Personality Series, Seeger does not confine himself to criticism of the performances; instead he prefers to emphasize the processual features displayed by the recordings, thus integrating functional and structural approaches: "The albums are . . . of interest . . . as sources for the study not of 'what has been' but rather of 'what is coming to be.' For they represent one of the most potent means for the artful re-insemination of vast sections of the American people with a heritage of their own dominant majority, a process that cannot but affect profoundly the nature of what the folklorists of tomorrow will call 'folklore' upon the North American continent" (1949b:68). Seeger's interest in process is further demonstrated by his creation of a formula to evaluate the authenticity of folksingers: on a four-point scale from folk through hillbilly and citybilly to concert, he sees most singers as moving rapidly from the folk through to the concert end, with just a few, such as his son Pete, trying to go in the other direction (1948:216).

Seeger's interest in these interactive "ongoing processes" led inevitably to a recognition of the need to consider a total musical culture rather than just part of it. This had a marked effect on his critiques of and advice to fieldworkers who collected folksongs. In 1951 he reviewed three anthologies of folksongs: *Folksongs of Florida, Texas Folksongs,* and *Folksongs of Alabama.* Objecting to the implied claims of exhaustive coverage, he points out the localized nature of the actual coverage, the omission in the Texas book of songs from black and Mexican Texans and the omission from the Florida volume of the songs of the substantial Spanish-, Greek-, Slovak-, and Polish-speaking communities and its unequal treatment of African-American materials and informants. Seeger's desire for inclusiveness in such work surfaces in his instructions to Sidney Robertson as she set out on a field recording project for the Resettlement Administration. As she recalled years later,

> "Record EVERYthing!" he said as emphatically as he could. "Don't select, don't omit, don't concentrate on any single style. We know so little! Record *everything!*" What he was trying to do was to inoculate me against contagion from the local collectors I was to meet, for each of them as a matter of course picked and chose items for his collection according to some personal standard of authenticity, or taste, or esthetic quality, or topical interest. Charlie knew it was important to disabuse me of any notion I might have that any particular part of the tradition was more important than any other. Nothing should be omitted! (quoted in Pescatello 1992:141)

As to the second direction in which function leads Seeger, the consideration of the interaction of music and its extramusical background, this theme first appeared in his writings long before he began to pay serious attention to folk music. As early as 1924 he offers a preview of this preoccupation, when he observes of would-be musicologists:

The end for which we ought to strive to-day is an education which shall enable the workers in any field whatsoever to understand better how the object of their own activity is subordinated to more general problems. It is with a view not only toward a better integration of music and talking about music and toward a better integration of the art of music and the art of language, that a revised musicology should be oriented, but with a view also to the better integration of both arts in the social life they so largely condition. (1924:248)

In 1933 Seeger returns to this idea more succinctly: "Music is a phenomenon of prolonged social growth—a culture. It is not only a product of a culture but one of the means by which the culture has come to be what it is and continues" (148). This theme recurs thereafter in many publications, culminating in the highly theoretical works of Seeger's last few years (see, e.g., 1977l [1970], 1977m [1971]). One of his most articulate statements of this viewpoint comes in a late definition of the field of musicology: it is "the total music of man, both in itself and in its relationships to what is not itself . . . in terms both . . . of human culture and . . . of his relationships with the physical universe" (1977l [1970]: 108). The relationship between music and society is treated again and again in Seeger's academic publications. Some articles indeed present the relationship as their major subject matter (e.g., "Music and Society: Some New-World Evidence of Their Relationship" [1977c (1952)]; "Music and Class Structure in the United States" [1977e (1957)]).

Baranovitch (this volume) suggests that Seeger's expression of such ideas in his early writings may be attributed to his familiarity with contemporary anthropological thought. Clearly in contemporary folklore scholarship too, with which Seeger became increasingly familiar through the 1930s, functionalism was a hot topic. B. A. Botkin, a scholar whose writings Seeger came to know, was able to suggest in 1937 that "this functional view of folklore is now generally accepted" (Botkin 1937:465). D. K. Wilgus, writing in 1959, asserts that despite the paucity of information on the place and function of a folksong in its setting, nevertheless "interest in functionalism in recent years has pervaded the whole area of folklore study and has tended to unite it" (1959:336).[3] Wilgus goes on to cite scholars such as Emelyn E. Gardner, Vance Randolph, and Zora Neale Hurston, all of whom produced works in the 1930s emphasizing the social setting of folk music and folklore collected, and lists the questions posed in 1938 by George Herzog concerning the contextual and functional aspects of folksong, which read like a blueprint of Seeger's interests.[4]

Seeger's writings on folk music are frequently framed in these terms. The title of the important 1940 essay "Folk Music as a Source of Social History" specifically posits a relationship between folk music and social history and suggests that the "folk-music idiom" is the field in which anthropologists, historians, and musicologists can cooperate to best advantage to fill in "gaps [in social history] caused by overreliance upon written sources" (1940a:321). The opening of this essay puts the more global question, "why has the study of music-culture relationships been neglected?" (ibid.:316). Seeger goes on to give a definition of the task of musicology that lays great emphasis on the function of music in its extramusical environment: it is "the presentation in language of an account (1) of the nature of music-technical processes, (2) of the relation between the universe of music and the universe of discourse, and (3) of the function of the total field of music in the total field of culture" (ibid.: 320). The potential value of musical evidence from folk culture to understanding social developments is also explicitly stated in Seeger's discussion of contrapuntal style in three-voice shape-note hymns, in another 1940 article: he hopes for study "not only of the technical processes [the hymns] exhibit but also of the sociohistorical processes of which they were a part" (1977a [1940]: 250). Not surprisingly, for at least one brand of musicological researcher, the folk music specialist, he strongly recommends training in both musicology and anthropology (1977b [1949]: 324).

That the social dimension to music and musicology was not a merely academic concern for Seeger is well known; Reuss for one has explored the development of Seeger's social conscience with particular reference to his professional work with folk music (1979). This conscience, however, was already operative many years before he became involved with folk music. Despite his patrician upbringing and Harvard education, Seeger began showing concern for the impoverished lower classes as early as 1914, when the economist Carlton Parker took him on a tour of the hop fields and fruit ranches of northern California, and he saw for himself the wretched conditions of the migrant workers (Pescatello 1992:60). During his tenure in California he and his fellow teacher Herbert Cory came into contact with anarchist, socialist, and Wobbly philosophies and became friendly with local radicals; Seeger addressed the Radical Club of San Francisco on Wagner's role in the 1848 revolt in Germany (Reuss 1979:225). In 1916 he shocked a large audience at Harvard by admitting: "Well, here am I; you all know that I graduated here with honors in music and want to be a composer—but who wants my music? In other words, what's the value to society of my music?" (Seeger

1972:140). Later Seeger explained to Reuss, "in the late teens and early twenties, I [gave] up composition because I couldn't approve of the music I liked and I couldn't like a music that I approved, and I couldn't make either one of them connect in any way with the social situation I found" (quoted in Reuss 1979:226).

In November 1920 Seeger and his violinist wife Constance decided to do something about this and set off from New York in a trailer, intending to bring "good" music to the American people on their way to California. Wintering in North Carolina, they became friendly with local rural inhabitants and tried to interest them in their performances of Bach, Beethoven, and Mozart; the locals reciprocated with banjos and fiddles. Apparently neither side was particularly impressed with the music of the other; and eventually the Seegers ran out of money and returned by stages to New York, where in August 1921 they commenced teaching at the Institute of Musical Arts (Reuss 1979:226–27; Pescatello 1992:81–83).

Seeger's social conscience seems to have been dormant thereafter until the Great Depression, which propelled him into the arms of the Composers Collective, a radical group with informal ties to the Communist Party. The collective's classically trained members aimed at a new workers' music, revolutionary in form and content. Seeger became involved with the collective in 1932 but by fall 1935 dropped out, doubting its efficacy and worrying about government surveillance of the group (Pescatello 1992:109–19).[5] In November 1935 his own desperate need for steady employment meshed with his desire to use music to help the American people when he accepted an appointment with the Resettlement Administration, thus enabling him to salve his conscience with government work from then on. His idealism was allowed international rein in his later work for the Pan American Union, as a result of which he expressed the hope that all might use music as an instrument of international cooperation (Seeger 1941:65).

How, then, did this preoccupation with social welfare affect Seeger's views on folk music? Ironically, in view of his later emphasis on the importance of using the people's own music to help them, for a long time Seeger dismissed popular and folk musics. Commenting in 1977 on his North Carolina sojourn of 1920–21, he noted, "We looked down on popular music—folk music didn't exist, or except in the minds of a few very old people, who would die shortly and then there wouldn't be any. And this new thing that was coming, called jazz, was simply filthy—it was of the gutter and the brothel and wasn't fit to pay any attention to" (quoted in Pescatello 1992:81).

During the early 1930s Seeger came into increasing contact with folk music: he met Aunt Molly Jackson at the Composers Collective, was introduced by the painter Thomas Hart Benton to commercial hillbilly recordings, read George Pullen Jackson's *White Spirituals in the Southern Uplands* (1933) and other works on folk music, and became acquainted with the Lomaxes (Reuss 1979:230–31). Yet still it took him some time to find value in folk music. In his 1932 essay on Carl Ruggles he complains, "what a great unwieldy corpus this American Music is—great talent, great resources, great opportunities; but still a giant without head or feet—no folk-art for us to stand on, no head to direct us" (1932:591). In the program set out in the 1934 article "On Proletarian Music," Seeger completely ignores folk music, suggesting instead that "the obvious thing to do is to connect the two vital trends—proletarian content and the forward looking technic of contemporary art music" (1934b:124–25). Writing under his pen name of Carl Sands for the New York edition of the *Daily Worker* of January 16 that year, he doubts the value of much folk music to the proletariat, complaining that "not all folk-tunes are suitable to the revolutionary movement. Many of them are complacent, melancholy, defeatist—originally intended to make slaves endure their lot—pretty, but not the stuff for a militant proletariat to feed upon. Folk-music that shows clearly a spirit of resentment toward oppression or vigorous resistance to it are [*sic*] valuable" (1934a:5). Later that year he did appear more enthusiastic on the subject: criticizing the black American composer William L. Dawson for the "sterile intellectualization" of his *Negro Folk Symphony,* he actually advises him to turn to folk music for inspiration: "Dawson is a Negro, a member of an exploited and humiliated race. The folk-music of that race expresses most eloquently its suffering and its aspirations, its gayety and its vitality. . . . It is a pity that this composer is still enmeshed in the love of old and dead gods. Perhaps some day he will hear one of the revolutionary songs of the Negro workers. . . . Perhaps it will awaken him. Perhaps he has it in him to . . . become a true son of his people" (1934c:5).

Seeger's initial dismissal but later acceptance of folk music as a positive social force was paralleled by a similar shift in viewpoint of other members of the collective and of the American Communist movement. The first songbook produced by the collective, in 1934, contains no folksongs; the second, from 1935, has two "Negro songs of protest"; while the third, *Songs of the People* (1937), emphasizes labor and political songs set to familiar folk and popular tunes. More thoroughgoing left-wing intellectual enthusiasm for folksong as a vehicle for revolutionary ideas appeared only in the late 1930s (Reuss 1971; Dunaway 1979:9–13; Zuck 1980:125–34; Lieberman 1989:30–31).

Seeger himself described his shift in view: "I began to see the point: people make the music that they want to make. . . . I didn't see this at once, it was very gradual. The transition took me three, four, five years." His move into New Deal government work facilitated this transition: "by the time I had worked through the Collective, I had my program all ready in my mind for the Resettlement Administration. Then the invitation came in November, 1935. I went down to Washington and was perfectly sure that what we should do would be to work in the vernacular: folk, popular, or mixed, whatever it was. . . . Not what I could superimpose upon people, but what they already had and which just needed to be encouraged and put to social use" (quoted in Dunaway 1980:167). This precept was clearly enunciated by Seeger in the principles he laid down for Special Skills Division music workers sent into resettlement communities in 1936. Despite the disappointing results and brief duration of the project as a whole, he must have been encouraged by the successful and flexible application of his principles by Margaret Valiant, his most effective worker (Seeger and Valiant 1980 [1937]; Warren-Findley 1979–80).

Continuing in this vein in a 1939 paper discussing music and government, Seeger endorses a statement by Dr. Carl C. Taylor of the Department of Agriculture, to the effect that "the wisest course for planning is to cooperate with the inevitable trends of culture and to seek to put intelligent guidance into the channel through which life normally flows" (1944:17). This has obvious consequences for the place of music in applied musicology. At the Conference on Inter-American Relations in the Field of Music, Seeger gave a paper entitled "The Importance to Cultural Understanding of Folk and Popular Music," suggesting that "if we wish to have music serve the ends implicit in this conference we shall do well if our major emphasis is upon folk and popular idioms, with fine art and primitive musics playing respectively the roles of dominant and recessive minorities" (1940b:8).

Given his activities with the Composers Collective and subsequently for the government, it is hardly surprising that even where Seeger is not overtly promulgating a program of applied musicology, a pronounced class consciousness nevertheless exists in many of his writings on folk music. He is strongly inclined to equate folk music with a predominantly rural lower class and to view the changing fortunes of folk and art music in the United States against the backdrop of a "tug of war between the development of a neo-European class structure and cultivation of a classless, Euro-American, equalitarian society." Indeed, he says, by 1750 "a sufficiently large urban class of status, wealth, and fashion began to require something more than a musical art upon a folk level" (1977e [1957]: 224). This article's title, "Music and Class Structure in the United States," indicates the lens through which Seeger views music. He does not hesitate to speak disparagingly of the "make America musical" movement, which attempted to impose "good" music (i.e., European art music) on the American population, regardless of the desires of that population.[6] The movement's members, as he observes, came from the well-to-do; he decries it as "authoritarian" and contrasts it with the "truly democratic, but unwritten . . . Euro-American and emerging American folk and folk-popular idioms" (ibid.:228).[7] Thus it can be seen that Seeger's sociopolitical views not only led him to seek the use of folk and other music to help the people, but also formed an ideational lens through which he viewed musical phenomena and their social context.

Seeger's at least partially ideologically derived disdain for the "make America musical" movement leads conveniently into the next theme that permeates his work, namely, his enthusiasm for the creation of American music and an American national musical identity in preference to the traditional reliance on European importations. With regard to art music, Seeger frequently deplores reliance on European models. In his 1932 essay on Carl Ruggles he complains of the "tragedy of American Music"—"that it has this opportunity for a short time before the imitation of European gods descends upon us and fixes us in a traffic of ten miles an hour—a stale neo-Romanism." Indeed, "crutches and guide-books we borrow uncritically from Europe and think we are dancing finely!" (1932:584, 591).[8] By 1939 Seeger explicitly advocates "Grass Roots for American Composers," in which he points out the immense vitality of American folk and popular music and the need for an American composer to know his musical roots (1939a). The combination of his anti-European stance and his rather left-wing political views leads to his definition of "positive acculturation" as "potential Americanism" and "negative acculturation" as "neo-Europeanism whose stronghold was always in the bourgeoisie of the cities" (1977h [1961]: 206).

Folk music is often cited as having a role to play in creating a national musical identity. That it cannot do this unassisted is something Seeger admits even in his last publication: "it cannot be said that there exists or ever has existed 'an' American or 'a' United States folk music" (1980:436). On the other hand, it can be employed to this end: in 1949 Seeger pointed to the potential for the study of American folk music to create a "more unified continental music culture for North America" (1977b [1949]: 328). He does not clarify to which of the idioms this unified music culture will belong, who will bring it about, or what he expects will happen to competing musical forms. Nevertheless, to achieve this goal, Seeger advocates "American Music for American Children," approving "the adherence of the music educators of the United States to the principle that one essential basis of music education in a country is the folk music of that country" (1942:11). Such was his interest in the teaching of folk music that he devoted an entire article to the subject, "Folk Music in the Schools of a Highly Industrialized Society," in which he presses for instruction by quasi-traditional oral means and the authentic performance by children of folksongs (1977d [1953]).[9]

Of all Seeger's interests perhaps the most obsessive is the relationship between music and speech and the problems of "speech knowledge" of music (i.e., talking about it rather than making it and thus knowing it from the inside). This is addressed as early as 1923 ("Music in the American University") and 1924 ("On the Principles of Musicology") and is, of course, a major focus of several subsequent articles. In "The Music Compositional Process . . ." he ties the speech-music dichotomy to the structure-function dichotomy, suggesting that on the parameter of speech semantic variance, "speech about music would seem to operate in an area near the structure limit, music itself, in one near the function limit." To maximize the possibilities of discussing music in terms of itself, he even goes so far as to suggest that mathematical speech, which he considers predominantly functional, would be the most efficient instrument for dealing with music (1977j [1966]: 143).

This particular theme in Seeger's writings, the relationship between speech and music and the problems of using the one to communicate about the other, offers a good example of the treatment of folk music as part of a broad, underlying trend of thought. Seeger's frequently voiced dissatisfaction with people obtaining only a "speech knowledge" of music must contribute to his constant enthusiasm for getting people to play music rather than just talk about it. On the subject of scholars studying the phenomenon of folk music, he is adamant that they should learn how to play it themselves, on the basis that "a certain minimum of competence in performance *of* folk music is necessary for the evaluation of the knowledge *about* the idiom that is the essential stuff of the study" (1977b [1949]: 325). To express it in terms of the structure-function dichotomy, they can only have a partial knowledge of the idiom if this knowledge is solely of the structurally inclined discursive speech dis-

course variety: an intrinsic music knowledge is essential to an understanding of the functional aspects. Both the theorizing that supports this
view and the practical form it takes are really no more than a modification
of Seeger's gut reaction to his Harvard music courses: "we went through
practically everything except the History of Music, which I didn't take
because it was talking about music and I thought that was a ridiculous
thing to do" (1972:24). The concrete realization of this conviction occurs
in such items as the arrangements for voice and piano of the songs in John
and Alan Lomax's *Folk Song USA* (1947), which the Seegers, as music
editors, deliberately kept simple to encourage amateurs of all standards
to perform them.

∾

So far these examples have concerned the way that Seeger's writings on
folk music can be seen to fit into the overarching theoretical preoccupations that pervade his scholarship as a whole from its earliest years. Also
worth consideration, however, is the active contribution that Seeger's
increasing knowledge of folk music made to some of the most sophisticated theoretical concerns of his later years.

In several late articles Seeger wrestles with the issue of the compositional process and the related problem of musical identity. He wants to
get away from the usual view of the "Western world, [that] music is talked
about to a greater extent in terms of structure—concrete structures, at
that—with immutable beginnings, endings, and inner construction"
(1977j [1966]: 140). Although he does not state it explicitly at this point,
this reads like a blueprint for the analysis of the scores of the Western art
music tradition he grew up with, in which the piece is effectively an artifact whose every note is predetermined. Analysis of folksongs, however,
proves beyond doubt that they do not have immutable beginnings, endings, and inner construction. This variability in folksong is treated in the
seminal 1966 article "Versions and Variants of 'Barbara Allen,'" in which
Seeger queries the parameters within which different realizations of a
folksong are recognized as constituting performances of the same song.
With an insight born of long experience of listening to and transcribing
recordings, Seeger summarizes the surprises in store for an (art music–
trained) outsider encountering the Anglo-American folksong tradition:

> Suppose . . . one hears three, four, or more separate singings of [a] tune,
> sometimes with different titles or words or both by as many different
> singers. The name finally adopted for the lot will be found to cover an

increasing number of differences. Probably each singer has sung the tune in his individual way; most, perhaps, slightly differently with each singing. The more separate singings one has heard, the more differences may be noted among both words and tunes. These may be so marked that one may discover that more than one tune has been used to deliver almost identical texts and that almost identical tunes have been used to deliver the words of entirely different songs—children's songs, political songs, and even hymns. (1977k [1966]: 273–74)

As he phrases the question, "how much can two singings differ and still be singings of the same tune? Or, conversely, how little can they vary and still be singings of different tunes?" (ibid.:275). He concludes that "no such entity as '*the* "Barbara Allen" tune' can be set up other than for temporary convenience" (ibid.:316).

This awareness of variability and shifting identity, derived at least in part from his own intensive analysis of certain folksongs, informs Seeger's approach to the problem of the compositional process. From the same year, 1966, comes the major theoretical article mentioned above, "The Music Compositional Process. . . ," which discusses the music-extrinsic and -intrinsic factors in the compositional process. For the purposes of cross-reference with "Versions and Variants . . . " the most pertinent section is that describing the music-intrinsic process: "To produce a 'piece' of music . . . tonal and rhythmic elements . . . are enchained so as to exhibit a certain *form* . . . traditional in a repertory. . . . The same elements . . . can be regarded as necessary variables . . . of a stream of sound in time that an individual or group *forms* . . . into music in accord with a tradition of formation whose norms of style have evolved historically as a function of a culture" (1977j [1966]: 157–58). Although the different compositional processes involved in Western art music and folk music are not invoked here by way of illustration, they have already been addressed in a theoretical article from 1960, "On the Moods of a Music Logic," in which the differences in music-intrinsic rationale between art music and folk traditions, and the contextual reasons for those differences, have already been set out in clear, if idiosyncratic form:

The degree of uncertainty in a comparatively stabilized idiom, cultivated within a small, homogenous society with few or no acculturative impacts is naturally less than in a rapidly changing idiom cultivated in a highly diversified society and across political boundaries. For example, in Turkey Creek, North Carolina, around 1900, the predictability of the successor to the melodic pattern or mood delivering "In scarlet town" (which continues "where I was born") was undoubtedly higher than that of the second measure of Brahms's Symphony No. 2. (1977g [1960]: 65)

Recognizing these differences, Seeger insists that "the key question remains: *how* is the inward forming done and how does what is thus formed perform the functions attributed to it?" (1977j [1966]: 158). It is difficult to imagine that he could have come up with this question had his musical experience been confined solely to the Western art music tradition that dominated his youth.

A second theoretical issue, related to the problem of the compositional process, emerges in several middle- and late-period writings: the relationship between oral and written traditions. There is no doubt that Seeger views folk music traditions as "typically . . . inherited, cultivated, and transmitted without the art of writing" (1965:133), and that for him the use of printed material for formal instruction represents an undesirable departure from the traditional medium of transmission (1977d [1953]: 334; 1977i [1966]: 337). He underlines the vital role played by the practically immutable scores of Western art music in defining the identity of pieces in that tradition and by contrast the equally vital role played by the lack of scores in ensuring the variability of songs in the folksong tradition (1977k [1966]: 275). In addition he finds an identifiable effect on Western art music produced by the de-emphasis in recent centuries on oral processes: "musicians recognize 'playing by ear' and 'singing by rote' . . . ; but traditions of both, together with the allied art of improvisation, are utterly dead in professional life" (1949a:826).

On the other hand, Seeger is well aware of evidence from both art and folk music traditions that suggests that oral and written traditions are not necessarily mutually exclusive: indeed he points out that each may function as an accessory to the other and cites by way of illustration the "tradition" of the violinist Joachim and the "ballet book" of some folksingers (1945:290). Put more fully, "the terms 'folk music' and 'oral traditions' are not necessarily synonymous. There is a real dependence upon unwritten techniques in the fine art of music as well as in the popular art, where both written and unwritten techniques are almost equally employed. It must not be forgotten that all techniques of writing are traditional and are absolutely dependent upon 'oral' transmission for their reading" (1965:133).[10]

A third theoretical issue that occupies much of Seeger's attention in his later publications is that of the shortcomings of conventional Western notation, especially for purposes of transcription. This is strongly related to Seeger's awareness of the role of oral tradition even in predominantly written musical idioms. One may trace this concern as it develops through a series of reviews of folksong anthologies from 1947 to 1958. In his reviews from the late 1940s of the four volumes of Vance Randolph's *Ozark Folksongs,* Seeger consistently queries the reliability of the transcriptions—some, he complains, are "frankly, unbelievable" (1947–50 [1947:331]). By 1951 he clarifies his position: not only is he worried about the professionalism of the transcriptions in another folksong anthology, but about what they *intend to represent:* "whether they purport to be a hypothetical or logical skeletonizing of the tunes, a full representation of the musically perceptible tonal and rhythmic norms and nuances, or some compromise between the two; or, indeed, whether these alternatives have been clearly envisaged by the transcribers" (1951:523). By 1952 he has moved a step further, to doubt the validity of Western art music notation for transcribing other traditions. Reviewing Bartók and Lord's *Serbo-Croatian Folk Songs,* he praises Bartók's "skillful and painstaking" techniques of transcription and his awareness "of the shortcomings of our ordinary music notation" (1952:133). However, he goes on to anticipate a major argument of his well-known 1958 article "Prescriptive and Descriptive Music Writing" (1977f [1958]). Bartók uses essentially the notation devised for Western art music; yet

> its use depends upon a highly specialized tradition, mostly oral in transmission from teacher to pupil, by which it is written and read. This specialized oral tradition enables its carriers to "put back" into the reading of the notation what was "left out" in the writing of it. . . . What happens in the reading of a notation of a folk song is quite another thing. First, the writing communicates to the reader only those factors in the folk songs that resembled factors in the fine art. Second, the reading puts back (in the performance) not what was left out of the folk song but what is conventionally left out in the notation of the "art" song. (1952:134–35)

In other words, a notation only works if the donor and recipient of the song carry the same tradition—that of which the notation system is a part.

Later Seeger homes in also on the possible biases of the transcriber when transcribing a tradition not his or her own. In a 1958 review he suggests that Cecil Sharp, despite his skill as a notator, "is open to suspicion of favoring the archaic." The problem is, Seeger explains, that "in transcribing folk song to ordinary notation one is continually faced with both tonal and rhythmic ambiguities that can be interpreted variously and notated accordingly. If one regards a folk music as a dying survival, one naturally tends to interpret an ambiguity as an archaism; if one regards it as a current tradition, one tends, equally naturally, to interpret it as a current convention" (1958a:400).

It is these shortcomings of conventional visual representations that lead Seeger to differentiate *prescriptive* from *descriptive* music writing. Prescriptive notation is the blueprint from which musicians who carry a predominantly written tradition work: it exists before any given performance occurs and functions to guide it. Descriptive notation by contrast is the precipitation onto paper of a musical performance that has already happened; and its goal is to capture as accurately as possible what has already occurred. In the seminal "Prescriptive and Descriptive Music Writing," Seeger brings together the issues raised in the book reviews discussed above and emphasizes that the underrated oral components of a tradition are the mortar that holds the bricks of a notation together. When attempting to use Western fine art notation to make a descriptive representation of any other kind of music,

> First, we single out what appear to us to be structures in the other music which resemble structures familiar to us in the notation of the Occidental art and write these down, ignoring everything else for which we have no symbols. Second, we expect the resulting notation to be read by people who *do not carry the tradition of the other music.* The result can be only a conglomeration of structures part European [fine art], part non-European [fine art], connected by a movement 100 percent European [fine art]. To such a riot of subjectivity it is presumptuous indeed to ascribe the designation "scientific." (1977f [1958]: 170)

In this article, however, rather than merely warning of the problem, Seeger actually proposes a solution: to supplement conventional notation by using an electronically produced graph to provide a more objective visual representation. In his later discussion of the tunes of "Barbara Allen," he does in fact employ graphs made by the Model B Melograph to help solve the problems of notation and analysis of Anglo-American folksong. Not only do they allow for more accurate measurement of pitches and proportional values, a particularly valuable property where so individually variable a tradition is concerned, but they also impose an element of objectivity: Seeger notes with satisfaction that while such graphs sometimes support subjective judgements, often they are able to provide a quite contrary perspective (1977k [1966]: 296).[11] In this case the cycle has come full circle: a concern developed largely in response to the peculiarities of folk and other non–art music traditions has resulted in the precipitation of a concept and analytical tool that feed straight back into the study of those traditions.

Finally, one essay perhaps more than any other epitomizes the inter-relation of Seeger's empirical musical experience and his theorizing about larger issues: "The Folkness of the Nonfolk and the Nonfolkness of the Folk," revised in 1977 from the 1966 original. The title is a play on that of B. A. Botkin's article "The Folkness of the Folk" (1937), and its overt objective is to examine with musical examples the definition of the largely rural, pristine "folk" and their inherent defining characteristics, or "folkness," and to contrast this with those who are not classifiable as "folk" and their distinguishing characteristics, or "nonfolkness." Further-more, as the title suggests, Seeger posits that these categories are not watertight and that folk and nonfolk elements are present in everyone. In addition this article addresses broader issues, in particular the struc-ture-function dichotomy as applied to the folk music revival movement, the fact-value dichotomy inherent in nonfolkness and folkness, and the urban-rural cultural divide. What is striking is that Seeger employs con-crete musical examples to illuminate wide-ranging issues of a nonmusi-cal nature: it is perhaps the best example of Seeger's using his knowl-edge of folk music specifics to ponder more general matters.

For example, the "authenticity formula" from the 1948 record review, by which Seeger evaluates a folksinger's shift from folk to concert per-formance practice, reappears in this essay, at least implicitly, as he de-scribes the rapid progress away from the folk style of Aunt Molly Jack-son, Leadbelly, and Woody Guthrie, who "almost swamp[ed] his native talent in Greenwich Villagese" (1977i [1966]: 339). Brushing aside the lamentations of folklorists over this state of affairs, Seeger draws on this musical evidence to note that "the avidity of the hillbilly most remote from the city for the city's nonfolkness is quite as self-propelled as that of the city-billy most remote from the country for the country's folkness." In fact, given the activities of the media in disseminating commercial versions of music and of the "make America musical" movement in pushing respectable classical music, "there must exist few, if any, persons left ratable as 100 percent either folk or nonfolk" (ibid.). As an example of the meshing of folk and nonfolk elements, Seeger cites the folk music revival movement, which he describes as "an American shotgun wed-ding of oral (folk) and written (fine and popular art) idioms" (ibid.:338).

Perhaps inevitably, he ends up positing a continuum with folkness at one end and nonfolkness at the other—incidentally, a situation remarkably similar to his "authenticity scale" for folksingers.

This leads immediately to the question of how one defines "folkness" and "nonfolkness." After a couple of capricious attempts to define each of these in terms of the other, Seeger comes down in favor of "folkness is a concept referent to a property of cultural structures and functions whose weight increases in direct proportion to the decrease in logic and increase in pure, mystical belief, which is close to saying: the less something is pinned down to the factual and to objective reality and the more to the valual and to subjective reality, the more it partakes of the nature of folkness" (ibid.:339). In other words, nonfolkness may be identified with scientific, logical, fact-based thinking and folkness with value-based thinking not grounded in conscious rational deliberation. While Seeger does not himself say so explicitly, there is the implication that oral, partially improvisatory music traditions partake more of folkness than do written high art ones.

Although there is a constant subtheme in this article of the rural-urban divide, Seeger eventually makes it clear that he is not associating folkness exclusively with rural dwellers or nonfolkness with city populations; and his comments on the mixed rural and urban origins of the folk music revival provide musical evidence for this view. To drive the point home still further, he argues that folkness in the sense defined above is found in every activity of social man—as much in science, government, and scholarship as in quaint rural beliefs (ibid.:340).

In its own, idiosyncratic manner this one essay draws together all the strands that commonly occur in Seeger's writings on folk music; and though it is centered on the folk and folklore rather than music per se, it is *musical* phenomena that provide the illustrations on which his arguments are based. Given that Seeger was first and foremost a musicologist and that most of his contact with the "folk" was through the medium of music, it seems very likely that his perceptions of folkness and nonfolkness and their carriers, from which he was able to launch off into even more wide-ranging ideas, were in large measure shaped by his empirical musical experience.

≈

From the evidence discussed above, it is obvious that Seeger's "philosophic worldview" as expressed in the leitmotivs already established in his publications before 1940 strongly influenced the way he wrote about folk music, especially in its contextual and applied aspects. Equally, as Reuss suggests, the empirical experience with folk music garnered over many years by Seeger—and Crawford Seeger—was a major contributor to some of the theoretical issues that define much of his later work—in particular, though not exclusively, that part of his output that deals with music sound. The presence of folk music in Seeger's armory was, of course, in addition to that of Western art music; of concepts in non-Western musics with which he became familiar; of input from his reading in areas outside music; and of his substantial experience in applied musicology.

In conclusion, therefore, an analysis of some of Seeger's writings, both on folk music and on general musicological matters, does bear out his contention that he was not a student of folk music per se; one quibble with Seeger's own assessment of the situation is that, instead of describing folklore and folk music as "temporary bypaths" for him, perhaps it is preferable to refer to them as "tributaries": trickling in at different times and in different amounts, but contributing their contents to the mainstream of his thought.

NOTES

I wish to thank Judith Tick for her suggestions for this essay. I am also grateful to the Regents of the University of California and the University of California at Los Angeles Oral History Program, Department of Special Collections, Charles E. Young Research Library, for permission to quote from "Reminiscences of an American Musicologist," © 1972 by the Regents of the University of California. All rights reserved. Used with permission.

1. The Composers Collective of New York was a group of radically inclined professional musicians, some of whom belonged to the Communist Party, who hoped to use their music to help the working class. Seeger participated for about three years, from 1932 to 1935. A detailed description of the collective and Seeger's changing role in it is given in Pescatello (1992:109–19); see also Reuss (1971).

2. Indeed Seeger adds a third dichotomy: that of "fact" and "value," explaining "history tries to tell us how things came to be as they are: system, how things are coming to be what they will be. *What* they are, as of now, may be viewed variously according to the unique structural-historical-factual and functional-systematic-valual imbalance that characterizes the behavior of each one of us" (1977i [1966]: 341).

3. Wilgus defines the functionalist's approach as laying "stress on the meaning of the material and its use in and to the community and the singer," and contrasts it with "the historical-comparative approach" (1959:343).

4. "How and why do songs concerned with actual local happenings become localized elsewhere, so that other places and other actors become substituted for the original ones? What songs does the singer like, which ones does he care less for, and why? . . . Does he play some particular role in his community? Is music something that endows him with social prestige? . . . How does one become an accomplished singer? How does one learn songs? What are the standards of criticism? What are the attitudes of the audience?" (quoted in Wilgus 1959:339). Judith Tick notes that Seeger definitely knew this article by Herzog (personal communication).

5. This was Seeger's most avowedly left-wing period, and it was to cause him trouble in the 1950s, when he was investigated by the FBI and, in 1953, denied a passport despite his position as a UNESCO representative (Pescatello 1992:208).

6. Seeger attributes what he terms the "make America musical" movement to the efforts of the urban upper classes of the nineteenth century, who, in order to assure cultural respectability, sought to "'make America musical' in the exact image of contemporary Europe as they saw it" (1977e [1957]: 225). These were the people Seeger saw as responsible for the propagation of European classical music to the detriment of American-born forms.

7. Similar treatment of folk music may be found, for example, in "The Cultivation of Various European Traditions of Music in the New World" (1977h [1961]). A more sophisticated treatment of some of these issues may be found in "The Folkness of the Nonfolk . . ." (1977i [1966]), discussed later in this essay.

8. An idea of contemporary intellectual trends in this area may be gained from *American Composers on American Music,* edited by Cowell (1933).

9. Judith Tick points out the influence of Seeger's second wife, Ruth Crawford Seeger, on his thought in this area. Ruth Crawford Seeger's arrangements of folksongs for children are well known (e.g., *American Folk Songs for Children in Home, School, and Nursery School* [1948] and *Animal Folk Songs for Children* [1950]). An overview of her life and work may be found in the biography by Tick (1997).

10. Practically the same point is made in "Oral Tradition in Music" (1949a) and in "The Music Compositional Process . . ." (1977j [1966]: 154).

11. Seeger kept up an interest in the improvement of graphic writers: note his review of Karl Dahlback's *New Methods in Vocal Folk Music Research* (1960).

REFERENCES CITED

Botkin, B. A. 1937. "The Folkness of the Folk." *English Journal, College Edition* 26 (6): 461–69.

Cowell, Henry, ed. 1933. *American Composers on American Music: A Symposium.* Stanford, Calif.: Stanford University Press.

Dunaway, David King. 1979. "Unsung Songs of Protest: The Composers Collective of New York." *New York Folklore* 5 (1–2): 1–19.

———. 1980. "Charles Seeger and Carl Sands: The Composers' Collective Years." *Ethnomusicology* 24 (2): 159–68.

Jackson, George Pullen. 1933. *White Spirituals in the Southern Uplands.* Chapel Hill: University of North Carolina Press.

Lieberman, Robbie. 1989. *"My Song Is My Weapon": People's Songs, American Communism, and the Politics of Culture, 1930–1950.* Urbana: University of Illinois Press.

Lomax, John A., and Alan Lomax, comps.; Charles Seeger and Ruth Crawford Seeger, music eds. 1947. *Folk Song USA.* New York: Duell, Sloan and Pearce.

Pescatello, Ann M. 1992. *Charles Seeger: A Life in American Music.* Pittsburgh: University of Pittsburgh Press.

Reuss, Richard. 1971. "The Roots of American Left-Wing Interest in Folksong." *Labor History* 12 (2): 259–79.

———. 1979. "Folk Music and Social Conscience: The Musical Odyssey of Charles Seeger." *Western Folklore* 38 (4): 221–38.

Seeger, Charles Louis. 1923. "Music in the American University." *Educational Review* 66 (2): 95–99.

———. 1924. "On the Principles of Musicology." *Musical Quarterly* 10 (2): 244–50.

———. 1932. "Carl Ruggles." *Musical Quarterly* 18 (4): 578–92.

———. 1933. "Music and Musicology." In *Encyclopedia of the Social Sciences.* Vol. 11:143–50. New York: Macmillan.

———. 1934a. "A Program for Proletarian Composers." *Daily Worker* (New York edition), January 16, 5.

———. 1934b. "On Proletarian Music." *Modern Music* 11 (3): 121–27.

———. 1934c. Review of William L. Dawson's *Negro Folk Symphony. Daily Worker* (New York edition), November 23, 5.

———. 1938. "Music in America." *Magazine of Art* 31 (7): 411–13, 435–36.

———. 1939a. "Grass Roots for American Composers." *Modern Music* 16 (3): 143–49.

———. 1939b. "Systematic and Historical Orientations in Musicology." *Acta Musicologica* 11 (4): 121–28.

———. 1940a. "Folk Music as a Source of Social History." In *The Cultural Approach to History.* Ed. Carolyn F. Ware. 316–23. New York: Columbia University Press.

———. 1940b. "The Importance to Cultural Understanding of Folk and Popular Music." In *Conference on Inter-American Relations in the Field of Music: Digest of Proceedings.* Washington, D.C.: U.S. Department of State.

———. 1941. "Inter-American Relations in the Field of Music: Some Basic Considerations." *Music Educators Journal* 27 (5): 17–18, 64–65.

———. 1942. "American Music for American Children." *Music Educators Journal* 29 (2): 11–12.

———. 1944. "Music and Government: Field for an Applied Musicology." In *Papers Read at the International Congress of Musicology Held at New York, Sep-*

tember 11–18, 1939. 12–20. New York: Music Educators National Conference for the American Musicological Society.

———. 1945. "Music in the Americas: Oral and Written Traditions in the Americas." *Bulletin of the Pan American Union* 79 (5–6): 290–93, 341–44.

———. 1947–50. Review of the four volumes of *Ozark Folksongs,* collected and edited by Vance Randolph (Columbia, Missouri: State Historical Society of Missouri, 1946, 1948, 1949, 1950). In *Notes,* 2d ser. 4 (3) (1947): 330–32; 5 (4) (1948): 576; 6 (3) (1949): 469; 7 (3) (1950): 469–70.

———. 1948. Review of four folksong records: *Listen to Our Story: A Panorama of American Ballads,* edited by Alan Lomax (Brunswick Radio Corporation, American Folk Music Series, Album B-1024, 1947); *Mountain Frolic: Square Dances and Hoedowns from the Southern Mountains,* edited by Alan Lomax (Brunswick Radio Corporation, American Folk Music Series, Album B-1025, 1947); *Sod Buster Ballads: Folk Song of the Early West* (Commodore Records, Album CR-10, 1947); and *Deep Sea Chanteys and Whaling Ballads* (Commodore Records, Album CR-11, 1947) In *Journal of American Folklore* 61 (240): 215–18.

———. 1949a. "Oral Tradition in Music." In *Standard Dictionary of Folklore, Mythology, and Legend.* 825–29. New York: Funk and Wagnalls.

———. 1949b. Review of four releases in Decca's Personality Series: *A Collection of Ballads and Folk Songs,* by Burl Ives (Album A-407, 1945); *Ballads and Folksongs,* vol. 2, by Burl Ives (Album A-431, 1947); *Ballads and Blues,* by Josh White (Album A-447, 1946); and *American Folk Music Series,* by Richard Dyer-Bennett (Album A-573, 1947). In *Journal of American Folklore* 62 (243): 68–70.

———. 1951. Review of *Folksongs of Florida,* collected and edited by Alton C. Morris (Gainesville: University of Florida Press, 1950); *Texas Folksongs,* by William A. Owens (Austin: Texas Folklore Society, 1950); and *Folksongs of Alabama,* collected by Byron Arnold (University: University of Alabama Press). In *Notes,* 2d ser. 8 (3): 523–25.

———. 1952. Review of *Serbo-Croatian Folk Songs,* by Béla Bartók and Albert Lord (New York: Columbia University Press, 1951). In *Journal of the American Musicological Society* 5 (2): 132–35.

———. 1954. "Folk Music: USA." In *Grove Dictionary of Music and Musicians.* 5th ed. Vol. 3:387–98. New York: St. Martin's Press.

———. 1958a. Review of *The Music of the Ballads,* edited by Jan Philip Schinhan (Durham: Duke University Press, 1957). In *Notes,* 2d ser. 15 (3): 399–401.

———. 1958b. "Singing Style." *Western Folklore* 17 (1): 3–11.

———. 1960. Review of *New Methods in Vocal Folk Music Research* (Oslo: Oslo University Press, 1958). In *Ethnomusicology* 4 (1): 41–42.

———. 1965. s.v. "Folk Music." *Collier's Encyclopaedia.* New York: Crowell, Collier and Macmillan.

———. 1972. "Reminiscences of an American Musicologist." Oral History Program, University of California at Los Angeles.

———. 1977a [1940]. "Contrapuntal Style in the Three-Voice Shape-Note Hymns of the United States." In *Studies in Musicology, 1935–1975.* 237–51. Berkeley: University of California Press. (Reprinted from "Contrapuntal Style in the Three-Voice Shape-Note Hymns," *Musical Quarterly* 26 [4]: 483–93.)

———. 1977b [1949]. "Professionalism and Amateurism in the Study of Folk Music." In *Studies in Musicology, 1935–1975.* 321–29. Berkeley: University of California Press. (Reprinted from *Journal of American Folklore* 62 [244]: 107–13.)

———. 1977c [1952]. "Music and Society: Some New-World Evidence of Their Relationship." In *Studies in Musicology, 1935–1975.* 182–94. Berkeley: University of California Press. (Revised from *Proceedings of the Conference on Latin American Fine Arts, June 14–17, 1951.* 84–97. Austin: University of Texas Press.)

———. 1977d [1953]. "Folk Music in the Schools of a Highly Industrialized Society." In *Studies in Musicology, 1935–1975.* 330–34. Berkeley: University of California Press. (Reprinted from *Journal of the International Folk Music Council* 5:40–44.)

———. 1977e [1957]. "Music and Class Structure in the United States." In *Studies in Musicology, 1935–1975.* 222–36. Berkeley: University of California Press. (Reprinted from *American Quarterly* 9 [3]: 281–94.)

———. 1977f [1958]. "Prescriptive and Descriptive Music Writing." In *Studies in Musicology, 1935–1975.* 168–81. Berkeley: University of California Press. (Reprinted from *Musical Quarterly* 44 [2]: 184–95. Kassel: Bärenreiter.)

———. 1977g [1960]. "On the Moods of a Music Logic." In *Studies in Musicology, 1935–1975.* 64–101. Berkeley: University of California Press. (Reprinted from *Journal of the American Musicological Society* 13:224–61.)

———. 1977h [1961]. "The Cultivation of Various European Traditions of Music in the New World." In *Studies in Musicology, 1935–1975.* 195–210. Berkeley: University of California Press. (Reprinted from "The Cultivation of Various European Traditions in the Americas." In *Report of the Eighth Congress of the International Musicological Society, New York, 1961.* 364–75.)

———. 1977i [1966]. "The Folkness of the Nonfolk and the Nonfolkness of the Folk." In *Studies in Musicology, 1935–1975.* 335–44. Berkeley: University of California Press. (Revised version of "The Folkness of the Nonfolk vs. the Nonfolkness of the Folk." In *Folklore and Society: Essays in Honor of Benj. A. Botkin.* Ed. Bruce Jackson. 1–9. Hatboro, Pa.: Folklore Associates.)

———. 1977j [1966]. "The Music Compositional Process as a Function in a Nest of Functions and in Itself a Nest of Functions." In *Studies in Musicology, 1935–1975.* 139–67. Berkeley: University of California Press. (Reprinted from "The Music Process as a Function in a Context of Functions." *Yearbook, Inter-American Institute for Musical Research* 2 [1]: 1–36.)

———. 1977k [1966]. "Versions and Variants of 'Barbara Allen' in the Archive of American Song to 1940." In *Studies in Musicology, 1935–1975.* 273–320. Berkeley: University of California Press. (Reprinted from "Versions and Variants of the Tunes of 'Barbara Allen,'" *Selected Reports* [University of California at Los Angeles, Institute of Ethnomusicology] 1 [1]: 120–67.)

———. 1977l [1970]. "Toward a Unitary Field Theory for Musicology." In *Studies in Musicology, 1935–1975*. 102–38. Berkeley: University of California Press. (Reprinted from *Selected Reports* [University of California at Los Angeles, Institute of Ethnomusicology] 1 [3]: 171–210.)

———. 1977m [1971]. "Music as Concept and as Percept." In *Studies in Musicology, 1935–1975*. 31–44. Berkeley: University of California Press. (Reprinted from "Reflections upon a Given Topic: Music in the Universal Perspective." *Ethnomusicology* 13 [3]: 385–98.)

———. 1980. "United States of America. II: Folk Music." In *New Grove Dictionary of Music and Musicians*. Vol. 19:436–47. London: Macmillan.

Seeger, Charles Louis, and Margaret Valiant. 1980 [1937]. "Journal of a Field Representative." *Ethnomusicology* 24 (2): 169–210. (Reprinted from the Resettlement Administration [Washington, D.C.] publication by the same name.)

Seeger, Ruth Crawford, comp. 1948. *American Folk Songs for Children in Home, School and Nursery School*. Garden City, N.Y.: Doubleday.

———, comp. 1950. *Animal Folk Songs for Children*. Garden City, N.Y.: Doubleday.

Tick, Judith. 1997. *Ruth Crawford Seeger: A Composer's Search for American Music*. New York: Oxford University Press.

Warren-Findley, Jannelle. 1979–80. "Musicians and Mountaineers: The Resettlement Administration's Music Program in Appalachia, 1935–37." *Appalachian Journal* 7 (1): 105–23.

Wilgus, D. K. 1959. *Anglo-American Folksong Scholarship since 1898*. New Brunswick, N.J.: Rutgers University Press.

Zuck, Barbara A. 1980. *A History of Musical Americanism*. Ann Arbor, Mich.: UMI Research Press.

5

Ruth Crawford, Charles Seeger, and "The Music of American Folk Songs"

Judith Tick

In my own life I try to reproduce Charlie's extraordinary synthesis of theory and practice, of thought and action. . . . Of course, he had to provide a foil to Dio [Ruth] as you would well know—anything he did was a combination of the two temperaments, so a tribute to him would have to be a tribute to Dio as well.
  —Peggy Seeger, quoted in Pescatello 1992:258

Sometime in the mid-1970s, when I was wading through graduate school in musicology, a very old Charles Seeger, sitting erect on a high-back chair in a conference-hotel lobby, nodded politely in my direction once. I noticed the dapper ascot draped around his wrinkled neck. He most likely did not hear my name, spoken at fortissimo level by Gilbert Chase, his former student and my mentor, who was honoring me with this introduction. The ritual was over in a moment.

Little did I suspect then how much time I would take getting to know this elder statesman of ethnomusicology. Because Ruth Crawford[1] (1901–53) fell in love with her teacher, married him in 1932, and stayed married to him until she died, as her biographer, I have smiled at pictures of six-year-old Charles dressed like a Victorian prince, shed tears over his love letters, read his business correspondence, and watched the faces of people who knew him light up with memories (see Tick 1997). While other scholars grappled with this challenging musical philosopher, I scrutinized Charles Seeger as the husband to a woman honored as a major figure in the post-Ives generation of American modernist composers.

If I choose to write about the husband now, it is because of the question of influence, a process so often confused with control and power. I do not think it an overstatement to say that until fairly recently most writers have assumed that the trajectory of influence generally flowed from Seeger to Crawford; as if Ruth, like her biblical namesake, followed the precept: "whither thou goest, I will go."[2] Because in some senses she did "goest"—moving to Washington, for example, when Seeger was hired by the Resettlement Administration, only obliquely did I come to recognize how much influence flowed from wife to husband. Charles Seeger rarely acknowledged this influence in public. Nevertheless I now believe that in his scholarship in traditional music he depended on Ruth Crawford's practice-based research and insight just as much as she depended on his theoretical mind.

Pete Seeger often remarked how his father and Ruth "thought like a team."[3] The two shared so much in their evolution from modernist warriors, battling for what Crawford called "modern American dissonant music,"[4] to urban folksong revivalists that Seeger's prescription for new music in the 1920s fits the texture of their odyssey: "Sounding apart while sounding together" (Seeger 1930:28). This phrase, which Seeger used to express his vision of an ideal modernist polyphony based on dissonance, captures the range of interactions within the intellectual counterpoint of this marriage: language shared, sources cited, subjects repeated, ideas borrowed, projects jointly undertaken. Their collaboration as music editors for John and Alan Lomax's *Folk Song USA* (1947) is only one case in point. Their intellectual intimacy is evident in excerpts from their various writings. This chapter draws heavily on Crawford's unpublished work "The Music of American Folk Songs" and focuses on two important areas of inquiry in folksong scholarship—transcription and singing style.

The Ideological Bond: Tradition as Opposition

The team of Crawford/Seeger shaped their cultural politics about traditional music after 1936. It is not necessary to review in detail Charles Seeger's role in the urban folk music movement that so many have chronicled elsewhere (e.g., Cantwell 1996; Cohen 1990; Lieberman 1989). A better focus is to recapitulate two points that appear early on in Crawford's contributions: (1) the role of national tradition in the training of classical musicians; and (2) the relationship between tradition and modernity.

While Seeger worked for the Resettlement Administration (1936–37), Crawford produced a set of piano arrangements of folk tunes (ca. 1936–38), designed for classical piano pedagogy; they have only recently been published as *Nineteen American Folk Tunes for Elementary Piano* (1995 [1936–38]). She prefaced them with a miniature manifesto for the urban folk revival movement, still in its early stages of formation. She urged an enlightened nationalism, that is to say, self-knowledge about one's own culture as a necessary prelude to knowledge of other cultures: "It is the belief of this composer that, just as the child becomes acquainted with his own home environment before experiencing the more varied contacts of school and community, so should the music student be given the rich musical heritage of his own country as a basis upon which to build his experience of the folk and art music of other countries" (ibid.: n.p.). Seeger shared and articulated this foundational value as well. Publishing his article "Grass Roots for American Composers" in 1939, he pressed the same self-knowledge on his colleagues. Many years later he applied this to music education in "World Musics in American Schools: A Challenge to Be Met": "From a musical point of view, the prime concern in education would seem to be acquisition of competence in one's own music, . . . just as, from a linguistic point of view, the prime concern is acquisition of competence in one's own language" (1994c [1972]: 427). Although his language is more abstract and the switch from Crawford's "home environment" to "language" germane, the classic folk revival precept of cultural self-knowledge before knowledge of others endures.

The Crawford/Seeger team also proposed a bond between modernism and tradition. This point is a bit more complicated, depending on an understanding of a shift away from the paradigm of folk music as the essence of simplicity toward a new model of folk music that emphasized its musical sophistication and stylistic otherness. Their position emerged from the music itself and their mutual discovery of the repertory discussed in George Pullen Jackson's *White Spirituals in the Southern Uplands* (1933). Crawford quickly perceived how the shape-note repertory was oppositional to common tonal practice of fine-art music. Had not Bartók championed Hungarian peasant music as antiromantic in much the same way? Both Crawford and Seeger adopted indigenous American hymnody as a symbolic ally in their attempts to destabilize the hegemony of Eurocentric aesthetics. If conventional classical music marginalized folk and avant-garde musics, then perhaps musical affinities between the two outsider musics validated them both. In her preface to *Nineteen Ameri-*

can Folk Tunes, Crawford explained how her piano arrangements illustrated their common practices. Her goal was:

> to present this music [her new arrangements of folk tunes] in an idiom savoring as much as possible of the contemporary, preferring a bareness rather than a richness of style, and accustoming the student's ear to a freer use of the fifth, fourth, seventh, and second intervals so abundantly used in most contemporary music. Curiously enough, there is part-singing widespread throughout the southeastern states, and has been for the past hundred years, which revels in these characteristics of "modern music." (1995 [1936–38]: n.p.)

The repertory of "part-singing" to which she alluded was studied by Seeger in his article "Contrapuntal Style in the Three-Voice Shape-Note Hymns" published a few years later. There similar points made in similar language evoke Crawford's preface in subtle ways: "Now, it is a curious but significant fact that European art music since before 1900 has employed increasingly a number of devices, including parallel intervals, which characterize the hymns I have been considering. The restrained melodic line and the spare tonal fabric have been gaining more and more adherents" (1977a [1940]: 249).

Our Singing Country and "The Music of American Folk Songs"

During the late 1930s the Crawford/Seeger partnership deepened as they approached cultural mediation with different emphases. Seeger administered various federal programs, initially traveling as a supervisor in the field and doing some collecting; in his public role associated with highly visible political institutions, Seeger could do battle. As Herbert Halpert recalled, "Charlie had courage, he was fighting the whole music group, trying to get folksong accepted"[5] by a resistant musical establishment.

Crawford concentrated on music and practice-based research that relied heavily on field recordings. She began with transcription, and it is here that one finds the wellsprings of her greatest influence on Charles Seeger. Between 1937 and 1941 she worked as music editor for *Our Singing Country* (1941), the second anthology of American traditional music based on the materials collected by John and Alan Lomax. Since *Our Singing Country* was what Bess Lomax Hawes has called a "family book," with the book came the family: John, his wife Ruby Terrill; Bess, then fifteen; and his son and heir apparent, Alan, then working at the Archive of American Folk Song. Ruth, occasionally Charles, and the Lomaxes gathered around a phonograph in a room at the Library of Congress to cull material from the field recordings of past and recent Lomax expeditions across the country.[6]

To Bess Lomax Hawes is owed an account of the seduction of a modernist composer. Crawford "was completely excited by the coherence and elegance of the different musical systems that Father and Alan had recorded, by the complexity of American folk music. She was really aesthetically very moved by this." When they "deliberately set out to talk about the United States as a place with enormous musical creativity; . . . [she] encouraged this by helping them pick out the most exotic and esoteric of the tunes."[7] In the "Music Preface" to *Our Singing Country*, Crawford would later celebrate: "a work song in 5/4 meter, a Cajun tune consistently in 10/8 throughout, a Ravel-like banjo accompaniment, a ballad of archaic tonal texture, a Bahaman part-song of contrapuntal bareness" (1941:xviii).

Alan Lomax paints this vivid portrait of the challenge posed by the task at hand—turning oral tradition into Western notation. He called Crawford "a musico-intellectual lambkin gamboling in the lion's jaws." Several decades later he told Mike Seeger, "I was witness to that struggle, the struggle of the conservatory-trained musician. We had given her the chance, and she, in total youthful wonderful confidence, set out to take the terrible European notational system and to do it, to make it communicate the ultimate originality of a living tradition."[8]

No wonder that a project scheduled to take one summer stretched into three years and what was supposed to be a small music appendix expanded into a serious highly technical monograph called "The Music of American Folk Songs." And no wonder that Macmillan, the publisher of *Our Singing Country*, refused to add such a work of scholarship to a trade book. Bitterly disappointed by the neglect of what she felt was a unique treatment of American folksong, Crawford then condensed its main ideas into a ten-page deceptively simple music preface.

The story of how this experience working with Lomax material affected Crawford's life and work is told elsewhere (Tick 1997:chaps. 16–17). The main purpose here is to show how and why it proved to be a turning point in Seeger's intellectual development, as he himself acknowledged in private.[9] First, Crawford changed the way Seeger regarded the transcription process. Second, she brought the idea of singing style to the forefront of the research focus.

Transcription

Crawford discussed transcription as theory and practice fully in her impressive still-unpublished study "The Music of American Folk Songs."[10] The table of contents (figure 5.1) from the autograph typescript of about sixty pages immediately shows the depth and range of her systematic investigation, with separate sections on "Remarks on Transcription" and "Notes on the Songs and on Manners of Singing." Gone was the warm tone of the published music preface, designed for a general readership, its place usurped by the dispassionate prose of analytic discourse.

Through her labor of making three hundred or so transcriptions, Crawford arrived at a crucial distinction that Seeger would later make famous in the scholarly ethnomusicological literature. Transcription was a bridge between peoples, over which a "vital heritage of culture can pass." She described how the notational bridge might be constructed: "The manner of its building must be determined, for the most part, by the specific use to which the notations will be put. If they are to be used for strictly scientific study rather than for singing, the transcriber will wish to include in them all details—rhythmic, tonal, and formal—perceptible to him. If they are to be published in song books for school or community use, he will no doubt feel constrained to indicate only the outline, the bare skeleton of the song" (1940:9). In effect she initiated the distinction expanded by Seeger in his famous article "Prescriptive and Descriptive Music Writing," where he defines the difference between them: the former as the "blueprint of how a specific piece of music shall be made to sound" and the latter as "a report of how a specific performance of any music actually did sound" (1977b [1958]: 168).

Before Crawford's work on *Our Singing Country,* Seeger himself had treated transcription somewhat desultorily. Calling his song-sheet project for the Resettlement Administration the repopularizing of traditional music, he believed this process would be subverted by "fancy transcriptions." Better to give people a norm of the song in the simplest terms possible and then "let them make the inevitable variants when they make it on their own," he told his friend George Korson.[11] As Crawford problematized the transcription process, Seeger began to take it more seriously as an area of scholarly inquiry. It was in a sense an issue that crossed the boundaries between sound and representation, a kind of exercise in musical linguistics: just the sort of thing that fascinated him throughout his life. He acted as a sounding board and editor for Crawford's "The Music of American Folk Songs" just as she had taken that role earlier for

TABLE OF CONTENTS

I
REMARKS ON TRANSCRIPTION

1. The singer and the song
2. Phonographic recording of the song
3. Transcription of the song from phonographic recording
    a. Transcription from phonograph recording versus dictation direct from folk singer, player or intermediary
    b. Transcription through graph notation
4. The reader and the song
5. Music notation as a bridge ~~from singer to reader~~
6. Three basic types of transcription illustrated
7. Song-norm
8. Majority usage
9. Underlimits of amount of detail shown in notation, especially with regard to the simpler singing-styles
10. The model tune as representative of the song as a whole
11. The initial tune as model tune
12. The composite tune
13. The transcriber and a changing oral tradition

II
NOTES ON THE SONGS AND ON MANNERS OF SINGING

14. Adherence to a dynamic level throughout the song as a whole
15. Adherence to a dramatic level throughout the song as a whole
16. Adherence to the tempo set at the beginning of the song
    a. Infrequency of long ritardandos from the beginning to the end of the song as a whole
    b. Infrequency of short stereotyped ritardandos at ends of phrases and stanzas
17. Strict time and free singing-styles
18. Pulse and count
19. Anticipation and delay of beat
20. Simple and compound meter
21. Rest
22. Metrical irregularities - prolongation and contraction of measure
    a. Contraction of measure
    b. Prolongation of measure - the extended tone and the extended or inserted rest
    c. Underlimit of metrical irregularity shown in notation, especially with regard to extension of tone and extension and insertion of rest
    d. Manners of notating the extended tone and the extended or inserted rest
23. Metrical irregularities - divisions of beat and measure
24. Phrase patterns
    a. Number of measures to the phrase
    b. Number of phrases to the song
25. Interstanzaic variation
26. Manners of accommodating extra syllables of succeeding stanzas
27. Tone attack and release
28. Intonation
29. Scale and mode
30. Accompaniment

Figure 5.1. "The Music of American Folk Songs" table of contents

his own treatise, "Tradition and Experiment in (the New) Music" (1994a [1931]).[12] Crawford acknowledged this in a letter to John Lomax: "The Appendix has bloomed, been pruned, added to, pruned again, tightened up and filled in, til even Charlie (who has had to have it talked at him, read to him, and thought out to him, with plenty of suggestions from him and ideas and new angles resulting) thinks it is pretty good."[13]

It seems likely that one such suggestion concerned the use of a mechanical graph to produce descriptive notation. As is well known, Seeger
advocated the mechanical graph for descriptive notation. Comments
about the graph and its diagrams are in his hand as well as hers in the
sketches for the document. Two quotations from their respective writing illustrate their shared language. Here is Crawford on transcription
through graph notation:

> The most accurate techniques of transcription from phonograph record-
> ing are, of course, the modern graphing techniques, now perfected for
> laboratory use but not generally available. [This is followed by reference
> to Milton Metfessel's *Phonophotography in Folk Music* (1928) and the mu-
> sical example "Swing Low, Sweet Chariot."] . . . These show a thing which
> musicians have always vaguely felt to be true—namely, that a tune is a
> stream of sound whose variations in pitch and in time can be represented
> on paper as a curving line. . . . Figure 5 represents within a margin of error
> of approximately .1 second, metrical irregularities observed in the origi-
> nal singing. (R. Seeger 1940:3–6)

As he would reiterate this point many times throughout his life,
Seeger relied on this language as well:

> On the one hand, let us agree, melody may be conceived . . . as a succes-
> sion of separate sounds, on the other, as a single continuum of sound—
> as a chain or as a stream. . . . Where the individual notation may give too
> much norm and too little detail, the individual graph may easily give too
> little norm and too much detail. . . . For the present, I am inclined to set . . .
> 1/10 of a second as fair margins of accuracy for general musicological
> use. [Then follow examples of Metfessel, "Swing Low, Sweet Chariot."]
> (1977b [1958]: 169, 179)

Other details deserve mention. Notes in Seeger's hand on sheets
among early draft material suggest that he apparently contributed the
idea of demonstrating different levels of transcription complexity through
examples that showed several versions of the same tune in varying de-
grees of elaboration. From precise to "skeletal," to use Crawford's term:
what was lost, what was gained—the reader witnessed scholarly judgment at work by watching foreground details slowly yield to alternative
versions. Figure 5.2 gives four versions of one phrase from the African-
American holler "Trouble, Trouble." (The published transcription used
version B.) Such observations immediately led to method theory about
the process of representation or, to put this another way, the problem of

the one and the many: what was the relationship of one field recording to the many versions of the tune that existed in tradition? What was typical and what was idiosyncratic? Might not a skeptic maintain that complex variants were exceptions to the rule? Several theoretical terms tackle solutions to these thorny issues: the "model tune"—the tune of one single stanza of one song as sung in one performance; "song-norm" referred to the "basic tune pattern" of an individual piece, which could then serve as a guide to understanding the contributions of individual singers in shaping variants; "majority usage" referred to a particular "variation being representative, within that musical function and at that point in the tune of the song in its entirety." Some editorial sketches suggest that Seeger contributed the term "song-norm." Later he adopted her term "majority usage," replying to a question about its provenance as follows: "I must admit that the term 'majority usage' was, to best of my knowledge, an invention of my wife Ruth's when she was working on the transcriptions of *Our Singing Country;* but maybe Cecil Sharp or even Percy Grainger used it."[14]

Singing Style

Without doubt Seeger's scholarship on Anglo-American folk music owes its greatest debt to Crawford's research when his work concerns singing

Figure 5.2. Four transcriptions of one phrase from the African-American holler "Trouble, Trouble"

style. A primary insight appears in the music preface, where she writes: "No one who has studied these or similar recordings can deny that the song and its singing are indissolubly connected—that the character of a song depends to a great extent on the manner of its singing" (1941:xviii). Producing written notation, so appealing to classical musicians who typically regard a score as the authoritative statement of music as object, was a point of departure, not an end in itself. The relationship between notation and performance demanded stylistic mediation that could only result from hearing the music. Therefore Crawford issued caveats to the city readers of her work that resound with the passion of advocacy: "It is often to be noticed that the city-person, unacquainted with folk idioms, will endow a folksong with manners of fine-art or popular performance that are foreign to it, and will tend to sentimentalize or to dramatize that which the folk performer presents in a simple straightforward way" (ibid.).

She elaborated this position further in a section she titled "The Reader and the Song" in her study "The Music of American Folk Songs." The following quotation written by Crawford will sound familiar to readers of Seeger's later work:

> The majority of those who read this book will, in all probability, be city or town people. They will be used to reading books, and may be able to read music notation more or less well. They must be warned however, that *it is only to the extent to which they are, or become familiar with the idiomatic variations of American folk singing that they can expect to put approximately the right kind of flesh, blood, and nerve fibre back on this skeleton notation*. . . . There will be a tendency to fill in the notation with approximations, not of folk singing, but of popular and fine-art music. This is partly because well-educated Americans have been taught that only fine-art music is "music" or "good music," and partly because they tend to associate music notation only with the mannerisms of fine-art music, for which idiom it was designed. (1940:3–4)

Here is Charles Seeger on the same point: "we must remember that this notation was developed for the purposes of composition and performance in the tradition of the professional, 'high,' elegant, elite, or fine art of Occidental music, not for performance of the folk art" (1977c [1966]: 287). And similarly:

> In employing this mainly prescriptive notation as a descriptive sound writing of any music other than the Occidental fine and popular arts of music, we do two things, both thoroughly unscientific. First, we single

out what appear to us to be structures in the other music which resemble structures familiar to us in the notation of the Occidental art and write these down, ignoring everything else for which we have no symbols. Second, we expect the resulting notation to be read by people who *do not carry the tradition of the other music.* (1977b [1958]: 170)

Crawford studied transcription at just that point in the urban folk revival when the Archive of American Folk Songs would begin to issue recordings available to the public at large. Even if she anticipated that new recorded-sound technology would make trade-book anthologies of transcribed melodies obsolete, she nevertheless seized the moment to validate the idea of singing style as a worthy area of investigation and, most importantly, a rival to textual scholarship. She made this manifest by documenting each aspect of musical style as fully as possible. For every observation she cited multiple examples from Anglo-American and African-American tradition. Indisputable authority emerges with the control she demonstrates over her material.

Here are two cases in point. Figure 5.3 pertains to the relationship between conventional metric notation and oral tradition. She is discussing the well-known song "Little Bird, Go Through My Window," which she transcribed using both 2/8 and 3/8. She explained the context of her decision precisely: "Notable illustration of alternation of meters can be

Figure 5.3. "Roll on, Babe" and "Little Bird, Go Through My Window"

heard throughout the singing of the many stanzas and choruses of '[Oh] Roll on, Babe' as also of the several repetitions of the stanza of 'Little Bird, Go Through My Window.' In the former, the *patterns* of alternation exhibit a considerable amount of interstanzaic variation. In the latter, variation in phrase occurrence of the eighth rest (interpolated, it would seem, for intake of breath), provides the principal interstanzaic variation with respect to meter" (1940:48).[15]

Figure 5.4 illustrates the consequences of choice over meter and rhythm by comparing an inferior to a superior transcription. In the published transcription of the spiritual "Choose You a Seat 'n' Set Down," a small metric shift from 2/4 to 3/4 in the chorus notates an irregular rhythm as something other than a conventional syncopation. Such a small moment but so alive. One need only compare the oversimplified version in 2/4 that she wrote as a foil with two other transcription options: the first, a highly complex version; and the second, an elegantly nuanced version she used for publication. She explained the issue at length:

> It might be of interest in presenting one further example (taken from the chorus of "Choose You a Seat 'n' Set Down") to include two types of transcription. Type B was chosen in publication. The pattern of metrical alternation is maintained almost without change through the four recurrences which comprise each singing of the chorus, as well as throughout all the repetitions of the chorus. [This] notation can be said to represent

Figure 5.4. Handwritten transcription options for "Choose You a Seat 'n' Set Down," reproduced from "The Music of American Folk Songs": (a) a complex transcription; (b) a moderately complex transcription published in *Our Singing Country;* and (c) an oversimplified transcription

more or less accurately the individual metrical norm felt to have been established in this particular singing of this particular song as a whole. (1940:49)

Crawford's insight and exactitude satisfied the twin aspects of Seeger's intellectual temperament—the macrotheorist and the micromethodologist. Increasingly hampered by hearing loss, he nevertheless followed along the path she charted in "The Music of American Folk Songs." In "Versions and Variants of 'Barbara Allen,'" Seeger used a similar kind of technical culture-specific analysis that Crawford had developed for transcribing many songs as a way to study variants for one song. Without diminishing the brilliance of his ability to link detail to abstraction, her influence is latent but significant.

It is far more apparent in Seeger's article "Singing Style," where he gave "a brief but well-rounded account of the problems met in the study of singing style" by explicitly drawing on her work (1994b [1958]: 404). Crawford had treated all parameters of oral tradition with precision and technical zeal, making observations that have held up over the decades about such matters as dramatic and expressive patterns, off-beat rhythms, vocal timbre, invariance of dynamics, tempo, metric irregularities, and nondiatonic intonation. Seeger reiterated them as entirely his own work. Rather than cite examples within the body of this paper, the relevant sections on the topics of dramatic level, dynamics, tempo, and meter follow in the appendix to this chapter. As the reader will see, the text comparisons speak for themselves.

∿

Why Seeger chose this route probably speaks in part to his attitude toward systematic theory as opposed to research. In letters of May 20 and June 18, 1971, to Richard Reuss in Seeger's later years, he explained: "I do not regard myself as a scholar, I am a systematist. The two are very different. For one thing, the scholar is primarily interested in knowing everything he can of other people's work; the systematist, in appropriating everything he can lay his hands on in the continual task of fortifying his World View" (quoted in Pescatello 1992:284). In this respect the systematist behaved like an artist, treating ideas as collective creative or intellectual property.

During the active years of Crawford's composing and Seeger's involvement in the musical avant-garde, husband and wife often discussed the nature of creativity and its inevitable dependency on the stimulation of other people's work. She regarded her work with Seeger and her assimilation of dissonant counterpoint as a major turning point in her own development. Before their marriage and at a crucial point in her life, he helped her break free from constraining self doubts with eloquent generosity.

Living in Berlin in the fall and winter of 1930–31, a lonely young American composer, Ruth Crawford, was just embarking on her most famous composition, the String Quartet. She was beleaguered by a recriminating friend (the Hungarian composer Imre Weisshaus), who accused her of stealing his ideas. In a series of letters she turned to her former teacher and absent lover for help: "Am I not inclined to take hold of someone else's idea—many of yours, two of Imre's—and call them mine? Of course, the music that comes out is different from what you would have written, or what Imre writes—I have noticed that, and am thankful for at least this sign of individuality. But is the appropriating of the idea condonable, even though the result projects a personality which is myself and not someone else?"[16] Seeger reassured her as fast as possible. He regarded the need for artistic ownership as a contemporary curse, sharing an alternative model of creativity with Crawford at a pivotal moment, which emphasized his belief in the true relational essence of art. What mattered was not originality but identity—the stamp of personality and expressiveness that each artist imparted to a work as a medium or a technique was absorbed and assimilated, reinvented and reimagined. In a letter of February 7, 1931, he bolstered her with these words:

> As to appropriating other people's ideas etc., I wish I could assure you that no one I have ever known gives more fair treatment to the people from whom he appropriates than you do. . . . It is no small job, these days, to strike a balance between what one must get from others and what one must contribute of oneself. There is too much striving for originality. We must work from now on more collectively. If there is anything you know you have from me, for God's sake use it if it is of any use to you. And if there are things you are unconscious of owing to me—use those too. Art is as much if not more a social thing than an individual one. . . . Appropriate all you can. All may not be fair in love or war—but in art it is; if you can take another person's idea the situation is very easy to evaluate. The originator's presentation and the appropriator's stand eventually side by side. The best is the best. Who should bother about the origin? How can we tell that the "originator" did not swipe somebody else's idea anyway? Oh I could punch Imre in the solar plexus.[17]

Such liberating words for them both.

Yet the issue of credit and debt touched certain private grievances. Seeger's relationship with Henry Cowell, for example, required his putting aside resentment at the way he was edited out of Cowell's book *New Musical Resources* (1930). His letter continues: "Bah. The idea of patenting musical ideas. Naturally I feel badly when Henry almost goes out of his way to omit my name from the list of those to whom he owes much of his stuff—even the titles, form and character of definite works. But he acknowledges it [my influence] even more by concealing it."

Perhaps this applies to his own reticence about Crawford's scholarly work. Even if Seeger would remember the extraordinary partnership he shared with Ruth Crawford in interviews he gave about her toward the end of his life, surely it is not only the partisanship of a biographer that leads to the feeling that Crawford's achievement could have been given more public acknowledgment.

The history of the urban folk revival movement would have been better served as well. Because Crawford published trade books for children, her brilliant introductions for *American Folk Songs for Children* (1948) and *Animal Folk Songs for Children* (1950) have been somewhat neglected by historians today. Had her scholarship been acknowledged in print by such a respected figure as Charles Seeger, her work might not have been so marginalized. Only recently did Robert Cantwell cite the introduction to the first book as "one of the master texts of the expanding folk revival" (1996:278).

All are borrowers and lenders. It seems plausible that Seeger did not acknowledge Crawford as his partner in some of his now-classic folksong scholarship because the idea did not occur: perhaps his own contributions to Crawford's work allowed him to rationalize this omission; or perhaps the nature of the Crawford/Seeger marriage beguiled him into thinking it would have been like crediting another part of himself. In an interview with Crawford's first biographer, Matilda Gaume, ostensibly about Ruth Crawford, Charles Seeger said: "I'm afraid this session I'm talking about myself more than I'm talking about Ruth. You see, the thing is, we had such a perfect union I can't tear myself apart from her."[18] His was the entitlement of a certain kind of intellect and a certain kind of love. If he was not quite able to let her sound apart, then perhaps it was because for so many years they had sounded together.

Appendix: Comparisons between the Writings of
Ruth Crawford and Charles Seeger

1. On Tempo

"Adherence to the tempo set at the beginning of the song
    "a. Infrequency of long ritardandos from the beginning to the end of the song
as a whole.
    "The singer, once he has set his tempo, usually sticks to it throughout the song
without substantial deviation. . . .
    "b. Infrequency of short stereotyped ritardandos at ends of phrases and stan-
zas.
    "The practice of making short, frequent, stereotyped ritardandos at ends of
phrases and stanzas—a convention so common among sophisticated singers—
is rarely found in these recordings." (R. Seeger 1940:29)

"(e) Tempo
    "While examples of fairly free or vacillating tempo can be found—as, for ex-
ample, in the field holler—I hazard the proposition that the tradition normally
maintains a steady tempo. The unit is the sung syllable, not the counted measure of the professional or fine art. Once established, the tempo is not changed.
Gross retardations and accelerations are entirely foreign to the style. The 'city-
billy' can be identified almost without fail by his slowing down at the cadences."
(Seeger 1994b [1958]: 403)

2. On Dynamics

"Adherence to a dynamic level set at the beginning of the song
    "With few exceptions, the singers of these songs maintain approximately the
same level of loudness or softness from phrase to phrase and from stanza to
stanza throughout the song. The calculated gradations of broad dynamic levels
so characteristic of fine-art performance, with emphasis on climax and morendo,
is not typical of folk singing recorded on these disks." (R. Seeger 1940:27)

    "Loudness is comparatively unorganized. It is customarily regarded as a char-
acteristic of the way a whole piece or substantial part of it is performed. . . . Even
by the elite, the professional or fine art musician, loudness is not articulated beyond the somewhat vague steps of *pp, p, mp, mf, f, ff*, and so on. None of these
has any significance in traditional ballad singing. Thus, while continual variance
in loudness is the rule in twentieth-century concert music (and in the singing of
folk songs by professional or professionally influenced performers), in the folk
art the tendency is to invariance." (Seeger 1977c [1966]: 284–85)

    "(c) Loudness. The singing style of Anglo-American folk song does not permit
of deliberate variation of loudness among sung syllables, phrase-breaths, or melody-
stanzas. Some singers sing more loudly than others. But once established, a dynamic

level is maintained with as little variation as possible, not only in one and the same song but in the whole repertory of the singer." (Seeger 1994b [1958]: 403)

3. On Meter

"Simple and compound meter

"One difficulty in the transcription of folk songs into the notation of fine-art music is the long standing ambiguity in fine-art practice of the concept of measure. . . . It can be said, however, that, although a few of the recordings from which these songs have been transcribed admit of wide and largely subjective choice in the selection of meter, the great majority of them present fairly obvious metrical patterns.

"In notating meters which would be most accurately represented by metrical signatures of 1/4, 1/2 or 1/3, compromise has been felt to be advisable, in all but a few cases, with the less unusual metrical signatures of 2/8, 2/4, 3/8, and 3/4, since few people—indeed, few musicians—are comfortable with dealing with one beat per measure.

"The infrequent appearance of 4/4 meter on these recordings has already been noted." (R. Seeger 1940:37, 40, 44)

"The combination of these traits [accentuation and syllabic shifts], added to those given above for tempo and proportion, indicate a pattern of single stress, or *ritmo di una battuta*—a strong 1-1-1 beat with negligible subordinate accents. According to the pattern theory of notation, the singing style is mainly characterized by meters of 4/4, with 3/2 for many of the older ballads and 3/4—even 9/8—for some recent intrusions of the popular idiom. . . . I aver, to the contrary, that the pattern theory grossly misrepresents the style in its delivery of the vast majority of the songs in the repertory. In most cases, instead of one measure of 4/4, we should write four of 1/4." (Seeger 1994b [1958]: 404)

4. On the Overall Expressive Aesthetic of Singing Style

"The reader and the song

"He [the reader of *Our Singing Country*] will, for instance, find that most of the singers on these recordings sing without 'expression'—i.e. expression in the manner of fine-art singing. He will miss the continual fluctuation of mood so prevalent in fine-art performance, the frequent formalized slowing down for 'effect' at ends of phrases and stanzas, the drama of constant change from soft to loud and back again, the rounded bel canto tone quality of the 'well-trained' voice. Upon repeated hearing, however, it is possible that such omissions may come to take on for him positive rather than negative value. He may begin to see in them signs of strength rather than of weakness. He may even discover that he likes this music for these very omissions. . . . Whether, finally he comes to define much of it in terms of epic quality is not of such import . . . as is the probability that [through hearing recordings and live performance], his re-creation from notation of similar songs in similar idioms will undoubtedly ring truer and 'come more natural' than before." (R. Seeger 1940:8–9)

"Adherence to a dramatic level throughout the song as a whole

"With few exceptions, the singer sets the dramatic mood at the beginning of the song and maintains that mood throughout. Dramatization in the conventional style of fine-art performance, with emphasis on fluctuation of mood, is scarcely ever heard on these disks. The singer does not try to make the song mean more, or less, than it does. No special emphasis is given to words or details which the sophisticated singer would tend to point up. The strong dramatic conviction with which the singer begins his song underlies each stanza from first to last; the gay stanza, or the comic, is sung in precisely the same manner of musical expression as the tragic and the dignified. The tune makes no compromises, is no slower nor faster, no softer nor louder. There is no climax—the song 'just stops.'" (R. Seeger 1940:27)

"It is difficult for urban Occidentals to recognize the fact that although variance may be the spice of life, invariance may be the meat. . . . The attitude, then, typical of the most admired traditional singer toward the song, tends to the serene and detached, however much force or gentleness may impel the line from its beginning to its end. Singing seems to be a natural thing for one to occupy himself with if he wishes. It requires of him no special preparation, effort, or pretense of an organized sort. . . . It is not a vehicle for pathos but seems to meet accepted requirements of an ethos. In spite of the often romantic words, an almost classic reserve is maintained." (Seeger 1977c [1966]: 286–87)

Notes

1. I use the surname "Crawford" in the text for the sake of clarity and literary convenience. Parenthetical citations use "R. Seeger" as entries appear in the references cited list under "Seeger, Ruth Crawford."

2. See, for example, Mellers's comment: "For Ruth Seeger abandoned composition to devote herself to her husband's related causes, those of American folk music and radical politics" (1987:xv).

3. This comment was made during various conversations with Pete Seeger, including a telephone interview by the author on June 3, 1990.

4. Archival materials of the Folklore Institute of America, Second Session, June 19–August 16, 1946, Indiana University. This includes "Informal Notes on Transactions and Lectures" and Mrs. Charles Seeger, "Uses of Folklore in Nursery Schools."

5. Telephone interview with Herbert Halpert by the author on September 26, 1989.

6. Interview with Bess Lomax Hawes by the author on July 13, 1984.

7. Ibid. See also Hawes 1995 for a fuller account of this project.

8. Interview of Alan Lomax by Mike Seeger and Judith Tick on January 6, 1983. The phrase "musico-intellectual lambkin gamboling in the lion's jaws" is in a letter from Alan Lomax to Ruth Crawford Seeger, July 12, 1938, Ruth Crawford Seeger Papers, Music Division, Library of Congress, Washington, D.C.

9. Seeger called it a "turning point" in an interview with Ed Kahn on November 9, 1971. The author wishes to thank Ed Kahn for permission to quote from his interviews.

10. Larry Polansky and I have embarked on a publication project for this manuscript. A brief summary of the materials includes the source for this essay, a sixty-one-page typescript entitled "The Music of American Folk Songs by Ruth Crawford Seeger. Music Appendix to Our Singing Country by John A. and Alan Lomax and Ruth Crawford Seeger, based on observations made during transcription of three hundred American folk songs from phonograph recordings in the Archive of American Folk Song of the Music Division of the Library of Congress." This typescript is in the possession of the Seeger Estate. The Ruth Crawford Seeger Papers at the Library of Congress includes a draft of a shorter "Appendix to the Music," another forty-seven-page draft of the "Music Appendix," and a twenty-four-page draft labeled "Introduction." Editorial notations by both Ruth Crawford and Charles Seeger occur throughout these drafts.

11. Letter from Charles Seeger to George Korson, May 17 (?), 1937, George Korson Folklore Archive, King's College, Wilkes-Barre, Pa.

12. Pescatello's introduction to *Studies in Musicology II, 1929–1979* (1994) fully documents Crawford's contributions.

13. Letter from Ruth Crawford Seeger to John Lomax, July 7, 1940, Ruth Crawford Seeger Papers.

14. Letter from Charles Seeger to Judith McCulloh, February 8, 1970, Ruth Crawford Seeger Papers.

15. "Oh, Roll on, Babe" is a work song transcribed by Crawford in *Our Singing Country* on p. 264; "Little Bird, Go Through My Window" is transcribed on p. 74.

16. Letter from Ruth Crawford to Charles Seeger, January 29, 1931, in the Seeger Estate. Cited by permission of Mike Seeger.

17. Letter from Charles Seeger to Ruth Crawford, February 7, 1931, in the Seeger Estate. Cited by permission of Mike Seeger.

18. Interview of Charles Seeger by Matilda Gaume on October 7, 1974, Music Division, Library of Congress, Washington, D.C.

REFERENCES CITED

Cantwell, Robert. 1996. *When We Were Good.* Cambridge, Mass.: Harvard University Press.
Cohen, Norm, ed. 1990. *Folk Song America: A 20th Century Revival.* Washington, D.C.: Smithsonian Collection of Recordings.

Cowell, Henry. 1930. *New Musical Resources.* New York: Alfred A. Knopf.

Hawes, Bess Lomax. 1995. "Reminiscences and Exhortations: Growing Up in American Folk Music." *Ethnomusicology* 39 (2): 179–92.

Jackson, George Pullen. 1933. *White Spirituals in the Southern Uplands.* Chapel Hill: University of North Carolina Press.

Lieberman, Robbie. 1989. *"My Song Is My Weapon": People's Songs, American Communism, and the Politics of Culture, 1930–1950.* Urbana: University of Illinois Press.

Lomax, John A., and Alan Lomax, comps.; Ruth Crawford Seeger, ed. 1941. *Our Singing Country.* New York: Macmillan.

———, comps.; Charles Seeger and Ruth Crawford Seeger, music eds. 1947. *Folk Song USA.* New York: Duell, Sloan and Pearce.

Mellers, Wilfrid. 1987. *Music in the New Found Land.* 2d ed. New York: W. W. Norton.

Metfessel, Milton Franklin. 1928. *Phonophotography in Folk Music: American Negro Songs in New Notation.* Chapel Hill: University of North Carolina Press.

Pescatello, Ann M. 1992. *Charles Seeger: A Life in American Music.* Pittsburgh: University of Pittsburgh Press.

———. 1994. "Introduction." In Charles Louis Seeger, *Studies in Musicology II, 1929–1979.* Ed. Ann M. Pescatello. 1–16. Berkeley: University of California Press.

Seeger, Charles Louis. 1930. "On Dissonant Counterpoint." *Modern Music* 7 (4): 25–31.

———. 1939. "Grass Roots for American Composers." *Modern Music* 16 (3): 143–49.

———. 1977a [1940]. "Contrapuntal Style in Three-Voice Shape-Note Hymns." In *Studies in Musicology, 1935–1975.* 237–51. Berkeley: University of California Press. (Reprinted from *Musical Quarterly* 26 [4]: 483–93.)

———. 1977b [1958]. "Prescriptive and Descriptive Music Writing." In *Studies in Musicology, 1935–1975.* 168–81. Berkeley: University of California Press. (Reprinted from *Musical Quarterly* 44 [2]: 184–95).

———. 1977c [1966]. "Versions and Variants of 'Barbara Allen' in the Archive of American Song to 1940." In *Studies in Musicology, 1935–1975.* 273–320. Berkeley: University of California Press. (Reprinted from "Versions and Variants of the Tunes of 'Barbara Allen,'" *Selected Reports* [University of California at Los Angeles, Institute of Ethnomusicology] 1 [1]: 120–67.)

———. 1994a [1931]. "Tradition and Experiment in (the New) Music." In *Studies in Musicology II, 1929–1979.* Ed. Ann M. Pescatello. 93–273. Berkeley: University of California Press.

———. 1994b [1958]. "Singing Style." In *Studies in Musicology II, 1929–1979.* Ed. Ann M. Pescatello. 397–405. Berkeley: University of California Press. (Reprinted from *Western Folklore* 17 [1]: 3–11.)

———. 1994c [1972]. "World Musics in American Schools: A Challenge to Be Met." In *Studies in Musicology II, 1929–1979.* Ed. Ann M. Pescatello. 427–34. Berkeley: University of California Press. (Reprinted from *Music Educators Journal* 58 [October]: 107–11.)

Seeger, Ruth Crawford. 1940. "The Music of American Folk Songs." Typescript. Ruth Crawford Seeger Papers, Music Division, Library of Congress, Washington, D.C.

———. 1941. "Music Preface." In *Our Singing Country.* Comp. John Lomax and Alan Lomax. Ed. Ruth Crawford Seeger. xvii–xxiv. New York: Macmillan.

———, comp. 1948. *American Folk Songs for Children in Home, School, and Nursery School.* Garden City, N.Y.: Doubleday.

———, comp. *Animal Folk Songs for Children.* Garden City, N.Y.: Doubleday.

———. 1995 [1936–38]. *Nineteen American Folk Tunes for Elementary Piano.* New York: G. Schirmer.

Straus, Joseph N. 1995. *The Music of Ruth Crawford Seeger.* Cambridge: Cambridge University Press.

Tick, Judith. 1997. *Ruth Crawford Seeger: A Composer's Search for American Music.* New York: Oxford University Press.

6

Seeger's Unitary Field Theory Reconsidered

Lawrence M. Zbikowski

As musicians, we are aware of a certain tension between making music—through composition, performance, or ritual—and talking about music. Making music is immediate, absorptive, and consuming, a torrent that sweeps us along in its path. Talking about music walls in the torrent, and the trickle that remains sometimes scarcely resembles that which has enraptured us. This opposition is not all there is to the relationship between language and music—the two modes of communication are far too rich to submit to such a simple reduction—but it is central to understanding the tension between making music and talking about music. This tension stems from two problems of the application of language (i.e., natural language) to music. First, language is not very good for describing processes. Language can be *part* of a process, as in the case of a play or a poem, but that is another thing. In general what one gets out of an application of language to phenomena is the fixed and immutable, even in situations where neither is to be expected. Second, it must be recognized that there are some concepts proper to music and distinct from language. To explain a little: sound images are part of the central business of what we call music. Part of what it means to be a musician is to try to express things in sound that cannot be expressed in words. And for these things that cannot be expressed in words—what I call properly musical concepts—language is simply inadequate. I shall develop the notion of a properly musical concept in greater detail in the latter half of this essay; in my own work it has been fundamental to addressing the question of how it is we structure our understanding of music and for developing an account of the relationship between language and music.

Charles Seeger wrestled with the relationship between language and music throughout his long life. In 1913, only a year after he took charge of starting a music program at Berkeley, he wrote, "The term 'Musicology' comprises, in its widest sense, the whole linguistic treatment of music—the manual instruction, the historical study, the music-research of the psycho-physical laboratory, the piece of music criticism. . . . Music is not founded upon language or upon language studies. But its conduct in our day depends customarily on an extensive use of language" (Seeger 1913: n.p.).

In later years Seeger situated the paradox of music's dependence on language at the musicological juncture. Speaking to the Society for Ethnomusicology in 1976, Seeger described the musicological juncture as "the situation we place ourselves in when we talk about music and particularly when, as now, we talk about talking about music" (1977a:180). The essays of Seeger's final two decades repeatedly explored this situation, examining the way speech was used generally, how it was applied to music specifically, and the differences and similarities between the two modes of communication. Again and again he worried the problem of the ways in which speech and language (terms he used interchangeably) constrain an understanding of music. However, in his proposal for a unitary field theory for musicology, which first appeared in print in 1970, and then (with slight revisions) in *Studies in Musicology*, he suggested a reversal of conceptualization that was telling. Seeger argued, "It is true that speech and music are very unlike in many ways, but they are very like in others. One can try to use agreement on the latter to help agreement upon the former's *account* of the latter" (1977c:104).[1] That is, knowledge of music should be used to refine the way one applies language to music.

In the time that remained to him Seeger was unable to take full advantage of the reversal he proposed. However, as part of the groundwork for this proposal he outlined a system of independent yet related conceptual domains that together formed what he called a unitary field. Speech was one such domain, music another. Conceptual domains of a strikingly similar sort have played an important role in recent accounts of linguistic structure and appear to be important for understanding cognition as a whole. In this chapter I would like to consider briefly the main points of Seeger's unitary field theory as he developed it for musicology and then offer an interpretation of aspects of this theory based on recent research in linguistics and cognition. I shall also draw on some of my recent work on the processes involved in conceptualizing music. What I hope to accomplish is a revitalization of Seeger's essential vision by considering closely the cognitive and semantic issues raised by talking about music.

Seeger's Unitary Field Theory

Seeger gave the first version of his unitary field theory for musicology in a paper read in December 1944. The theory was to have had a function analogous to that of Einstein's unified field theory: the explicit task was the definition and systematization of musicology. Apparently no typescript of this paper has survived. However, an abstract was published in the *Bulletin of the American Musicological Society* (Seeger 1947), and it is this abstract that served as a point of departure for the 1970 version of the theory, which was written as a dialogue between Seeger, Boris Kremenliev, and a student named Jim Yost.[2]

Seeger began his definition and systematization of musicology with the notion of a "world view." Each person, he proposes, has a worldview, a highly conceptualized account of how things appear, the product of reflection on the world without and the world within. Although a worldview is taken to be "highly conceptualized" it is not necessarily systematic; in the unattributed prologue to the 1970 version of the theory, a worldview is described as "that which is not language" (Seeger 1970:171). This description, and the perspective that it entails, is useful for understanding the unitary field theory, and in the following the assumption is that a worldview is unsystematized and nonlinguistic.

Extending the notion of a worldview a little, we can think of each scholarly discipline as incorporating a particular worldview of its own (Seeger 1977c:105). Although the concept of a worldview is easy enough to grasp, coming to terms with its empirical referent is rather more difficult. To facilitate the process, Seeger suggests the heuristic of a structural universe, a complex of empirical entities to which the worldview refers. In brief, each structural universe comprises the plurality hidden in the apparent unity of its respective worldview. The structural universe also permits a systematic account, through language, of the nonlinguistic worldview. Thus the worldview of musicology has as its empirical referent the structural universe of musicology, a universe that contains a number of subuniverses. For the purposes of this chapter only the first five subuniverses introduced by Seeger need be considered; the sixth, the subuniverse of value, is introduced much later in the dialogue and is not essential to understanding the basic outlines of Seeger's unitary field theory. The discussion of value also engages a host of important issues that occupied Seeger throughout his career but that are not central to the concerns here.

The first subuniverse proposed by Seeger is that of the physical, phenomenal, external world, the domain of science and fact, represented by a P on figure 6.1. The second subuniverse is that of discourse, or speech, represented by an S on figure 6.1. This domain includes all three modes of speech recognized by Seeger: the affective, or mystical; the reasoned, or logical; and the discursive, or commonsensical (1976, 1977b). The third subuniverse is that of music, represented by an M on figure 6.1. Seeger argues "if there is a universe of speech, which is one way men communicate by mediums of sound, why should there not be one of the other mediums of communicating by sound—music? As musicians, we know that music communicates something that speech does not" (1977c:106–7). The fourth subuniverse is a personal one, a sort of half-conscious, experiential domain just prior to, or perhaps just beyond, verbalization or representation. Seeger summons this domain with a rhetorical question: "When you run into a snag in what you are writing about or are composing, don't you ever feel that there is a fund of knowledge, feelings, and purposes rumbling around inside you that is definitely yours and no one else's . . . , but it is not quite in the order you could wish it to be so as to enable you to clarify the passage you are working on; and that by exploring it a bit deliberately or resting and letting yourself dream you either solve the problem satisfactorily or give up and make a fresh start?" (107) This subuniverse is represented by an I on figure 6.1. The fifth subuniverse is that of culture, which in its social

Figure 6.1. Seeger's representation of the subuniverses of the structural universe of musicology (Reprinted with permission from Charles Seeger, *Studies in Musicology, 1935–1975*, 108, © 1977 by the Regents of the University of California)

organization and traditions provides an essential framework for the very possibility of music; it is represented by a C on figure 6.1.

It is upon these five subuniverses that Seeger builds his comprehensive definition of musicology. In his words,

> musicology is (1) *a speech study* [S], systematic as well as historical, critical as well as scientific or scientistic; whose field is (2) *the total music* [M] of man, both in itself and in its relationships to what is not itself; whose cultivation is (3) *by individual students* [I] who can view its field as musicians as well as in the terms devised by nonmusical specialists of whose fields some aspects of music are data; whose aim is to contribute to *the understanding of man*, in terms both (4) of human *culture* [C] and (5) of his relationships with the *physical universe* [P]. (1977c:108)

And it is at this point that we come to the unitary aspect of Seeger's theory, for he asserts that there is a special relationship that obtains among the five domains: *each subuniverse includes all the others.* He illustrates the inclusion relations with a figure drawn from the practices of formal logic, shown in figure 6.2.

Seeger clearly intends this assertion to be somewhat paradoxical (Boris Kremenliev responds, "Oh, come now!"). Having described musicology as an amalgamation of the unique characteristics of five discrete subuniverses he now proposes a reflexive inclusion among the subuniverses based on a commutativity of relationships not evident in his account of their structure. However, a type of reflexive inclusion does in fact follow from the function of these subuniverses within Seeger's theory. Let us retrace the steps that brought us to this paradoxical situation.

The point of departure for Seeger's theory is the notion of a worldview (that is *un*systematized); the worldview has as its empirical referent a structural universe (that *is* systematized). Each structural universe is understood to be a complex, systematic plurality. One aspect of this

Figure 6.2. Seeger's representation of inclusion relations among the five subuniverses (Reprinted with permission from Charles Seeger, *Studies in Musicology, 1935–1975*, 109, © 1977 by the Regents of the University of California)

complex plurality is that the structural universe is itself made up of a number of subuniverses; these subuniverses are one way of bringing order to the wealth of information represented by the structural universe. The crux of the paradox concerns the relationships between these sub-universes, for priority among the subuniverses is not assigned: any subuniverse can be taken as a primary referent relative to which the other subuniverses are interpreted. Of course, each interpretation will change the topography of the structural universe of musicology. For instance, speech could be given priority; after all, speech is where the other four subuniverses are named and where interrelationships between them are established (this relationship is represented in figure 6.2a). Or music could be taken as primary, and the other four subuniverses interpreted in terms of music (figure 6.2b). From another perspective it is the universe of the individual that is primary, for it is here that the other subuniverses are actually experienced (figure 6.2c). There is certainly a perspective where culture is the primary referent, and the other subuniverses are contained within its encompassing embrace (figure 6.2d). And, finally, is it not the case that the constitutive phenomena of each subuniverse are part of the physical universe (figure 6.2e; Seeger 1977c: 109–10)?

Although it is possible to explain the idea of reflexive inclusion systematically, this does not necessarily resolve the problem practically. What sense is there in saying that music can be regarded as a subdomain of speech *and* speech can be regarded as a subdomain of music? Is this paradoxical situation simply a manifestation of Seeger's love of system (which is represented throughout his writings), or does it point to more profound insights into the relationship between speech, music, and other aspects of human experience?

There is little doubt that aspects of the unitary field theory for musicology reflect Seeger's love of system, a love graphically demonstrated in the elaborate fold-out table that accompanied his essay. However, the paradox of self-inclusion is not so much an accident or a hierarchical inconsistency as it is detritus left by Seeger on the battlefield of speech and music. Seeger was unwilling to surrender his crucial insight that there was a world of music within which theorizing, creativity, and understanding could take place. He was also unable to surrender certain priorities of meaning construction that he had inherited from the writings of early twentieth-century semioticians. And so Seeger could not grant final priority to either music or language, but instead set them spinning around one another like paired stars (Seeger 1977c: 113).

In recent years musicians have frequently looked to linguistics and semiotics to expand the possibilities for developing accounts of music (Powers 1980; Lerdahl and Jackendoff 1983; Nattiez 1990; Agawu 1991; Hatten 1992, 1994). Linguists and semioticians have less often met the challenge to their theories presented by the apparent asymmetry between music's syntactic and semantic development, or considered the possibilities music presents as a nonlinguistic domain for conceptualization and communication (see Eco 1976:10–11, 88–90; for a less ambitious but perhaps more honest consideration see Langacker 1987). However, linguists *have* recently come to consider how meaning construction comes about, and the linguistic theories that have resulted are particularly useful for dealing with Seeger's paradox. In the following I want to focus on an influential theory of meaning construction originally proposed by Gilles Fauconnier. This theory can be used to make the relationship between the domains of language and music explicit and thereby provide a way around the complications of Seeger's unitary field theory. Fauconnier's theory also touches upon general cognitive activities that appear to be *prior* to language (but of which one is not necessarily conscious). I take the position that there is a basic level of cognitive activity prior to *both* language and music. This position, only a few aspects of which can be sketched here, affords a perspective that places Seeger's theory within a broader theory of cognition. This broader theory can not only accommodate Seeger's fundamental insights, but takes them as cornerstones upon which to build an understanding of the process of conceptualizing music.

Recent Theories of Linguistic and Cognitive Structure

Fauconnier's Mental Spaces

Gilles Fauconnier developed his theory of meaning construction as a means of accounting for the multiple mental representations to which a given grammatical construction can give rise. For instance, the sentence

s1.0: *Plato is on the top shelf*

could be the basis for a number of mental representations, including:

mr1.1: Plato (his body) is on the top shelf
mr1.2: The books by Plato are on the top shelf
mr1.3: The bust of Plato is on the top shelf

It follows that the construction process for these mental representations is underdetermined by the grammatical instructions provided by a given sentence: one sentence can yield multiple mental representations (Fauconnier 1994:2). Because a different meaning is attached to each mental representation, a given sentence can thus have more than one meaning.

It is important to note that, while the construction processes for each mental representation are underdetermined, they are not *un*determined. The sample sentence would not normally give rise to the mental representation *Your duck is on the top shelf* unless your duck were named Plato. One goal of Fauconnier's study is to explore the possibilities for and the restrictions on the construction of mental representations from language.

In the case of the first example, one sentence gave rise to a number of mental representations. Multiple mental representations may also be implicit within a single sentence. Consider example S2.0:

S2.0: *In Len's painting, the girl with blue eyes has green eyes.*

Here two mental representations are summoned: first, the world of Len's painting, which contains a girl with green eyes, and second, the real world, which contains a girl with blue eyes who has served as a model for the image in Len's painting. Connection between the two worlds is based on the highly pragmatic assumption that the prepositional phrase "In Len's painting" sets up a world of images based on real world models.

The notion of "the real world" plays an important part in this account—it is, after all, the source for the images in the painting. However, this does not necessarily entail that the real world is the primary referent for language. For the sentence

S3.0: *Bruce believes that Aristotle and Plato are the same person*

the real world does not play an immediate part—the sentence instead refers to the world of Bruce's beliefs. In Fauconnier's theory of meaning construction, reality is not a privileged domain, but simply another mental representation (Fauconnier 1994:15). In this Fauconnier echoes Erving Goffman's theory of frame analysis (the influence of which Fauconnier acknowledges). Some ten years earlier Goffman had recognized multiple, and occasionally simultaneous, realms of being, among which what we call reality was but one (Goffman 1974:564). In both cases the status of objects in the real world is not the main issue, nor is the accuracy with which a mental representation or frame correlates with or describes the real world. What is at issue is the character and properties of the mental entities themselves, as reflected in the way we talk and think.

Fauconnier calls a mental representation evoked by language a *mental space*.[3] Mental spaces are constructs distinct from linguistic structures but built up in any discourse according to guidelines provided by the linguistic expressions. Mental spaces can be thought of as structured, incremental sets—that is, sets that are constituted of elements and relations between elements (Fauconnier 1994:16). Mental spaces are also highly dynamic and are constantly modified as thought unfolds.[4]

A bit of technical terminology will facilitate the discussion of Fauconnier's theory. The linguistic expressions that establish mental spaces are called *space-builders*. Typical space-builders may be prepositional phrases, adverbs, connectives, or underlying subject-verb combinations. Space-builders always have their foundation in a larger space, the *parent space*. The parent space may be inferred pragmatically from previous discourse or may be explicitly indicated by the syntactic embedding of space-builders. For example, in *"Bruce believes that in John's story Aristotle is Plato,"* the mental space of *John's story* is a part of (or is included in the mental space of) *what Bruce believes* (Fauconnier 1994:17).

Some (but not necessarily all) of the elements of the *daughter space* are pragmatically connected to the parent space. To describe this process, Fauconnier uses the notion of *triggers, targets,* and *connectors* (1994:4). The trigger is an element in the parent space: in example S2.0, the trigger is *the girl with blue eyes*. The target is an element in the daughter space— *the girl with green eyes*. The daughter space was of course established by a space-builder—here, *in Len's painting*. The connector is defined as a *pragmatic function:* such a function links dissimilar objects for psychological, cultural, or locally pragmatic reasons (1994:3). In general, connectors reflect the cognitive organization basic to meaning construction (discussed in more detail below). In example S2.0 the pragmatic function is an image connector, which links models to images. The two mental spaces, their elements, and the connection between them are represented schematically in figure 6.3; similar diagrams are given in figures 6.4 and 6.5 for the sentences of examples S1.0 and S3.0.

To summarize: in Fauconnier's theory of mental spaces, linguistic expressions introduce (or build up) mental representations, called mental spaces. Each mental space consists of elements and relations between these elements. A mental space is connected to other mental spaces by pragmatic functions, or connectors, that link mental objects for psychological, cultural, or locally pragmatic reasons. We move from one mental space to another by means of these connectors, attributing a different meaning to the linguistic expression with each different space. Fun-

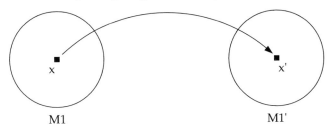

In Len's painting, the girl with blue eyes has green eyes.

x = the girl with blue eyes (*trigger*)   x' = the girl with green eyes (*target*)
M1 = speaker's reality (*parent space*)   M1' = Len's painting (*daughter space*)

F1 = model-to-image connector (*connector or pragmatic function*)

Figure 6.3. Schematic representation of a mental space structured by a model-to-image connector

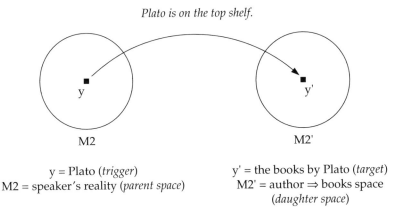

Plato is on the top shelf.

y = Plato (*trigger*)   y' = the books by Plato (*target*)
M2 = speaker's reality (*parent space*)   M2' = author ⇒ books space
                                                      (*daughter space*)

F2 = author-to-books connector (*connector or pragmatic function*)

Figure 6.4. Schematic representation of a mental space structured by an author-to-books connector

Bruce believes that Aristotle and Plato are the same person.

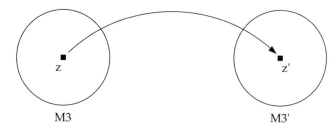

z = Aristotle (*trigger*)   z' = Plato (*target*)
M3 = Bruce's beliefs (*parent space*)   M3' = reality (*daughter space*)

F3 = beliefs-to-reality connector (*connector or pragmatic function*)

Figure 6.5. Schematic representation of a mental space structured by a beliefs-to-reality connector

damental to this theory is the view that linguistic expressions do not have one primary referent in the real world, but instead set up the *basis* for some form of reference by establishing a mental representation or group of representations.

Mental Spaces and Music

But what of music? A properly musical concept, in the most general terms, could be described as a concept-about-sound that stands apart from language. By definition, this is a mental representation that is *not* introduced or built up by a linguistic expression—in consequence it falls outside Fauconnier's theory. One way around this problem would be to relax (for present purposes) the reliance on linguistic expressions for the construction of mental representations, resulting in a modified version of the theory of mental spaces.[5] After all, it would appear that many mental representations (for constructs such as "It hurts when you bend my arm that way" or "That pan is very hot") do not require language for their introduction, since they can arise through direct experience. (The notion of mental representations that do not require linguistic expressions for their introduction also touches on the problem of the ultimate origin for the parent space, which is not discussed by Fauconnier.) In this modified version of the theory of mental spaces the domain of music (with its properly musical concepts) would be connected to the domain of speech through a music-to-speech connector. Conversely the domain of speech could be connected to the domain of music through a speech-to-music connector.[6]

This approach can then be used to resolve Seeger's paradox of reflexive inclusion. Each of the arrangements given in figure 6.2 could be seen as a reflection of the fluid possibilities for structuring the universe of musicology through the construction processes related to mental spaces. The primary subuniverse is equivalent to the parent space; the choice of parent space dictates the sort of connectors required to link this space (or subuniverse) with other spaces (or subuniverses). However, it should be mentioned that the notion of reflexive inclusion employed in Seeger's unitary field theory is changed with this interpretation. Although the music-to-speech connector is related to the speech-to-music connector, they are not equivalent. Because mental spaces are built and linked according to connectors, each connector must be understood to be of a unique type and to operate in only one direction.

Cognitive Structure, Meaning, and Musical Understanding

Although this modification of Fauconnier's theory provides one way of explaining the somewhat puzzling notion of the *unitary* aspect of Seeger's unitary field theory (by interpreting each subuniverse as mental space that can be connected to any other mental space), the account it provides is lacking in at least two respects: first, the cognitive status of a properly musical concept is unclear; second, the basis for the construction of and connection between mental spaces must be elaborated if the structuring of mental representations provided by connectors is to be more than arbitrary.

The basic notion of a properly musical concept is influenced by my own experience: I can remember having ideas and thoughts about music well before I discovered any way of describing them to others. At first blush, such a notion might seem uncontroversial, but the idea that there might be concepts that are independent of language is by no means universally accepted by those who discuss such issues. Ray Jackendoff, for one, has maintained that musical representations are not conceptual; in his words, "musical representations do not lead ultimately to the construction of conceptual structures" (1987:237). Jackendoff *does* place musical structure in correspondence with a nonconceptual level of mental representation that he calls *body representation*, which is related to the cognitive structure behind the control and appreciation of dance (1987:238–39). This is helpful although not entirely satisfactory, since the modified theory offers no account of the relationship of *body representa-tion* to concepts proper.

A somewhat broader definition of "concept" is preferable to that which Jackendoff employs, one not tied specifically to language. This definition has been influenced by the work of Gerald Edelman, who has been interested in developing a biological approach to consciousness. Edelman's definition of a concept is developed as a description of the capacities necessary for the control of complex interactions between an organism and its environment:

> An animal capable of concepts is able to identify a particular thing or action and control its future behavior on the basis of that identification in a more or less *general* way. It must act *as if* it could make judgments based on recognition of category membership or integrate "particulars" into "universals." This recognition rests not just on perceptual categori-zation (although a concept may have a highly sensory content) but, to some degree, *must also be relational*. It can connect one perceptual catego-rization to another even in the absence of the stimuli that triggered these categorizations. (1989:141)[7]

Thus to have concepts involves not only the process of categorization, but also recognizing relationships *between* categories.

This description is somewhat *too* general for the purposes here; in-deed Edelman's central program of developing a biological approach to consciousness requires that he give an account of prelinguistic concep-tual structures, which he takes to be connected with the emergence of primary consciousness in higher life forms, including but not restricted to mammals. However, his description does suggest the outlines of a notion of concept adequate to musical experience, what I call a "prop-erly musical concept."

A properly musical concept has three characteristics. First, it is a prod-uct of the various cognitive processes that give rise to categories. The properly musical concept is first and foremost a category in the general sense developed in recent work by Eleanor Rosch (1978), George Lakoff (1987), and Lawrence Barsalou (1992). Categories of this sort are not only fundamental to thought, but are also crucial to memory. Second, a prop-erly musical concept can be used to guide present and future actions. These actions thus constitute a sort of indirect evidence for a cognitive structure almost as ephemeral as music itself. Third, the properly musi-cal concept can be related to other concepts, including other musical concepts and concepts associated with bodily states (both physical and emotional), perceptual categories (including sound, which, after all, is not necessarily music), and linguistic constructs.

It must be noted that this definition is problematic in at least one important respect: a properly musical concept, so defined, includes both a melodic fragment and naturally occurring birdsong; both a six-note chord and a tiger's roar. However, basing a notion of a properly musical concept on an *a priori* definition of music is more problematic still, given the range of cultural products that can fall under the rubric "music." It is perhaps more accurate to speak of a properly musical concept as a cognitive structure that can be *specified* for what we call music, leaving both "we" and "music" undefined.[8]

The problem of the apparent arbitrariness of meaning that results from Fauconnier's theory is, if anything, more complicated than the cognitive status of nonlinguistic concepts, and the solution that seems most viable can only be sketched here. However, this sketch in itself is promising, for it connects this problem to issues at the heart of Seeger's thought.

The fundamental idea that meaning is dependent on a group of cognitive activities—for Fauconnier, these activities are the building and connection of mental spaces—has proven to be important for recent work in linguistics and cognitive science. Ronald Langacker comments, "Meaning is not objectively given, but constructed, even for expressions pertaining to objective reality. We therefore cannot account for meaning by describing objective reality, but only by describing the cognitive routines that constitute a person's understanding of it. The subject matter of semantic analysis is human conceptualization, and the structures of concern are those that a person imposes on his mental experience through active cognitive processing" (1987:194). Important to this active cognitive processing are the bundles of knowledge generally called *knowledge structures*. Knowledge structures represent knowledge in a schematized form, "that is, organized in chunks or packages so that, given a little bit of appropriate situational context, the individual has available many likely inferences on what might happen next in a given situation" (Abelson and Black 1986:1). Knowledge structures provide the context upon which inference and judgment are based; that is, the psychological, cultural, or locally pragmatic reasons for the linkage provided by Fauconnier's connectors.

Coming to terms with the properties and characteristics of knowledge structures is an activity that has occupied researchers in cognitive science and artificial intelligence for over twenty years. Over this time the conception and characterization of knowledge structures has varied widely.[9]

Among these the notion of a *cultural model* first proposed by Naomi Quinn and Dorothy Holland is particularly applicable for the cultural studies proper to ethnomusicology. The framework for this notion is based on an approach to anthropology that views culture as a body of shared knowledge: "not a people's customs and artifacts and oral traditions, but what they must know in order to act as they do, make the things they make, and interpret their experience in the distinctive way they do" (Quinn and Holland 1987:4). Given this framework, cultural models can be thought of as "presupposed, taken-for-granted models of the world that are widely shared (although not necessarily to the exclusion of other, alternative models) by the members of a society and that play an enormous role in their understanding of the world and their behavior in it" (ibid.).[10] Some of these models are specific to the cultural practices that give rise to music and provide the cognitive framework for connecting musical activity to other sorts of activity.

Another use of knowledge structures comes in the more overtly sociological approach to music for which Stephen Feld (1984) has argued. As part of his account of the dynamic nature of musical meaning Feld adopts Goffman's notion of a *frame*, which can be understood as a relatively simple set of conventional expectations that offers a means of understanding the events we experience (Goffman 1974:21–39). Goffman's frames are quite similar to the knowledge structures discussed above and, as noted earlier, also informed Fauconnier's theory of mental spaces. Feld uses Goffman's notion of a frame to explain the communication of highly patterned aesthetic orderings for a setting, style, performance, or musical moment; musical identity; and the integration of musical experience into experience as a whole (Feld 1984:12–13). He then uses the level of generality associated with the organization provided by frames to connect his own thought to that of Seeger. Feld writes, "Of the many things Seeger stressed, he often held that music is interesting because of the way generality entails many levels or overlaps of conscious discovery in listening. Here is where our views are most compatible. I would stress that the significant feature of musical communication is not that it is untranslatable and irreducible to the verbal mode, but that its generality and multiplicity of possible messages and interpretations brings out a special kind of feelingful activity and engagement on the part of the listener" (1984:13).

In both the program of cognitive anthropology and in Feld's argument for the dynamic nature of musical meaning knowledge structures— whether as cultural models or as frames—play an important part. Of course, the premises that music is fundamentally cultural and that music is about communication are two of the motivations for Seeger's unitary field theory for musicology. Knowledge structures such as cultural models and frames offer one way to systematize the sorts of relationships revealed by Seeger's theory and to connect our understanding of music to the more comprehensive endeavor of understanding our own understanding.

Conclusion: Words and Music

In his proposal for a unitary field theory for musicology, Seeger conceives of music as a mode of communication independent of speech; he then applies this conception to our understanding of the way speech is used, thereby setting up an environment within which language can be construed separate from other cognitive activities. A particular worldview need not be dependent on language; this is apparent in his descriptions of the subuniverses of music and the individual, both of which are theorized as standing apart from language. The conceptual domain proper to the subuniverse of the individual in fact anticipates aspects of Fauconnier's theory, for this domain is a construct distinct from linguistic constructs. The principal barrier to realizing the fruits of the unitary field theory lay in the sterility of reference to the objective world. The seeming inviolability of the link between language and the real world mitigates against assigning priority to any other conceptual realm, for to do so would sever our connections to reality: the dominance of speech is, for Seeger, inescapable. In an epilogue to the unitary field theory he writes, "speech alone poses the conditions of our lives in terms of problems, while its domination of us and our affairs is possibly the biggest problem of all. How can we expect to solve all problems in terms of the biggest problem of all—that of the linguocentric predicament—is quite a problem. As a problem, I believe it is insoluble" (1977c:133).

In the face of such a predicament the tension between music and language would appear to be irresolvable. David Burrows puts the situation in terms of near antagonism; he writes, "Music's own precisions of pitch and rhythm lie apart in a domain of relentless emergence that represents the threat of vagueness and dissolution to that tropism of the mind that seeks fixity and delimitation in the world, the tropism that has its fullest musical realization not in music itself but in music's metamorphoses into words and pictures" (1990:107). However, both Seeger and Burrows put too much trust in language. Language does not get meaning from reference to objective reality. Instead meaning is constructed through active cognitive processing. And so, when one applies speech to music one is not arriving at a greater truth, but mapping connections between different conceptual domains.

There will always be a certain tension between making music and talking about music, but it is a tension that results from an awareness of identity; its analog is the tension between our individual selves and the Other. Musical constructs are distinct from linguistic constructs. To reduce one to the other is to demand that the image of the girl with blue eyes be only and absolutely a girl with blue eyes. It is a more promising endeavor to come to terms with the way we structure connections between the two domains. By making our assumptions explicit we can better understand what it is we are talking about and how our ways of talking fail us. As musicians who talk about music we are in the middle of these two domains. With courage and humility it is a place we may abide.

NOTES

Portions of this chapter were presented in a paper read at the Society for Ethnomusicology National Meeting in Oxford, Mississippi, October 29, 1993. I thank the participants in that session for their comments. I also received comments from members of my seminar at the University of Chicago during the winter of 1994 and participants in the Ethnomusicology Workshop at the University of Chicago during that same year. Finally, Nicholas Cook and Richard Cohn read drafts of this essay, and their comments were also extremely helpful. I am grateful to the University of California Press for permission to reproduce figures 6.1 and 6.2.

1. The majority of references are to the version of the unitary field theory that appeared in the 1977 *Studies in Musicology*. It would be somewhat presumptuous to say that this is the final version of the theory, but it is at least the latest.

2. With respect to this mode of presentation, Bonnie Wade, in a letter to Lucia Core, noted that Seeger's favorite activity was dialectic discussion and that "Toward a Unitary Field Theory" gave a clear picture of that style (see Pescatello 1992:254).

3. The idea of a mental space is not new; William James employed it in his discussion of mental constructs (1890:289). Wittgenstein appears to have used the term in a fashion similar to that of Fauconnier; this is discussed by Bertrand Russell in an evaluation of the typescript for Wittgenstein's *Philosophische Bemerkungen* (Russell 1969:297, 300–301).

4. For further work on mental spaces see Fauconnier and Sweetser (1996) and Fauconnier (1997).

5. Fauconnier currently embraces the idea that mental spaces are very general and are constructed for many cognitive purposes and that they are not necessarily built up solely from language (personal communication). This perspective is also represented, somewhat less explicitly, in Fauconnier (1997).

6. Elsewhere, I discuss connections between a variety of mental spaces for music (1991:48–64). For a discussion of language and music that takes as its point of departure the notion that music is indeed ineffable, see Raffman (1993). For another view of connections between the two, see Swain (1997).

7. For a more concise expression of this notion of a concept see Edelman (1992:108).

8. Elsewhere I describe the processes through which categories of cultural products are defined as individual musical works, representatives of musical genres, and music in general (1998, n.d.:chap. 6).

9. Analogues for knowledge structures include the *frame* (Minsky 1975, 1985); *mental models* (Johnson-Laird 1983; Barsalou 1992; Gentner and Stevens 1983); *idealized cognitive models* (Lakoff 1987; McCauley 1987); and *cognitive domains* (Langacker 1987, 1992). My approach to knowledge structures is sketched in Zbikowski (1997) and developed in more detail in Zbikowski (1991:chap. 5, n.d.:chap. 4).

10. See also the work of Roy D'Andrade (1995), D'Andrade and Claudia Strauss (1992), and Bradd Shore (1996).

REFERENCES CITED

Abelson, Robert P., and John B. Black. 1986. "Introduction." In *Knowledge Structures.* Ed. James A. Galambos, Robert P. Abelson, and John B. Black. Hillsdale, N.J.: Lawrence Erlbaum Associates.

Agawu, V. Kofi. 1991. *Playing with Signs: A Semiotic Interpretation of Classical Music.* Princeton, N.J.: Princeton University Press.

Barsalou, Lawrence W. 1992. *Cognitive Psychology: An Overview for Cognitive Scientists.* Hillsdale, N.J.: Lawrence Erlbaum Associates.

Burrows, David. 1990. *Sound, Speech, and Music.* Amherst: University of Massachusetts Press.

D'Andrade, Roy G. 1995. *The Development of Cognitive Anthropology.* Cambridge: Cambridge University Press.

D'Andrade, Roy G., and Claudia Strauss, eds. 1992. *Human Motives and Cultural Models.* Publications of the Society for Psychological Anthropology. Cambridge: Cambridge University Press.

Eco, Umberto. 1976. *A Theory of Semiotics.* Bloomington: Indiana University Press.

Edelman, Gerald M. 1989. *The Remembered Present: A Biological Theory of Consciousness.* New York: Basic Books.

———. 1992. *Bright Air, Brilliant Fire: On the Matter of Mind.* New York: Basic Books.

Fauconnier, Gilles. 1994. *Mental Spaces: Aspects of Meaning Construction in Natural Language.* 2d ed. Foreword by George Lakoff and Eve Sweetser. Cambridge: Cambridge University Press.

———. 1997. *Mappings in Thought and Language.* Cambridge: Cambridge University Press.

Fauconnier, Gilles, and Eve Sweetser, eds. 1996. *Spaces, Worlds, and Grammar.* Chicago: University of Chicago Press.

Feld, Stephen. 1984. "Communication, Music, and Speech about Music." *Yearbook for Traditional Music* 16:1–18.

Gentner, Dedre, and Albert L. Stevens, eds. 1983. *Mental Models.* Hillsdale, N.J.: Lawrence Erlbaum Associates.

Goffman, Erving. 1974. *Frame Analysis: An Essay on the Organization of Experience.* Cambridge, Mass.: Harvard University Press.

Hatten, Robert S. 1992. Review of Agawu, *Playing with Signs,* and Nattiez, *Music and Discourse. Music Theory Spectrum* 14 (1): 88–98.

———. 1994 *Musical Meaning in Beethoven: Markedness, Correlation, and Interpretation.* Bloomington: Indiana University Press.

Jackendoff, Ray. 1987. *Consciousness and the Computational Mind.* Cambridge, Mass.: MIT Press.

James, William. 1890. *The Principles of Psychology.* 2 vols. New York: Henry Holt and Company.

Johnson-Laird, Philip N. 1983. *Mental Models: Towards a Cognitive Science of Language, Inference, and Consciousness.* Cambridge, Mass.: Harvard University Press.

Lakoff, George. 1987. *Women, Fire, and Dangerous Things: What Categories Reveal about the Mind.* Chicago: University of Chicago Press.

Langacker, Ronald W. 1987. *Foundations of Cognitive Grammar: Theoretical Prerequisites.* Stanford, Calif.: Stanford University Press.

———. 1992. *Foundations of Cognitive Grammar: Descriptive Application.* Stanford, Calif.: Stanford University Press.

Lerdahl, Fred, and Ray Jackendoff. 1983. *A Generative Theory of Tonal Music.* Cambridge, Mass.: MIT Press.

McCauley, Robert N. 1987. "The Role of Theories in a Theory of Concepts." In *Concepts and Conceptual Development: Ecological and Intellectual Factors in Categorization.* Ed. Ulric Neisser. 288–309. Cambridge: Cambridge University Press.

Minsky, Marvin. 1975. "A Framework for Representing Knowledge." In *The Psychology of Computer Vision.* Ed. Patrick H. Winston. 211–77. New York: McGraw-Hill.

———. 1985. *The Society of Mind.* New York: Simon and Schuster.

Nattiez, Jean-Jacques. 1990. *Music and Discourse: Toward a Semiology of Music.* Trans. C. Abbate. Princeton, N.J.: Princeton University Press.

Pescatello, Ann M. 1992. *Charles Seeger: A Life in American Music.* Pittsburgh: University of Pittsburgh Press.

Powers, Harold. 1980. "Language Models and Musical Analysis." *Ethnomusicology* 24 (1): 1–60.

Quinn, Naomi, and Dorothy Holland. 1987. "Culture and Cognition." In *Cultural Models in Language and Thought.* Ed. Dorothy Holland and Naomi Quinn. 3–40. Cambridge: Cambridge University Press.

Raffman, Diana. 1993. *Language, Music, and Mind.* Cambridge, Mass.: MIT Press.

Rosch, Eleanor. 1978. "Principles of Categorization." In *Cognition and Categorization.* Ed. Eleanor Rosch and Barbara B. Lloyd. 27–48. Hillsdale, N.J.: Lawrence Erlbaum Associates.

Russell, Bertrand. 1969. *The Autobiography of Bertrand Russell.* 3 vols. Boston: Little, Brown, and Co.

Seeger, Charles Louis. 1913. "Toward an Establishment of the Study of Musicology in America." Ms. Seeger Collection, Library of Congress, Washington, D.C.

———. 1947. "Toward a Unitary Field Theory for Musicology." *Bulletin of the American Musicological Society* 9–10:16.

———. 1970. "Toward a Unitary Field Theory for Musicology." In *Selected Reports* (University of California at Los Angeles, Institute of Ethnomusicology) 1 (3): 171–210.

———. 1976. "Tractatus esthetico-semioticus: Model of the Systems of Human Communication." In *Current Thought in Musicology.* Ed. John W. Grubbs. 1–39. Austin: University of Texas Press.

———. 1977a. "The Musicological Juncture: 1976." *Ethnomusicology* 21 (2): 179–88.

———. 1977b. "Speech, Music, and Speech about Music." In *Studies in Musicology, 1935–1975.* 16–30. Berkeley: University of California Press.

———. 1977c. "Toward a Unitary Field Theory for Musicology." In *Studies in Musicology, 1935–1975.* 102–38. Berkeley: University of California Press.

Shore, Bradd. 1996. *Culture in Mind: Cognition, Culture, and the Problem of Meaning.* New York: Oxford University Press.

Swain, Joseph P. 1997. *Musical Languages.* New York: W. W. Norton.

Zbikowski, Lawrence M. 1991. "Large-Scale Rhythm and Systems of Grouping." Ph.D. dissertation, Yale University.

———. 1997. "Conceptual Models and Cross-Domain Mapping: New Perspectives on Theories of Music and Hierarchy." *Journal of Music Theory* 41 (2): 193–225.

———. 1998. "Of 'Jazz' and 'Rhythm': An Approach to Musical Categories." Ms.

———. n.d. "Conceptualizing Music: Cognitive Structure, Theory, and Analysis." Ms.

7

Anthropology and Musicology:
Seeger's Writings from 1933 to 1953

Nimrod Baranovitch

In 1933, almost twenty years before comparative musicology turned into ethnomusicology and exactly twenty-seven years before Alan P. Merriam defined the new field as "the study of music in culture," Charles Seeger suggested that "music is a phenomenon of prolonged social growth—a culture" (1933:148). In this statement Seeger also anticipated by half a century a more recent development in ethnomusicology, namely, the view of scholars such as John Blacking, Steve Feld, Norma McLeod, Marcia Herndon, Anthony Seeger, Ruth Stone, and Christopher Waterman that music should be studied not *in* culture but *as* culture, not *in* context but *as* context. Like these scholars Seeger argued that music is not merely a product of culture and does not only reflect culture, but it is also a formative factor that shapes and constructs culture and contributes to its development (ibid.).

Seeger's 1933 statement, which some might take for granted today, marked the beginning of a new line of thought in musicology. It was indeed one of the seeds that later developed to become the field of ethnomusicology. The concept of culture and the notion that music is an integral part of culture and should be studied as such were borrowed from anthropology.[1] Seeger was exposed to anthropological ideas at least as early as 1912, when he became a professor at Berkeley. There he participated in various seminars given in different departments, including anthropology. He got to know Alfred Kroeber and Robert Lowie, two of America's leading anthropologists, who also taught at Berkeley at that time (Pescatello 1992:53, 62). This early acquaintance with anthropological thought eventually bore fruit in his musicological writings: from 1933 on, the influence of anthropological ideas becomes unequivocally apparent.

This essay examines several of Seeger's writings published between 1933 and 1953, which was approximately when the new field of ethnomusicology came into being. It points to specific anthropological ideas that Seeger appropriates and analyzes the development of anthropological influence in his writings on music.

The State of Anthropology in the United States
in the First Half of the Twentieth Century

American anthropology of the first half of the twentieth century owes its general theoretical framework to Franz Boas. Seeger's Berkeley colleagues Kroeber and Lowie, together with Ruth Benedict and Margaret Mead, were among the most famous American anthropologists of the first half of this century; all were trained by Boas. The Boasian school made major contributions that continue to shape the field of anthropology to this day; among the most important were the redefinition of the concept of culture, the introduction of the idea of cultural relativism, and the rejection of nineteenth-century unilinear evolutionary theories.

The Boasians established the concept of culture as a universal human phenomenon, in the sense that it is equally possessed by all human beings—or, as Kroeber put it, "All men are totally civilized" (Kroeber 1915:286). This concept replaced the traditional notion of culture, which had been understood as the exclusive possession of higher class Europeans and white Americans. The most important implication of the concept of cultural relativism was the rejection of the idea that some cultures are superior or inferior to others and of the practice of viewing other cultures in terms of Western categories and standards. The Boasian embrace of cultural relativism inevitably led to a strong emphasis on objectivity and on the notion of fact as the basis for theorizing. For this reason Boas is frequently referred to as the scholar who turned anthropology into a science.

The new concept of cultural relativism was also tied to the rejection of contemporary unilinear evolutionary theories. Developed in the nineteenth century under the influence of Darwinism, such theories assumed both a single universal sequence of stages through which all societies are thought to develop and, inevitably, that the industrialized West represented the most advanced stage. Thus Kroeber stated, "The so-called savage is no transition between the animal and the scientifically educated man. . . . There is no higher and lower in civilization for the historian" (1915:286).

In addition Boas established the idea that in order to understand a certain cultural trait of a particular society, one needs to examine it in the context of its own particular history, environment, and other cultural traits, rather than comparing it to other societies. This approach of the Boasian school is referred to today as "historical particularism." Boas was also among the earliest modern scholars to introduce the idea that culture is integrated—in other words, that every cultural phenomenon is related to other cultural phenomena, affecting them and being affected by them.

Both in the United States and in Europe social scientists were in general agreement early this century that culture is a social phenomenon rather than an individual one. Kroeber, for instance, who is known for his rather extreme view regarding the place of the individual in society and culture, stated that "the personal or individual has no historical value, save as illustration" (1915:284). Marvin Harris traces Kroeber's lack of interest in the individual back to the early nineteenth century: "It has of course been clear at least since Hegel that a scientific approach to sociocultural phenomena must proceed on the assumption that individual choices are the products of and not the originators of social forces" (1968:332). In his discussion of the French social scientist Emile Durkheim, who was active before and after the turn of the century and had similar views regarding the role of the individual in society and culture, Harris points to another intellectual ancestor for these ideas—Karl Marx. As he puts it, "Durkheim, like Marx, believed that individual states of consciousness were molded by social conditions of which the individual remained unaware" (1968:471).

Anybody familiar with Seeger's writings will see parallels between the concepts discussed above and their reappearance in Seeger's work. Moreover Seeger had firsthand contact with some of these major thinkers and their writings. Apart from his personal acquaintance with Kroeber and Lowie, he also studied Hegel during his early years at Berkeley (Pescatello 1992:62); and he was obviously influenced by Marx at least from the early 1930s, when he adopted Marxist ideology and became involved in various left-wing groups such as the Composers Collective. Harris points out that all the Boasians were politically associated with the left (1968:298). Similarly Seeger's interest in social theory and the new ideas that dominated American anthropology during the first half of the century was closely related to his political views.

Kroeber and "The Superorganic" (1917)

One of Kroeber's most important works, his 1917 essay "The Super-organic," offers direct discussion of music and suggests the possibility of a direct influence on Seeger. It also illustrates the general anthropo-logical view of music at the beginning of the century.

Kroeber's main purpose in this essay is to establish a "superorganic" status for culture. This concept posits that culture has its own develop-ment independent from the individual human beings who carry it. Con-sequently one of the main concerns of the essay is to disprove Galton's "great men" theory, which offers a biological explanation for develop-ments in culture and suggests that great people, or geniuses, are the mainspring of civilization. It is in reference to this theory that Kroeber writes: "The reason why mental heredity has nothing to do with civili-zation, is that civilization is not mental action but a body or streams of products of mental exercise. . . . Any demonstration concerning . . . [men-tal activity] consequently proves nothing whatever as to social events. Mentality relates to the individual. The social or cultural on the other hand, is in its very essence non-individual. Civilization, as such, begins only where the individual ends" (1917:192–93).

To illustrate and support his argument, Kroeber refers to the domain of music: "Bach born in the Congo instead of Saxony," he writes, "could have composed not even a fragment of chorale or sonata. . . . The con-tent of the invention or discovery springs in no way from the make-up of the great-man, or that of his ancestors, but is a product purely of the civilization into which he with millions of others is born as a meaning-less and regularly recurring event" (ibid.:195–96). Furthermore, "the march of history . . . [and] the progress of civilization is independent of the birth of particular personalities" (ibid.:202); and "the concrete effect of each individual upon civilization is determined by civilization itself" (ibid.:205). In 1940 Seeger too started to refer to the "great men theory"; and in 1941, in his essay "Inter-American Relations in the Field of Mu-sic," he made the same point that Kroeber is making here. Also like Kroeber he illustrated it by referring to Bach.

Throughout his essay Kroeber treats the terms "society," "history," and "culture" almost as if they were synonyms. He defines "historian,"

for instance, as one "who wishes to understand any sort of social phenomena" (1917:183–84), and later he suggests that the term "social science" is "equivalent to history" (ibid.:206). This close relationship between anthropology and history is also assumed by Robert Lowie, who,
when discussing the anthropologist, writes: "To put it tersely, whatever
else the investigator of civilization may do, he must be an historian" (1947
[1920]: 4). It is important to keep in mind that this integration between
anthropology and history existed in the first half of the century; otherwise the main point of Seeger's 1940 essay "Folk Music as a Source of
Social History" may be overlooked or even misinterpreted.

Kroeber further states that a clear distinction should be made between
culture and biology. Culture, he suggests, is what distinguishes humans
from other living creatures. Then, referring to language and music as two
of the most important and obvious manifestations of culture, he asserts
that "human speech or human music . . . accumulate and develop from
age to age . . . [and] inevitably alter . . . from generation to generation by
fashion or custom. . . . It is impossible for [them] to remain the same: in
other words [they are] a social thing" (1917:172). This statement is representative of the general anthropological view of music past and present,
which sees it as a part of culture, a human and social phenomenon, and
consequently treats it in conjunction with other sociocultural phenomena such as language.

Seeger adopted this view of music in 1933, when he stated that "music is a phenomenon of prolonged social growth—a culture." Four years
later, in 1937, almost forty years before John Blacking published his
influential book *How Musical Is Man?* (1973), Seeger would write: "Every person is inherently musical, and music can be associated with any
human activity" (quoted in Pescatello 1992:145). It took almost twenty
years for Seeger to explore fully the implications of his statement and for
others to accept it, before it became one theoretical foundation for the
field of ethnomusicology.

Historical Musicology and Comparative Musicology
in the First Half of the Twentieth Century

Until recently historical musicology was mainly concerned with the
study of a relatively small number of "masterpieces," composed by a
relatively small number of European individuals, mainly between the
sixteenth and early twentieth century. Several assumptions have conven-
tionally underlain the study of music by historical musicologists, espe-

cially during the first half of this century. One such assumption was that music is transcendental and autonomous, in the sense that it has very little to do with the general world around it. Another was that European art music is better, or more advanced, than other musics and is therefore the only one that deserves study. The first assumption manifested itself in the narrow scope and orientation of scholarly inquiry: until recently this was limited mainly to music itself, more specifically the musical text and the individual composer who created it, as if both stood above society and culture. The second assumption still manifests itself in the narrowness of the repertoire commonly studied, as if the term "music" applies to European art music alone.

Comparative musicology differed from historical musicology mainly in its focus on non-European musics. The extension of geographical scope, however, did not always mean giving up the assumption that European art music is the best or the most advanced. Non-European cultures have been studied by anthropologists from at least the mid-nineteenth century. Yet at least until the turn of the century in America and even later in Europe, they were usually seen through the lens of the West—which, as mentioned above, was perceived as representative of the most advanced stage in the universal unilinear evolutionary scale. More often than not non-European musics were studied not in their own right, but rather as the living representations, or survivals, of the early evolutionary stages in the history of Europe. Many comparative musicologists believed in uniform unilinear evolution at the beginning of the twentieth century, and some even held to this theory as late as the middle of the century.[2]

Finally, and no less important, comparative musicology, like historical musicology, dealt mainly with the study of music itself—although primarily with sounds rather than texts—while very little attention was paid to context. Seeger's introduction of anthropological thought in his writings on music must be viewed against this intellectual background.

"Music and Musicology" (1933)

In this essay Seeger discusses various subjects under separate subtitles: "Music and Language," "Musicology," "Criticism and Music," and "Musical Science." One single theme, however, connects the separate discussions, and that is the relationship between music and society. Not surprisingly this essay was published in the *Encyclopedia of the Social Sciences* and was written during the Great Depression, when Seeger was active in the Composers Collective—a group of left-wing intellectuals who aimed to use music as a social tool for the betterment of the working class. In the first section of this essay Seeger discusses the relationship between music and language—an issue he explored ceaselessly for the rest of his life. Here, he states that the examination of this relationship is necessary to understand the social function of music (1933:143). He goes on to argue that music, like language, has social value, and he points to other cultures where music is highly integrated with other aspects of culture, such as statecraft and the "actual living of life" (ibid.:145). He then makes the seminal statement that "music is a phenomenon of prolonged social growth—a culture" and that it is not only a product of a culture but also a formative factor that contributes to the development of culture (ibid.:148).

In this essay, then, Seeger diverges from what he calls the "romantic individualism [which stands] at the basis of European and American musical thought" (ibid.:146) and treats music as a social phenomenon and part of culture that is related to other aspects of culture, such as language. He also challenges the view that music is a transcendental art or an end in itself, stating instead that it has a social function and that study of this function is worthwhile.

Seeger adopts at least in part the Boasian concept of cultural relativism. Bearing in mind that it was written more than sixty-five years ago, his comparison of Western art music with several other musical cultures is impressive in its objectivity. This treatment is also related to Seeger's notion of "musical science," explored in one of the essay's sections. Here the concept of cultural relativism manifests itself when Seeger refers to the tones of the piano, somewhat tongue-in-cheek, as being "out of tune" (1933:145), by which he means that the Western musical scale does not correspond to the "physically pure scale" (ibid.). This statement evokes Kroeber, who states in "The Superorganic" that "there is no natural human language" (1917:175). Both scholars challenge the ethnocentric belief that was prevalent in the West at that time that Western culture—language, music, kinship patterns, etc.—is natural and therefore universal, or better than any other culture. Seeger even goes a step further and suggests that "there are two respects at least in which occidental music is behind some of the other musics of the world": in the dulling effect of mass production and virtuosity, and the simplistic treatment of rhythm (1933:150). In this statement he challenges the whole idea of unilinear evolution with the West placed at the most advanced stage. He explains,

"Men have manipulated the raw materials of music in a manner deemed by them . . . to be socially useful and valuable. . . . Each great culture has become habituated to a particular kind of manipulation of the material, so that their musics are quite as distinctive as their languages" (ibid.:148).

"Music and Government: Field for an Applied Musicology" (1939)

In this essay, read at an International Congress of Musicology in 1939 but not published until 1944, Seeger starts to explore some of the implications of his statement that music is a cultural phenomenon. He suggests here that "both government and music are functions of a culture," and later he adds that "although music is nearly a billion-dollar industry, we know very little about music as a cultural function" (1944:15). Clearly a believer in the anthropological concept of culture, Seeger inevitably also subscribed to the notion that culture is integrated and that music is related to other cultural phenomena—in this case specifically politics and economics. Such a view was of course diametrically opposed to the still prevalent idea of music and the other arts as autonomous entities blessedly disengaged from the vulgar world of business and government affairs.

Indeed, in suggesting that "we know very little about music as a cultural function," Seeger implies that there is an alternative way to study music or at least a possibility to extend the scope and orientation of scholarly inquiry beyond the customary narrow concerns of humanities-oriented research. As Seeger made clear in later writings, to study music as function means two things: first, to study it not as an object but as a process; second, to study it not as an independent self-contained entity, but as part of a larger system encompassing extramusical phenomena.

Later in this essay Seeger comments on the place of musicology among the other disciplines. He asserts boldly that "prediction has not been developed as a scientific technique by musicologists. Yet it has been developed and found generally useful by the social sciences, among which musicology is to be classed" (1944:16). This provocative statement is a direct development of his pronouncements from 1933 discussed above. If music is a social phenomenon, Seeger reasons, it is only natural that the study of music be placed among the social sciences. The desired divorce from the humanities implied in this statement is also related to Seeger's wish to turn musicology into a science. He suggests, then, that the field should aim to develop the ability to predict and use statistical methods and experimental techniques.

"Folk Music as a Source of Social History" (1940)

Seeger opens this important essay with two questions: "(1) Why has the study of music-culture relationships been neglected? and (2) How shall we go about remedying the situation in which we are at present?" (1940:316). He then points to four gaps in the study of music that need to be filled, two of which are of relevance to the present discussion. The first is "a concept of music as a social and cultural function," and the second is the "utilization by musicologists of current concepts of total culture" (ibid.:318). While these two observations do little more than summarize what he has suggested in earlier writings, the following statement marks a significant new stage in the Seegerian bridging of the gap between anthropology and musicology. He writes: "The inner, technical operations of the art of music cannot adequately be studied without consideration of the outer relations of music and the culture of which it is a part" (ibid.). In 1939 Seeger implied that it is possible to understand and study music in a new way. Now he goes a step further and argues that one cannot gain a full understanding of music itself if one does not consider the context. Seeger here introduces anthropological functionalism.[3] This statement is perhaps the earliest articulation of the principle of the study of music in context, which later became one of the cornerstones of ethnomusicological theory.

Seeger goes on to point out the difficulty in implementing this principle, because "the musicologist is . . . well accustomed to regarding music as a thing apart from, rather than bound in with the worlds of daily life" (1940:318). He then states that "the social historian can still be of considerable help in persuading . . . [musicologists] that music exists in the here and now more than in some kind of 'other world'" (ibid.:319). This assertion and the comment that "the alignment of music-historical and general historical fields may perhaps best be sought in respect to contemporary rather than past history" (ibid.:320) suggest that when using the term "history" Seeger does not refer to the field of history as often conceived today, but rather to the social sciences, and specifically to anthropology—which was perceived by many at that time to be inseparable from history. History as many think of it today does not study the "now" nor does it label itself "social history." The distinction between history and "social history" is of importance here since one of the main points in this essay is that musicologists should cease to occupy themselves exclusively with texts and start to deal with the real primary source, sound; they are also urged to pay attention not only to the past but also to the present. Seeger obviously has historical musicology rather than comparative musicology in mind when he makes these comments.

Just one year after saying that musicology should be classed among the social sciences, Seeger further suggests here that it is not only theory, concepts, methods, and techniques that musicology can share with anthropology, but also subject matter, sources, and aims. Thus another provocative idea in this essay is that knowledge about music per se is not necessarily the ultimate goal of musicology, but rather a means to understand and gain knowledge about human society and culture in general.

Seeger not only theorized about these issues but also applied some of them to the real world. The folk music recording project that he headed at this time for the Resettlement Administration saw him issuing almost Boasian instructions to one of his field collectors: just as Boas a few decades earlier had been conscientiously engaged in obtaining every possible piece of data on American Indians, knowing that their cultures were endangered, so did Seeger admonish Sidney Robertson to "record EVERY-thing! . . . Don't select, don't omit, don't concentrate on any single style. We know so little! Record *everything!*" (quoted in Pescatello 1992:141).

In "Folk Music as a Source of Social History," Seeger points to several reasons why folk music is valuable as a source of social history, two of which are its "universality" and "anonymity." Under "universality" Seeger writes: "As the musical vernacular of the 'common man,' its study compensates in part for the still strong temptation to tread the primrose path of prestige and great man theories. It constitutes the first hand approach to music materials, through which the other idioms can be seen in a truer perspective. It brings into the picture a new quantitative criterion to offset traditional overemphasis upon qualitative criteria that have so long dominated the field." Then under "anonymity" he adds: "[In folk music] one is dealing directly with a socially molded thing, with a deep-set cultural function expressing not so much the varieties of individual experience as the norms of social experience" (1940:320–21). Seeger introduces here the anthropological interest in the human, in society and culture, and suggests that it can substitute for, or at least expand, the traditional limited musicological interest in a few talented individuals, or great people. This is the first time that Seeger refers to the "great men" theory; it is also at this point that two related dichotomies, individual versus society and qualitative versus quantitative, start to appear in his writing. These two dichotomies were to occupy him for much of the following two decades; and the desire to give serious musicological consideration to the second halves of these dichotomies marked a radical departure from conventional historical musicology.

Earlier in the essay Seeger provides a sociohistorical contextual explanation to how Western art music came to be regarded as "good" music. This suggests that he acknowledges the relativity of this qualitative label. After criticizing musicology for treating music as if it were transcendental, he writes: "This centuries-old trend became grossly exaggerated during the last hundred years or so, when large-scale music organization required the support of wealth and fashion and so came to emphasize the rare rather than the common, the difficult rather than the easy, the *recherché* rather than the ordinary. It was during this time that fine-art music became 'good' music and other idioms either 'bad' music or not music at all" (1940:318). From this point on, when referring to Western art music, Seeger starts to place the "good" in "good music" in quotation marks in order to express his relativistic, objective, and scientific approach.

As for the "great men" theory, at this point Seeger does not explicitly apply the anthropological notion that music and musicians are a "socially molded thing" to European art music. It is only the anonymous folk tune that he perceives as such in this essay. It seems, then, that although Seeger keeps criticizing musicologists for treating music as if it were transcendental, he himself nevertheless still allows for individuality and transcendence where European art music is concerned. It would take one more year for Seeger to bridge this particular gap between musicology and anthropology and to acknowledge that European art music, too, is a "socially molded thing."

"Inter-American Relations in the Field of Music" (1941)

In writings up to 1940 most of Seeger's criticism is directed at historical musicology. This essay, by contrast, opens with criticism directed at comparative musicologists. Seeger complains that "scholars—a very few of them, known as comparative musicologists—have written a good deal on so-called 'primitive' music, on folk music, on the fine or high art musics of the world, and even something, though very little, upon one of the largest categories of music activity, popular music. But of the relationships among these, of their functions in the social orders they are found in, of their significance to us, and, least of all, of the problems of their social organization, comparative musicology tells us nothing" (1941:17). Besides articulating once again the need to study music in context, Seeger also expresses in this last statement his new sensitivity to social and quantitative factors, even suggesting that popular music, "one of the largest categories of music activity," deserves to be studied more thoroughly.

In earlier writings Seeger made it clear that he was not content with the state of what one calls today historical musicology. In this essay from 1941 his complaints about comparative musicologists suggest that he did not consider comparative musicology as then practiced a valid alternative. It appears that Seeger was after a completely new scholarly orientation, and at this point he started to lay the foundations for a new branch of musicology.

In section 2 of this essay Seeger presents and criticizes five assumptions that he perceives as underlying the conventional American conception of music: "(1) Music is a universal language. (2) By means of it the individual maker communicates with the individual listener. (3) Qualitative considerations are more important than quantitative. (4) Quality depends primarily upon inherent technical excellence and upon the emotional enjoyment it effects. (5) The best music is written music: the basis of music education is in written techniques and in the performance of written masterpieces" (1941:18). Committed as he is to the concept of cultural relativism, Seeger opens his criticism by dismissing the notion that music is a universal language. The point, of course, is to reject the prevailing view that it is European art music that is universal: "German and Italian authority was harnessed upon us firmly. . . . We rationalized this dependence by particular emphasis upon the belief in the universality of western European fine-art music. But we were fooling ourselves" (ibid.:64). Cultural relativism manifests itself also in Seeger's sensitivity to the evolutionary implications of the term "primitive music," sensitivity that leads him to place the word "primitive" in quotation marks.

Seeger also challenges the contemporary habit of viewing other musics through European eyes and of always comparing "us" and "them," with "us" as the yardstick. Helen H. Roberts's definition of comparative musicology can serve as a good illustration of the still strong ethnocentrism against which Seeger reacts. She writes: "The kind of studies that are now coming to be classified under the term 'comparative musicology' deal with exotic musics as compared with one another and with that classical European system under which most of us were brought up" (1937:233). Very much aware of his American identity, Seeger reacts against the habit of labeling all non-European musics "exotic"—which among other things suggests that the scholar is always taken for granted to be culturally European. Here Seeger deliberately

identifies the exotic in his essay with European art music itself. By doing so he suggests that European music can also be seen from the outside. It, too, can be perceived as exotic: it simply depends on where one
stands. Seeger's point, of course, besides stating his American identity,
is to question the exclusiveness of point of view.

Referring to the second popular assumption regarding music, that
"by means of it the individual maker communicates with the individual
listener," Seeger writes: "While it is true that the individual maker of
music communicates with the individual listener, the nature of this communication is at least as much a social as it is an individual thing. For
instance, the work of John [*sic*] Sebastian Bach stands before our public
as the work of one man. Bach inherited, however, forms of idiom, style,
technique, instruments, pedagogical methods, social organization of
music, which were the work of thousands of men over a period of centuries. The content, or meaning, of these forms was of a type indissolubly bound up with them, expressing attitudes, reactions, and aspirations
of a whole culture. In the absence of any conceivable measure, we must
admit that though the man may, in some cases, influence the times, it
must be a general rule that men make the man and the times too"
(1941:18). While a year earlier, in "Folk Music as a Source of Social History," Seeger confined the notion of music as a "socially molded thing"
to folk music alone, here he extends it to include the music of the "great
men." The anthropological influence is clear: both the thinking and the
choice of Bach as an example reflect Kroeber's essay "The Superorganic"
discussed above.

In his comments on the third popular assumption, that qualitative
considerations are more important than quantitative ones, Seeger elabo-
rates on the qualitative-quantitative dichotomy he introduced a year
earlier, which is related to another of his obsessively discussed dichotomies, that between value and fact (cf. Grimes's essay in this volume). He
writes: "Qualitative considerations are sometimes less important than
quantitative. It is a question whether occasional contact with what is
supposed to be the 'best' in music can compensate for more frequent
contact with the 'less good,' which has been condemned by the vogue
of hearing only the 'best.' Does not a candid view of our typical concert
audiences lead us inevitably to feel that pretended appreciation of the
classics may not represent either social or individual value equal to genuine grasp of a vulgar idiom?" (1941:18). This statement shows that despite all that he has said so far in this essay, Seeger is in fact unwilling to

adopt a complete relativistic view or, in other words, to avoid value judgment altogether and disregard his personal likes and dislikes. Although he puts all qualitative labels in quotation marks (except for "vulgar," which is telling), the formulation of the argument suggests that he still believes that "what is supposed to be the 'best'" is musically really the best, or at least good. Seeger is willing to go as far as to explain what makes other musics good, which is usually their function, or in general to argue that there are other criteria besides the quality of the music itself for determining its value. Yet, even the very first statement in the paragraph above, that "qualitative considerations are sometimes less important than quantitative [ones]," obviously implies that he accepts and shares the belief that, musically speaking, that which is considered to be of quality is indeed good.

Seeger has never given up his belief in the importance of value and criticism in the study of music; what he attempts to do here is to integrate this aspect with fact and scientism or, in other words, to reconcile the dichotomy between fact and value. His unwillingness to separate fact from value and his attempt to force integration both on fact and value and on quantity and quality lead to an argument that is problematic because of the two assumptions involved: first, that "less good" music is necessarily associated with "frequent contact," and the "best" music with "occasional" contact; and, second, that the "best" music is necessarily associated with "pretended appreciation," and "less good" music with "genuine grasp."

Despite this particular problematic attempt to integrate fact/value and quantity/quality, Seeger's engagement with these dichotomies is important because it results in the establishment of the value of quantity to the study of music. Thus the study of popular and folk music is legitimized and becomes valuable for the same reason that these musics were traditionally anathema to historical musicologists, namely, that they are associated with a large number of people. In 1953 Seeger would write, "The ultimate task of musicology is to contribute to the general study of man, what can be known of man as music maker and music user" (1953: 366). This was twenty years before Blacking's famous book *How Musical Is Man?* (1973), which is known for propagating this idea. The seed of this idea is found in Seeger's earlier essay "Folk Music as a Source of Social History" from 1940, where he acknowledges for the first time the value of studying the common rather than the rare, the human in music rather than "great men."

"Music and Musicology in the New World" (1946)

Concern with the integration of conceptual dichotomies persists into this next essay. Here Seeger outlines several fallacies that exist in musicological thought, two of which are relevant to the present discussion. Referring again to the fact-value, or quantity-quality dichotomy, he writes: "The second fallacy is to set in general a higher value upon value than upon fact, or vice versa. Quality and quantity are conditions for each other's existence and are not commensurable. The third fallacy, a corollary of the second, is to let determinations of value color our determinations of fact. Thus, the positions that only 'good' music is music, or the musicology of 'good' music is musicology, are untenable" (1977a [1946]: 213). Following on from his attempt five years earlier to integrate quality and quantity, Seeger suggests here that quality and quantity do not in fact stand in opposition to one another but are both equally necessary to the study of music. At the same time, however, his warning not to allow determinations of value to influence determinations of fact implies his belief that fact is indeed mistreated by musicologists.

Pointing, then, to the differences between the musician and the musicologist in terms of fact and value, Seeger writes: "The musician is more or less bound to confine his activity to the class of music he values most. The typical attitude of the musicologist is, however, to be able to submerge his own taste preferences at will, in order to be as objective as possible in the study of other people's taste preferences, or upon occasion, to study music data as free as possible of all critical considerations whatever" (ibid.:218). The distinction between fact and value and the question whether or not the scholar should make value judgments in his or her research have been major issues in anthropology from at least the late nineteenth century. As mentioned earlier, Franz Boas emphasized the primacy of fact and prescribed that anthropologists should collect facts and avoid value judgments. This prescription was related both to the concept of cultural relativism and to the Boasian wish to turn anthropology into a science. Seeger's statement in the last quotation, which obviously should be read as prescription rather than description, clearly shows again the influence of the Boasian program. Yet this is likely the only time in which Seeger moves to the extreme of suggesting that musicologists should, even if only "upon occasion," "study music data as free as possible of all critical considerations whatever" (ibid.). By contrast seven years earlier, in 1939, Seeger had called for increase both in scientism and in criticism, a holistic view that he would propagate from that point on.

The idea that music is part of culture, a social phenomenon, and that it should be studied as such, is expressed several times and in different ways in this essay. For example, Seeger argues that the study of "the place and function of music in human culture" should be central to musicological study (1977a [1946]: 217). In the last part of the essay Seeger advocates that "our knowledge of music in its relation to other things should be brought up to the standards of our knowledge of music as a thing in itself" (ibid.:220). Seeger introduces here the notion of "music as a thing in itself," or "music itself," which one uses so often today to make a distinction between music sound and the extramusical. Seeger, of course, needed this notion once the whole concept of music in context had been established in his writings.

"Music and Society: Some New-World Evidence of Their Relationship" (1951)

In this essay, read at a Conference on Latin-American Fine Arts in 1951 and first published in 1952, Seeger discusses the history of music in America from 1500 to 1950. His purpose is to present evidence of the influence of society on music. In this particular context Seeger readdresses the individual-society dichotomy:

> Music and society, we may agree, are both phenomena or functions of culture. So it is reasonable to assume that the various phenomena or functions of culture have definite relationships, one to another and to the whole collection. Society being the more comprehensive concept, one might claim that music must be dependent upon it. Yet in spite of this reasonableness and its support by evidence of some of the larger events and processes of history, there seems to be very little tangible in it when we come down to details. . . . So we fall back upon the "great man" theory of history—that things happen because great men make them happen. Let us concede that sometimes they do. But there are many things, we all admit, that do not happen because great men make them happen. It is with respect to these that the problem of music and society arises. (1952:84–85)

Seeger's revision of this essay amplifies and makes explicit his view of the situation in America, both south and north: "Individuals did, it is true, inherit, carry, and hand on the music traditions of their communities. But the whole 450 years is conspicuous for its lack of outstanding individuals, 'masters,' 'great men'" (1977b:186). Thus Seeger concludes: "In a virtually leaderless four and one-half centuries, our musicology, built upon the study of European leaders and the monuments they bequeathed us, can avail little. It is convenient, of course, that leaders are appearing, so that a man who may write a paper . . . in the year 2001 may have a somewhat more balanced scene to deal with" (1952:97). Seeger revises here the statement made ten years earlier in "Inter-American Relations in the Field of Music," where he wrote that "in the absence of any conceivable measure, we must admit that though the man may, in some cases, influence the times, it must be a general rule that men make the man and the times too" (1941:18). Whereas in 1941, as this last statement suggests, he concluded that as a general rule the influence of society on the individual is more significant than that of the individual on society, in 1951 he now takes a more balanced and holistic stand, accepting the equal possibility of both.

In his conclusion Seeger also softens his critical tone towards historical musicology. He no longer challenges the legitimacy and validity of this subdiscipline's approach to European art music but rather suggests that since it is used to deal exclusively with "great men," it cannot help in the particular case of the history of music in the New World and in other similar cases where "great men" did not exist.

Seeger faces in this essay a lack of theoretical framework for studying the relationship between music and society, and that results in his difficulty in dealing with the history of musical culture that lacks individuals. Again he does not blame historical musicology and its approach to the study of European art music but simply suggests that the study of music in other places in the world, such as America, will require a new approach and a new theory that he himself does not provide. "A complete theory of music and society," he writes, "will have to be done by other hands than mine" (1952:96).

At the time of publication of "Music and Society" Seeger was already in his mid-sixties. And although he would be fortunate to live and to be academically active for almost three more decades, there is a strong sense in the last statement of someone who leaves a charge to others. Seeger was plainly well aware of his pioneering role in bridging the gap between musicology and anthropology, and he recognized that by this point there were other people following in his footsteps. Thus in this will-like statement he acknowledges both his own contribution and the end of his pioneering role.

It was two years after the initial appearance of "Music and Society" that the first issue of *Ethno-musicology Newsletter* was published, and a new branch of musicology was born.

Conclusion

Seeger's persistent interest in dichotomies is clear to anyone who reads his writings. This essay has examined Seeger's engagement with some of the major dichotomies that he perceived to be related to the study of music: fact-value, quantity-quality, and society-individual. Historical musicology has traditionally paid attention mainly to value, quality, and the individual composer. Seeger's introduction of anthropological thought into musicology, and its application to music, initiated and legitimized a new approach to music, one that emphasizes the other element in this set of dichotomies, namely, fact, quantity, and society.

Twice in his writings Seeger goes to the extreme of suggesting that fact and society are more important to the study of music than value and the individual: first in the essay from 1941 in relation to the society-individual dichotomy, and second in 1946 in relation to the fact-value dichotomy. The supremacy of quantitative considerations over qualitative ones in the study of music is never suggested by Seeger. However, he explains why a larger quantity can be a quality—or, in other words, why the common or widespread can be valuable for the scholar; and thus he legitimizes an approach to music that puts emphasis on quantitative aspects.

After exploring the other side of the coin (the antithesis, to use the terminology of Hegel, whose influence on Seeger is most obvious in the latter's engagement with dichotomies), Seeger soon goes back to maintain a more holistic and balanced approach. This approach attempts, not always with success, to integrate or synthesize the two elements in all the dichotomies. Thus more often than not Seeger eventually ends up advocating the importance of both perspectives in all the above dichotomies to the study of music.

Ironically, in many people's minds Seeger is associated very much with the sound branch of ethnomusicology. The melograph project that he initiated and led from around the mid-1950s no doubt has contributed significantly to this inaccurate association. Another important factor that led to this erroneous view of Seeger is that during the 1960s and 1970s Seeger often expressed views closer to those entertained by historical musicologists, music theoreticians, and composers than to those espoused by ethnomusicologists.[4] This development in Seeger's later thought was a kind of reaction against the path that ethnomusicology took, which was mainly to subscribe to the second element (fact, quantity, society) in all the dichotomies mentioned above. Believing in reconciliation of all the dichotomies and always propagating a holistic approach to the study of music, Seeger's reaction should be understood as an attempt to remind ethnomusicologists that value and criticism, the role of the individual, aesthetics, and music sound, or "music itself," should not be neglected.

Charles Seeger is considered today to be one of the founders of ethnomusicology, and yet his contribution to the field has seldom been identified in concrete terms. Bruno Nettl articulates a common perception: "And so I am somewhat puzzled by Seeger's role in our history. Scholars are not really following his lead. The melograph has declined in influence. Vernacular musics are not treated as a unit. The philosophy of musicology has not emerged as a major area of discussion at meetings or in publications. That we still see Charles Seeger as a great leader is due to his charismatic style. . . . [We] look to him more for inspiration than for substantive instruction" (1991:269). This essay suggests that Seeger's contribution to the field of ethnomusicology was concrete and solid and not confined to abstract charisma and inspiration. When reading Seeger's writing from 1933 to 1953, while keeping in mind publications of other contemporary scholars, it is clear that Seeger laid the very foundations for the field: he introduced cultural relativism, functionalism, and objectivism; stressed the importance of the social, quantitative, and factual aspects in music; and promoted the idea that music can be understood only when studied in context.

Dieter Christensen writes that Seeger's name "is invoked probably much more than his works are read" (1991:207). The situation implied by this statement—that many have not read Seeger, or not thoroughly enough—is the primary reason why his important contributions pointed out in this essay have never been acknowledged. Seeger's writings have not been read with sufficient frequency and attentiveness for two main reasons. First, they can be difficult to follow. Second, in contrast to Alan Merriam's book *The Anthropology of Music* (1964), for example, in which the author formulates, develops, and introduces his ideas in a comprehensive, coherent, and complete manner in a single volume, Seeger's writings were published sporadically, one essay at a time, often without obvious links between them. No less important, many of them appeared in nonmusicological publications. Despite this Seeger is still considered one of the intellectual founders of ethnomusicology, as well as a leading light in the founding of the Society for Ethnomusicology and related organizations. Thus I suggest that he may have stimulated and influenced others mainly orally and that the concrete details of his influence may have been overlooked.

The future of our field, like its past, can benefit greatly from the rich ideas found in Seeger's writings. I would urge all students of music to read his writings for both inspiration and substantive instruction, as well as to gain a better understanding of the history of our field.

NOTES

I am grateful to Bell Yung, who introduced me to Seeger's writings and thought, for his comments on earlier drafts of this essay. I am also indebted to Nicole Constable and Lee Tong Soon for their valuable remarks on an earlier version of the essay. Sincere thanks are also owed to Helen Rees for helping to revise this essay.

1. "Anthropology" throughout this essay stands for American cultural anthropology.

2. A good example is Curt Sachs. The following representative statements are taken from *Our Musical Heritage: A Short History of Music* (1955 [1948]): "This, then, is the inevitable fact: whoever wants to know the origins and early rise of music must read them from fossil remains in primitive life of today. The branch of learning in charge of collecting and reading these fossil remains is none too adequately called Comparative Musicology or, better, Ethnomusicology. Astride between anthropology and the history of music, its students are concerned with the phonographic recording, the analysis, and the interpretation of primitive music in all its forms" (2). "Oriental music has on the whole been stationary . . . the ancient pentatonic scales . . . have tenaciously held their ground while Europe was consistently evolving from stages much earlier" (8, 9).

3. I use the term "functionalism" in a broad sense to mean, first, the idea that culture is integrated, and, second, a holistic approach to the study of culture.

4. In several articles written in the 1960s and 1970s Seeger considers the concept of the autonomy of music, which is anathema to many ethnomusicologists. A good example is found in "The Musicological Juncture: 1976," originally presented at the Society for Ethnomusicology meeting: "I run afoul of people who talk about meaning in music. If I understand rightly, the meaning of something is what it stands for, unless, by rare exception, it stands for itself, which is next to meaningless. I find that the imputed meaning of music is precisely that. Otherwise, meanings ascribed to the function of music in social contexts are speech meanings in speech contexts" (1977c:183). Seeger here addresses ethnomusicologists and seems to suggest in this article that they have surrendered to speech.

REFERENCES CITED

Blacking, John. 1973. *How Musical Is Man?* Seattle: University of Washington Press.

Christensen, Dieter. 1991. "Erich M. von Hornbostel, Carl Stumpf, and the Institutionalization of Comparative Musicology." In *Comparative Musicology and Anthropology of Music: Essays on the History of Ethnomusicology*. Ed. Bruno Nettl and Philip V. Bohlman. 201–9. Chicago: University of Chicago Press.

Harris, Marvin. 1968. *The Rise of Anthropological Theory.* New York: Harper Collins.

Kroeber, Alfred. 1915. "The Eighteen Professions." *American Anthropologist* 17:283–89.

———. 1917. "The Superorganic." *American Anthropologist* 19:163–213.

Lowie, Robert H. 1947 [1920]. *Primitive Society.* New York: Liveright.

Merriam, Alan P. 1964. *The Anthropology of Music.* Evanston, Ill.: Northwestern University Press.

Nettl, Bruno. 1991. "The Dual Nature of Ethnomusicology in North America: The Contributions of Charles Seeger and George Herzog." In *Comparative Musicology and Anthropology of Music: Essays on the History of Ethnomusicology.* Ed. Bruno Nettl and Philip V. Bohlman. 266–74. Chicago: University of Chicago Press.

Pescatello, Ann M. 1992. *Charles Seeger: A Life in American Music.* Pittsburgh: University of Pittsburgh Press.

Roberts, Helen. 1937. "The Viewpoint of Comparative Musicology." In *Proceedings of the Music Teachers National Association.* 31st ser. Ed. Karl W. Gehrkens. 233–38. Oberlin, Ohio: Music Teachers National Association.

Sachs, Curt. 1955 [1948]. *Our Musical Heritage: A Short History of Music.* New York: Prentice-Hall.

Seeger, Charles Louis. 1933. "Music and Musicology." In *Encyclopedia of the Social Sciences.* Vol. 11:143–50. New York: Macmillan.

———. 1940. "Folk Music as a Source of Social History." In *The Cultural Approach to History.* Ed. Carolyn F. Ware. 316–23. New York: Columbia University Press.

———. 1941. "Inter-American Relations in the Field of Music." *Music Educators Journal* 27 (5): 17–18, 64–65.

———. 1944. "Music and Government: Field for an Applied Musicology." In *Papers Read at the International Congress of Musicology Held at New York, September 11–18, 1939.* 12–20. New York: Music Educators National Conference for the American Musicological Society.

———. 1952. "Music and Society: Some New-World Evidence of Their Relationship." In *Proceedings of the Conference on Latin American Fine Arts, June 14–17, 1951.* 84–97. Austin: University of Texas Press.

———. 1953. "Preface to the Description of a Music." In *Kongressbericht, Internationale Gesellschaft für Musikwissenschaft, Utrecht 1952.* 360–70. Amsterdam: Vereneging voor Nederlandse Muzikgeschiedenis.

———. 1977a [1946]. "Music and Musicology in the New World, 1946." In *Studies in Musicology, 1935–1975*. 211–21. Berkeley: University of California Press. (Reprinted from *Proceedings of the Music Teachers National Association*. 40th ser. Ed. Theodore M. Finney. 35–47. Pittsburgh: Music Teachers National Association.)

———. 1977b. "Music and Society: Some New-World Evidence of Their Relationship." In *Studies in Musicology, 1935–1975*. 182–94. Berkeley: University of California Press.

———. 1977c. "The Musicological Juncture: 1976." *Ethnomusicology* 21 (2): 179–88.

8

From Modern Physics to Modern Musicology: Seeger and Beyond

Bell Yung

Physics and music are connected in people's minds only because a few well-known physicists have been amateur musicians. Notable examples are Albert Einstein the violinist and, closer to our time, Richard Feynman the drummer. Textbooks in acoustics may make references to music in their discussion of soundwaves and harmonic series. On the other hand, physics and musicology, defined as the scholarly study of music, are almost never linked and appear to have little in common. In writings on the philosophy of physics there is hardly any reference to music or musicology. An exception is *Physics as Metaphor* (1982), in which the physicist Roger S. Jones takes the position that scientific objectivity is an illusion and that measurement itself is a value judgment created by the human mind. Jones writes that "the scientized concepts of space, time, matter and number will be explored as metaphors, expressing the human need and ability to create meaning and value. These metaphors have an intuitive, mythic, life-giving character which completes and enhances their quantitative meaning and which is motivated by basic human fears and yearnings" (11). In short Jones argues that physical theories are metaphors of our intuitive perceptions of the universe or our means of coping with it, rather than an explanation of it. He dwells particularly on music as another kind of metaphor for the same universe.

In musicological literature, beginning with the ancient Chinese and

Greeks, philosophers and theorists have related music to, and even identified music with, mathematics, especially numerology. Most notable are numerical and arithmetical manipulations in the construction of musical scales. However, one can argue that most of these studies are not in fact about music but only about certain acoustic properties of musical sound: they have as much to do with music as spelling has to do with literature. In the early days of so-called comparative musicology in the late nineteenth and early twentieth centuries, non-Western music was studied by Western scholars who were trained in fields other than music such as anthropology, linguistics, folklore, psychology, mathematics, and even physics. These pioneering works laid the foundation for directing ethnomusicology toward the interdisciplinary study of music.

Charles Seeger is known for taking a broad approach toward the study of music. From his writings one can discern that he was well acquainted with several fields of intellectual inquiry, and many of his most provocative and influential ideas can be traced to, or are explicitly acknowledged by him as originating from, cognate and sometimes not-so-cognate scholarly disciplines. For example, he often referred to concepts from other humanistic disciplines such as philosophy and linguistics and from the social sciences such as anthropology and folklore. Little known is the influence of physical theories on some of his writings. In this regard two theories from modern physics are particularly important. They are the particle-wave duality in atomic physics and the special theory of relativity.[1]

Seeger's invocation of modern physics is significant, for beginning from his earliest writings, he was keenly aware of the need for a new approach toward the scholarly study of music. He devoted much of his intellectual activities throughout his life to the formulation of new philosophies, principles, and methodologies of musical research. Not surprisingly, he was attracted to revolutionary ideas in modern physics that, in the early twentieth century, drew the attention of scientists and scholars far beyond the realms of physics. Seeger found these ideas particularly appealing because they fit the letter and the spirit of a new approach toward musical research that he had been seeking.

Modern physics arose to a large extent as a result of the advancement in the techniques, and thus precision, of quantitative measurements of behaviors in the physical universe that had not been hitherto possible or even conceivable. Scientists were able to probe into ever smaller dimensions on the atomic and nuclear level and the ever-faster movement of subatomic particles with speeds approaching those of light. These data threw long-held theories into chaos and forced scientists to rethink the working of the physical universe on a fundamental level. Similarly the late nineteenth and early twentieth centuries saw an explosion of musical and musicological data from the far corners of the globe as well as from musical activities in one's own backyard that had not been taken seriously as music before. This information forced musicologists to rethink long-held concepts of music and of its relationship to society.

As Seeger was exposed to an increasing amount of diverse musical data, he must have been struck by the parallel between the need for new physical theories and the similar need for new musicological theories. The fundamentally revolutionary way of looking at the physical universe inspired him to take similarly revolutionary ways of looking at the musical universe. The invocation of the particle-wave duality and the special theory of relativity are concrete examples of his journey into the intellectual world of modern physics and application of some of the abstract ideas to his formulation of musical and musicological concepts.

Particle-Wave Duality

In classical, or Newtonian, physics, the physical universe is neatly divided into either particles or waves. Particles include falling apples, heavenly bodies, and everything in between; examples of waves are sound and light. Particles and waves have distinct properties. For example, a particle contains a definite amount of matter and has clearly measurable dimensions and a specific spatial position in relation to other particles. On the other hand, a wave is identified as the oscillatory behavior of a medium in the form of continuous movement. It behaves distinctly differently from particles under certain conditions, as in its ability to bend around corners as sound waves do. Thus particles and waves are acknowledged to be two very different entities in the physical universe, each obeying its own laws, sometimes contrasting ones.

This view of the universe was shattered when physicists began studying matters on the atomic level, where particles, such as electrons, are extremely small and move extremely fast. Physicists made the amazing discovery that an electron has the properties of a particle under certain conditions and of a wave under others. This dual nature as particle and/or wave led physicists to rethink the laws of classical physics and to formulate new ones in order to explain the apparent paradox. This gave birth to modern physics and more specifically to quantum physics, which proposes a model of the universe that is ambiguous, forcing one to accept polar opposites as existing in the same reality: in this case discrete particles and continuous waves. Fritjof Capra, in *The Tao of Physics*, writes: "The reality of the atomic physicist, like the reality of the Eastern mystic, transcends the narrow framework of opposite concepts. Force and matter, particles and waves, motion and rest, existence and non-existence—these are some of the opposite or contradictory concepts which are transcended in modern physics" (1975:154).

Seeger was apparently acquainted with both Eastern mystic philosophy and modern physics. Consider his article "Prescriptive and Descriptive Music Writing." Written as a theoretical treatise to contrast the "descriptive and objective" nature of the melograph and the "prescriptive and subjective" nature of traditional staff notation, he proposes two opposing representational models of a melodic line as follows: "On the one hand, . . . melody may be conceived . . . as a succession of separate sounds, on the other, as a single continuum of sound—as a chain or as a stream. Conception as a chain tends to emphasize structure and entities that move; conception as a stream, function and movement itself as a transmission of energy" (1977 [1958]: 169).

He is of course equating the "succession of separate sounds" or "chain" with the staff notation, in which a musical line is represented by discrete symbols denoting discrete pitch levels, which in turn leads to conceptualization of music as a succession of discrete sound events. In contrast, "a single continuum of sound" or "stream" is equated with the melograph output of a melodic line as a frequency-time continuous graph.

Seeger continues: "Neither, of course, tells the whole story as the musician knows it. Both distort this knowledge to extents we cannot precisely gauge. . . . these verbal constructions are not mutually exclusive opposites, but can be shown to have possibilities of serving as complements to each other. And the truth may lie somewhere between them" (ibid.).

Seeger understands the fundamental philosophy of quantum physics: that two opposing representational models can coexist for a single physical reality and that the indeterminacy of the physical reality in terms of these representational models is a fact. He borrows this philosophy and says that, in musicology, which is the "verbal construction" of music, one should acknowledge the possibility of opposing representational models of the same musical reality. In this case the musical reality is a single musical line; the two opposing representational models are "a succession of separate sounds" and "a single continuum of sound." Of course Seeger borrows more than the idea of apparent paradox, but he finds the opposing concepts of "discrete" and "continuous" in particle-wave duality perfectly applicable to the notational representation of a melodic line. It may be worthwhile to carry this line of comparison beyond what Seeger made explicit. In physics the opposing theories arise from and are verified by precisely controlled experiments on the physical universe. What do opposing theories in music arise from? What purpose do these opposing theories serve?

The physical universe is assumed to be a given; a fundamental assumption in physics is that the physical universe behaves in consistent ways that are beyond the control of human beings. The aim of physics is to discover the principles according to which the physical universe behaves. On the other hand, the musical "universe" is one created by human beings. Taking the broad definition of musicology, the musical universe consists not only of musical sound, but also of musical instruments, musical concepts and theories, and individual and social behaviors in musical activities. Furthermore one should also consider how these elements are historically transmitted, socially maintained, and individually perceived and created. How does this musical universe behave? What one cannot say is whether or not this complex musical universe follows certain principles consistently, the way the physical universe does. In view of the creative mind of the human being, it probably does not. What one *can* say is that, if such principles did exist and did play some role in the musical universe, they would be of such a complicated nature that it would be quite impossible to design and carry out controlled experiments analogous to those in physics.

If no experiments could verify the opposing theoretical viewpoints, what are the bases for those viewpoints? How does one justify them? These questions, however, are not addressed by Seeger in the above-mentioned article, which is primarily intended as a theoretical justification for the value of the melograph and its role as a complementary representation of music to staff notation. However, in other articles, particularly in "Preface to a Critique of Music" (1965), Seeger offers a clue as to what his possible answer will be: that music and musicology are an expression of a value system. Contrasting verbal constructions of the same musical phenomenon are but different means to express the values of the researcher and his culture. They are thus subjective rather than objective, evaluative rather than factual.

It is interesting to observe that some years later Jones proposed a similar view in *Physics as Metaphor* (1982). To him physical theories are but metaphors of our intuitive perceptions of the universe or our means of coping with it; they are not explanations of it. They are subjective, personal, and creative. Jones devoted many pages to the discussions of music as another, though different, kind of metaphor for the universe. What is proposed here is that musicology, defined broadly as an explanation of the musical universe, also consists merely of metaphors rather than true explanations.

Special Theory of Relativity

In addition to quantum theory Seeger also alludes to the special theory of relativity. The special theory of relativity arose from the consideration of the following hypothetical situation. What happens when a person in one frame of reference observes and measures a physical phenomenon that occurs in another frame of reference, if the two frames of reference are moving relative to one another? The typical example used in textbooks refers to measurements made from a moving train of some physical occurrences outside of the train, say, the time when two bolts of lightning strike.

Light travels fast, but it still takes a finite amount of time, however small, for the light to travel from the source to its observer. Therefore, *when* a lightning bolt strikes necessarily depends upon the movement of the observer relative to the lightning. If there are two observers on two trains moving in opposite directions, it is theoretically possible that to one lightning bolt A appears to strike first; to the other lightning bolt B may appear to strike first. Neither observer is wrong within his or her frame of reference. One may ask: is there an absolute answer as to which lightning bolt strikes first, independent of the observers on the trains?

The hypothetical situation and question posed above address a fundamental physical as well as a philosophical question: in the physical universe, is there an absolute and stationary frame of reference in which events can be said to occur in a definite time sequence? Physicists for centuries have taken for granted the existence of such a stationary and absolute frame of reference. By the late nineteenth century, however, experimental data seriously challenged them to examine this assumption more closely. Several experiments were specifically designed to test directly the existence of such an absolute frame of reference; they have all pointed to the conclusion that it does not exist. The most famous is a series of experiments carried out by Albert A. Michelson and Edward W. Morley over several years at the end of the nineteenth century in search of so-called ether, a substance that physicists had assumed to fill the universe and—if it existed—could serve as an absolute frame of reference. The Michelson-Morley experiments once and for all proved the nonexistence of ether and thus the nonexistence of an absolute frame of reference.

With such resounding experimental proof one is forced to accept a negative answer to the hypothetical question posed earlier: that the opposing claims about the relative sequence of the two lightning bolts are both valid—or both false. It was Einstein's genius to pose the paradox and resolve it by stating, and mathematically formulating, the special theory of relativity. The essence of the theory is that in the physical universe time and space are not independent of each other but must be considered as a unified whole. Time is not the absolute yardstick that it was long assumed to be; rather, how it behaves depends upon its relation with space—in other words, the movements of the frames of reference. One can no longer speak of space and time as if they were independent coordinates, because instead they are closely tied with one another. Einstein therefore proposes a physical universe that consists of four dimensions rather than three. In addition to the three spatial dimensions, he adds that of time. Thus one speaks not of space and time but rather of space-time, because one should not separate the two as if they were independent dimensions. One must keep in mind that the space-time concept is based upon the indeterminacy of whether any frame of reference may be considered as the stationary and absolute one.

What does all that have to do with Seeger and music? Seeger was particularly attracted to the space-time concept; that is, to the idea that space and time are inseparable dimensions of the physical universe. In his article "Systematic Musicology: Viewpoints, Orientations, and Methods" (1951), he specifically refers to the space-time concept in the physical universe, and then applies it to music. He proposes that a musicologist must recognize two universes: the general (or physical) universe, which he calls general space-time, and the music universe, which he calls musical space-time. The general space-time is a given, one in which all events occur, including musical-social, behavioral and acoustical phenomena. However, a musical event, while inevitably taking place in the general space-time, also exists in a musical space-time quite apart from the general space-time, with its own defining parameters and rules of behavior. He gives the example of the sense of beat in music (musical space-time), which is quite different from the ticking of a clock (general space-time). While general space-time is a given and beyond human control, musical space-time is created by human beings and may thus differ in detail from one culture to another, from one community to another, or even from one individual to another. Anyone with experience of music, whether in making it or perceiving it, will acknowledge the existence of a musical space-time in which music is perceived as something above and beyond simply a sequence or aggregate of sounds.

By general space-time he of course is referring to the concept of physical space-time in the special theory of relativity. But what does he mean by musical space-time? He explains that musical space refers to pitch, dynamics, and timbre, while musical time refers to tempo, movement, and duration. In combining space and time into a hyphenated word, he is clearly borrowing the concept from the space-time of the special theory of relativity, implying that musical space-time consists of six dimensions, but that these six dimensions are inherently related to each other and must be treated as such, just as the four dimensions in physical space-time are.

The distinction between the general and musical space-times becomes significant in what he calls the two viewpoints in musicological research: the music viewpoint and the general viewpoint. He proposes that the music viewpoint focuses on the musical event within musical space-time (the musical experience involving the six dimensions of pitch, dynamics, etc.), while the general viewpoint focuses on the musical event in general space-time (physical location of a performance, actual sound waves, social function of music, etc.).

On the detailed level Seeger's model of the six dimensions of musical space-time poses some problems because he did not define some of the dimensions clearly, particularly those that make up musical time. Furthermore, he gave them different names, equally unclear in their meaning. For example: tempo, accent, proportion (1994 [1913]: 86); tempo, movement, duration (1951:241); tempo (relative speed), accent (relative emphasis), proportion (relative duration) (1966:24).

However, on the conceptual level the model of musical space-time is significant, and the special theory of relativity as a source of inspiration is clear. In proposing a musical space-time, his obvious implication is that these six dimensions of musical sound cannot be separately perceived or analyzed and must be treated as a whole just as physical space and time have to be. Since the special theory of relativity and the space-time concept have been validated by many experiments, its use as an analogy states as strongly as possible the inseparableness of the musical space and musical time. Although he does not explicitly say so, Seeger uses the theory to comment on the kind of musical analysis that singles out one musical dimension, say harmonic structure, for discussion, without relating it to the other five dimensions. Just as in discussion of the physical space-time, such an analysis will distort the representation of a musical experience in musical space-time.

Furthermore, by proposing musical space-time and relating it to physical space-time in his model for musicological research, Seeger successfully constructs a model with a certain simplicity, balance, and elegance that echo the qualities of the special theory of relativity. It is often said of physicists that they are inherently artists in their search for physical theories that are simple and elegant. It has also been said of Seeger that as a musical scholar he sometimes allowed his creative and poetic urges to creep into his scholarly writing, and he let his search for simplicity and elegance of form influence his formulation of musicological concepts. His space-time concept and its role in his model for musicological research illustrate this observation well.

Seeger's detour into modern physics brought him invaluable insights and helped him formulate concepts in music and musicological research in ways that might otherwise have been less succinctly and powerfully expressed, or indeed might not have been forthcoming at all. But the significance of Seeger's contribution goes beyond these specific cases. By directly applying physical theories to the study of music, Seeger is tacitly proposing that, just as physics is a theoretical study of the physical universe, so musicology may be considered as a theoretical study of the musical universe. Such a line of thinking should inspire musical scholars into viewing their objects, approaches, and methods of study with fresh insights.

Beyond Seeger

Seeger's borrowing of the special theory of relativity stops short of calling attention to an astounding parallel between the development of modern physics and of (ethno)musicology. Both fields developed as a result of an awareness of the critical role of the frame of reference. The development of modern physics was based upon the breakdown of strongly held assumptions in classical physics, among which the most important was probably the gradual awakening to—and experimental proofs of—the fallacy of an absolute frame of reference in the physical universe. The history of so-called ethnomusicology in the West, or perhaps even the history of modern musicology in the West, may well be viewed in a similar light as an awakening to the fallacy of an absolute frame of reference in the musical universe, or, to use Seeger's words, in the musical space-time. As scholars gained increasing knowledge of musical systems and cultures in general outside of their own heritage, they gradually moved from highly ethnocentric views to an acceptance of the fact that all musical systems have their own place and value within their musical and cultural contexts and that any study and evaluation of such a musical system must take into consideration the musical and cultural frames of reference in which it lives. Such an acceptance of the relativity of musical and cultural frames of reference introduces an entirely new orientation toward the study of the concept of music, its scope, its function, and its value.

Furthermore, the timing of the development of both fields is worth noting. The series of Michelson-Morley experiments designed to prove the existence of ether, which eventually produced a definitive negative result, thus leading to the special theory of relativity, occurred between 1881 and 1887, while the celebrated article by Alexander Ellis on the intervalic structures of several musical systems around the world, in which he introduced the unit of the cent as a measuring yardstick of pitch interval, was published in 1884. The Michelson-Morley experiments are considered a landmark in the development of modern physics because they constituted the first concrete experimental proof that led to the breakdown of the concept of an absolute frame of reference in the physical universe. Ellis's article has been considered a landmark in the development of a global perspective of music because it was a definitive move away from an ethnocentric view of non-Western music and an important first step toward creating an objective method of comparing musical systems from different cultures. Is it a historical accident or an indication of something deeper and far-reaching in human intellectual development that both awakenings to the fallacy of an absolute frame of reference occurred at almost exactly the same time?

≈

It has often happened in physics that an essential advance was achieved by carrying out a consistent analogy between apparently unrelated phenomena. In these pages we have often seen how ideas created and developed in one branch of science were afterwards successfully applied to another. The development of the particle and wave theories (mechanical and field views) gives many examples of this kind. The association of solved problems with those unsolved may throw new light on our difficulties by suggesting new ideas. It is easy to find a superficial analogy which really expresses nothing. But to discover some essential common features, hidden beneath a surface of external differences, to form, on this basis, a new successful theory, is important creative work. (Einstein and Infeld 1961:272–73)

Einstein's wisdom as expressed in these words underscores the importance of an interdisciplinary approach in musicological research and specifically Seeger's intellectual journey into modern physics and his fruitful return to musicology. More important, it foretells the development of a global perspective in musicological research, because important creative work, in Einstein's words, arose out of the discovery of essential common features that might otherwise have remained hidden beneath a surface of external differences. By exploring the diversity in global musical phenomena and discovering the universal humanness in all, modern musicological research will move forward with new creative energy.

NOTE

1. For a simple and nontechnical explanation of some of the ideas of modern physics presented here, I recommend Einstein and Infeld's book *The Evolution of Physics* (1961).

REFERENCES CITED

Capra, Fritjof. 1975. *The Tao of Physics.* Boulder, Colo.: Shambhala Publications.
Einstein, Albert, and Leopold Infeld. 1961. *The Evolution of Physics.* 2d ed. New York: Simon and Schuster.
Ellis, Alexander. 1884. "Tonometrical Observations on some Existing Non-Harmonic Scales." *Proceedings of the Royal Society* 37:368–87.
Jones, Roger S. 1982. *Physics as Metaphor.* Minneapolis: University of Minnesota Press.
Seeger, Charles Louis. 1951. "Systematic Musicology: Viewpoints, Orientations, and Methods." *Journal of the American Musicological Society* 4:240–48.
———. 1965. "Preface to a Critique of Music." *Boletín interamericano de música* 49 (September): 2–24. (Reprinted with corrections and revisions from *Primera Conferencia interamericana de etnomusicología: Trabajos presentados.* Cartagena de Indias, Colombia, February 24–28, 1963. 39–63. Washington, D.C.: Pan American Union, 1965.)
———. 1966. "The Music Process as a Function in a Context of Functions." *Yearbook: Inter-American Institute for Musical Research* (Tulane University) 2:1–36.

————. 1977 [1958]. "Prescriptive and Descriptive Music Writing." In *Studies in Musicology, 1935–1975.* 168–81. Berkeley: University of California Press. (Reprinted from *Musical Quarterly* 44:184–95.)

————. 1994 [1931]. "Tradition and Experiment in (the New) Music." In *Studies in Musicology II, 1929–1979.* Ed. Ann M. Pescatello. 17–273. Berkeley: University of California Press. (Previously unpublished treatise.)

CONTRIBUTORS

Nimrod Baranovitch received his B.A. in musicology and Chinese studies from the Hebrew University in Jerusalem and his Ph.D. in ethnomusicology from the University of Pittsburgh with a dissertation entitled "China's New Voices: Politics, Ethnicity, and Gender in Popular Music Culture on the Mainland, 1978–1997." He teaches courses in ethnomusicology and Chinese culture at Bar Ilan University, Tel-Aviv University, and Hebrew University in Israel.

Taylor A. Greer is an associate professor of music at the Pennsylvania State University. He is the author of *A Question of Balance: Charles Seeger's Philosophy of Music* (1998) and editor in chief of *Theory and Practice*, the journal of the Music Theory Society of New York State.

Robert R. Grimes, S.J., is an associate professor of music at Fordham University and dean of Fordham College at Lincoln Center in New York City. He was an AMS 50 Fellow of the American Musicological Society in 1991–92 and is the author of *How Shall We Sing in a Foreign Land?: Music of Irish Catholic Immigrants in the Antebellum United States* (1996), which received the Irish in America Publication Award from the University of Notre Dame.

Helen Rees, an assistant professor in the Department of Ethnomusicology at the University of California at Los Angeles, specializes in ritual and tourist musics of southwest China. She is the author of *Echoes of History: Naxi Music in Modern China* (forthcoming).

Leonora Saavedra is an associate professor at Mexico's National Center for Music Research (CENIDIM). Her work on twentieth-century Mexican music and its relationship to ideology and to the Mexican state has been published in Mexico, Spain, and the United States. She is the author of *History of Mexican Music* (forthcoming).

Anthony Seeger is an anthropologist, ethnomusicologist, archivist, and record producer who currently serves as curator of the Folkways Collections and director of Smithsonian Folkways Recordings at the Smithsonian Institution. His father, John Seeger, was Charles Seeger's second son by his first wife, Constance.

Judith Tick is a professor of music at Northeastern University in Boston. She is the author of *Ruth Crawford Seeger: A Composer's Search for American Music* (1997), which won an ASCAP Deems Taylor Award and the Irving Lowens Prize for outstanding scholarship from the Sonneck Society for American Music. She is also coeditor of *Women Making Music: The Western Art Tradition, 1150–1950* (1986), which won an ASCAP Deems Taylor Award.

Bell Yung, who has Ph.D.s in physics (MIT) and music (Harvard), holds joint appointments as a professor of music at the University of Pittsburgh and as Kwan Fong Chair in Chinese Music at the University of Hong Kong. A recipient of a Guggenheim Fellowship (1996), his most recent publication is *Celestial Airs of Antiquity: Music of the Seven-String Zither of China* (1997).

Lawrence M. Zbikowski is an assistant professor of music at the University of Chicago, where he teaches courses in the theory, history, and analysis of music. His main research interests include the application of recent work in cognitive science to problems of musical understanding and the study of large-scale rhythm. During 1997–98 he was a Fellow at the Chicago Humanities Institute.

INDEX

103n1; in Mexico, 31; in United States, 31, 40, 52

Communist Party. *See* communism

comparative musicology, 150, 155, 159, 160, 161, 169n2, 173

composers and compositions: contemporary American, 1; modern, experimental, and avant-garde, 4, 6, 7, 13–16, 20–26, 31, 32, 35–39, 43–45, 49, 52, 58, 73, 75, 109, 111, 113, 121; teaching of, 32, 34, 36, 51

Composers Collective, 4, 29, 31, 39, 40, 47–52, 60n3, 65, 73–79, 85, 91–93, 103n1, 152, 156

compositional process, 32, 34, 35, 96–98

compositional theory, 14, 40

Conference on Inter-American Relations in the Field of Music, 93

Conference on Latin-American Fine Arts, 165

consonance and dissonance, 17, 18, 20

consonant tone quality, 26n5

Copland, Aaron, 31, 82n9

Core, Lucia, 146n2

Cornell University, 4, 10n3

Cory, Herbert, 90

Cowell, Henry, 4, 18, 24, 25, 26n6, 31, 32, 39, 57, 58, 82n9, 123

Crawford, Ruth, 4, 6, 8, 13–27, 39, 58, 103, 104n9, 109; compositions of: *Music of American Folk Songs*, 8, 109–27; *Piano Study in Mixed Accents*, 27n9; *String Quartet 1931*, 7, 18–27, 39, 58, 103, 109–27

criticism. *See* music criticism

cultural relativism, 9, 151, 156, 161, 164, 168

Daily Worker, 6, 46, 65, 73, 76–79, 82n11, 92

Darwinism, 151

Dawson, William, 82n13; and *Negro Folk Symphony*, 78, 92

Degeyter, Pierre, 82n12. *See also* Pierre Degeyter Club; Pierre Degeyter Club orchestra

discrete pitch levels/continuum of sound, 175

dissonant counterpoint, 25, 33, 122

dissonant tone quality, 26n5

dissonation, 23

Durkheim, Emile, 152

Edelman, Gerald, 142

Edson, Constance, 4, 39, 91

Einstein, Albert, 172, 178, 182; and Unified Field Theory, 132

Eisler, Hanns, 77, 81n8

Ellis, Alexander, 181

emotion, 32

Engles, Friedrich, 48

ethnomusicologists, 2, 169n4

ethnomusicology, 1, 3, 6, 9, 55, 109, 142, 144, 148, 149, 150, 154, 158, 167, 168, 173, 180

Ethno-musicology Newsletter, 167

fact/value dichotomy, 70, 101, 102, 103n2, 162, 164, 167

Fauconnier, Gilles, 8, 136–43, 146n3, 147n5

Federal Bureau of Investigation (FBI), 104n5

Federal Music Project, 5, 85

Feld, Stephen, 144, 150

Feynman, Richard, 172

fine art (as idiom), 75, 100, 101, 111, 118, 124, 125, 126. *See also* art music

fine-art music. *See* art music

folk art, 118

folk culture, 43

folklore, 2, 84, 88, 89, 102, 103, 173

folk music, 6, 7, 8, 38, 42, 50, 51, 52, 64, 78, 79, 84–104, 111, 113, 117, 126n2, 159–63; folk (music) revival, 100, 101, 102, 111, 119, 123; revivalists, 110

folk songs/tunes, 2, 5, 78, 84, 85, 88, 89, 92, 95–100, 104n7, 110, 112, 113, 118, 123–27

Folk Song USA (Lomax and Lomax), 96, 110

form and content, 73

frame, 144, 147n9; frame analysis, 137

frame of reference, 177–81

functionalism 9, 89, 103n3, 158, 168, 169n3

function of music, 86, 181. *See also* social function of music

function/structure dichotomy. *See* structure/function dichotomy

Galindo, Blas, 55

Galton, Sir Francis, 153

Gardner, Emelyn E., 89

Gaume, Matilda, 123

socialism, 31
Society for Ethnomusicology (SEM), 5, 131, 169, 169n4
sociology, 55
space and time, 178–80
special theory of relativity, 9, 173, 177–80
speech/music dichotomy, 7, 69, 95, 131, 135
Stone, Ruth, 150
Straus, Joseph N., 25
Stravinsky, Igor, 14, 73, 78
structure/function dichotomy, 86, 87, 95, 101, 103n2, 175
"Swing Low, Sweet Chariot," 116
systematic musicology, 1

Taylor, Carl C., 93
Terrill, Ruby, 112
transcriptions, 5, 98, 99, 110, 112–17, 119, 120, 125
"Trouble, Trouble" (holler), 116

UNESCO, 6, 104n5
University of California at Berkeley, 4, 13, 39, 65, 66, 68, 69, 85, 150–52,
University of California at Los Angeles (UCLA), 4, 13, 85

Valiant, Margaret, 93
value/criticism, 163, 168
value/fact dichotomy. *See* fact/value dichotomy
value theory, 68
value/valuing, 6, 7, 32, 34, 35, 36, 42, 43, 47, 52, 64–82, 90, 131, 154, 161, 172, 174, 181; aesthetic, 67; musical, 69, 70, 71, 74, 32, 35, 46, 79; of "good," "less good," and "bad" music, 94, 160, 163, 164
Varèse, Edgar, 4, 23, 36
Vivaldi, Antonio Lucio, 76

Wade, Bonnie, 146n2
Wagner, Richard, 36, 90
Washington, D.C., 5, 65, 93, 110
Waterman, Christopher, 150
Weiss, Adolph, 58
Weisshaus, Imre, 122
Wilgus, D. K., 89, 103n3
Wittgenstein, Ludwig Josef Johan, 146n3
workers' choruses, 51, 58
working class, 29, 31, 32; audience, 48; music, 46, 51
Works Progress Administration (WPA), 65
World War I, 68

Music in American Life

Typeset in 10/13 Palatino
with Palatino display
Designed by Paula Newcomb
Composed by Jim Proefrock
at the University of Illinois Press
Manufactured by Cushing-Malloy, Inc.

University of Illinois Press
1325 South Oak Street
Champaign, IL 61820-6903

www.press.uillinois.edu